"FRESH AND BEGUILING . . .

A beautifully crafted exploration of the power of passion and goodness to soothe past injuries and tame the demons in a man's soul."

—JENNIFER BLAKE

∽

By Christina Cordaire

Published by Fawcett Gold Medal

Books published by The Ballantine Publishing Group
are available at quantity discounts on bulk purchases
for premium, educational, fund-raising, and special
sales use. For details, please call 1-800-733-3000.

LOVING A LOWLY STRANGER

Christina Cordaire

FAWCETT GOLD MEDAL • NEW YORK

A Fawcett Gold Medal Book
Published by Ballantine Books
Copyright © 1997 by Christina Cordaire Strong

All rights reserved under International and Pan-American Copyright Conventions. Published in the United States by Ballantine Books, a division of Random House, Inc., New York, and simultaneously in Canada by Random House of Canada Limited, Toronto.

http://www.randomhouse.com

Library of Congress Catalog Card Number: 97-90126

ISBN 0-449-18335-1

Manufactured in the United States of America

First Edition: December 1997

10 9 8 7 6 5 4 3 2 1

To three of the kindest friends one could have—
in alphabetical order and in deepest gratitude

Jennifer Blake
Pat Potter
Mary Jo Putney

Prologue

⤲

HMS *Audacious*—at sea

Adrian Ashe stood at the rail of HMS *Audacious* and ignored the pain caused him when his sailor's tarred pigtail brushed the fresh welts on his shoulders. Anguish and fury rose in his throat like bile.

Savagely he crumpled the heavy vellum letter that informed him he was the new Earl of Haverford. *Too late.* With narrowed eyes and a grim expression he watched the cliffs of England draw nearer. *Why did it have to come now, when it's too damned late?*

Jamming the vellum into the wide leather belt at his waist, he permitted himself a twisted smile. Dame Fortune, deaf to his pleas during all the years she could have helped him save his family, had finally smiled on him, damn the bitch!

Haverford village, 1828

In the little churchyard on the hill, the respectful residents of Haverford village and surrounding farms had buried the district's most illustrious resident,

Martin Delacourte, Eighth Earl of Haverford only last week. And today they were burying one of its least illustrious—but a more respected man—Ethan Frost, a simple coal miner.

Lady Elise, the widowed Viscountess Danforth, was the only person besides the vicar who had attended both funerals. Being at this service brought back painful memories of yet another funeral, that of her husband.

Two years ago, her beloved Lawrence—who'd shared all his concerns with her and taught her to manage their estate, who'd treated her as an equal—had been killed, and she'd thought her life had ended. Without him, loneliness was like a cold stone in her heart.

Standing now at Ethan Frost's graveside, she hugged the dead man's orphaned daughter close. With her cloak, she shielded little Megan Frost from the light rain. With her heart, she shared her grief.

Except for the gentle voice of the vicar and the muted drip of the rain, the churchyard was so quiet that the sound of the sea came to them clearly from over a mile away. The first spadeful of earth landing on the coffin's lid was startling in its loudness and finality.

It was then that Megan let out a wild cry, and Elise gathered her even closer. This child was so slight . . . and so alone now. She smoothed the child's hair, then picked her up and carried her to the carriage.

In the snug interior, Elise held Megan in her lap, wishing she could bring the little girl to live with her.

But Danforth Hall was no place for a grieving child. Luxury was no substitute for loved ones.

Firmly she told herself that at the Limes', Megan would have other children to play with . . . and both a mother *and* a father. The arrangement was perfect.

Lawrence had taught her to be very good at making arrangements.

She drew a deep breath and bowed her head to kiss the child's blond curls. She would consider herself a very skillful arranger indeed if only she could manage to stop her own tears and Megan's.

Chapter One

∽

More money in the pocket of his cheap gray suit than he'd possessed in his entire life, Adrian Ashe entered Haverford village like an enemy scout.

His gaze took in the village street, passing over the row of tiny shops to the small inn at the far end. The inn's wide front porch invited him. Even at this distance, his sailor's eyes made out chairs, placed well back in the generous shade of the porch roof. Suddenly, he wanted to sit in one of those chairs for a while and simply watch what happened in this village—*his* village. With a brief smile, he decided to do just that. It felt good to stretch his legs after the long stagecoach ride from London. It felt even better to know the street he walked belonged to him.

His. This village was *his*. It *belonged* to him. To him, a man who but days before couldn't afford to replace the pipe some shipmate had stolen from him. He had to stifle an exultant laugh.

Smiling crookedly, he reached the end of the tree-shaded street and entered the inn.

He was welcomed by dark beams and white walls, a well-scrubbed floor and the smell of beeswax and turpentine from the huge, lovingly polished dresser that displayed the inn's best china. The innkeeper, a large man with an honest and genial face, stood behind a long bar on the far side of the spacious commonroom. With a limp linen rag as white as snow he rhythmically polished glasses, his huge hands dwarfing them. "Good morrow, sir. How may I serve ye?"

"Your best ale, landlord." After paying for it Adrian picked up his pint of ale, nodded his thanks, and went out to the porch as he'd planned. The village was peaceful, the sun was shining, and he had the porch to himself. Years spent in a crowded forecastle had given him a taste for solitude.

The village street lay quiet and dusty in the dappled sunlight. The tall, ancient elms lining both sides reached branches across to cool it with their shade.

Adrian lifted a chair and put it down again near the porch railing. He sat and, propping his booted feet on the rail of the porch, turned his thoughts to the responsibilities he faced.

Slowly he began to relax. This was journey's end for him, after all. Here in Haverford he'd end his days. End them as the Earl of Haverford. Ironic. The solicitors had told him that he'd inherited a coal mine in addition to the many farms belonging to the vast estate called Delacourte. That might prove interesting . . . and somewhat difficult.

As a boy on long visits to the estate of his mother's favorite brother, Cecil, Adrian had learned a great deal about farming and estate management. His uncle, at a loss to know what to do with him, had decided to teach him all about farms and the responsibilities of an English landlord. About mines, however, Adrian knew absolutely nothing—as Cecil had known absolutely nothing.

Adrian ran a hand through his thick dark hair. His eyes narrowed in thought. Maybe, just maybe, he should learn a bit about them before he admitted to owning one.

Languidly, he shifted his position. The marmalade cat that had been sunning itself on the porch rail sprang up and glared resentfully back over its shoulder at him. An instant later, it shot off its perch and ran across the street, a golden streak in the dust of the road.

One of the village dogs raised its head and watched the cat go, but didn't give chase. The hound yawned widely, dropped its nose back down on its forepaws, and after a contented groan, went to sleep again.

Adrian smiled and buried his own nose in his tankard of fine brown ale. Contentment settled over him like a velvet cloak.

Suddenly, the silence was broken by the sound of hoofbeats. Five or six horses, unless his ears deceived him. Instantly alert again, he turned his head in their direction.

Out of the leafy lane that entered the village on his right erupted a group of men on horseback escorting a single woman. They swept into the village, shattering the peace.

The sleepy street sprang to life. Chickens scattered, squawking and flapping frantically in a blurring rush. Dogs leapt up to run barking through the cloud of dust the riders raised and to snap at the horses' heels.

Taking his feet down off the rail, Adrian Ashe watched them warily. Here, no doubt, were the people among whom he was expected to make a new life— the local gentry. Gentry. Contempt welled up in him. No matter. Though he may have picked up rough ways in the past few years, he knew he'd fit. He'd had the constant tutelage of his gentle aristocrat mother throughout his young life and spent enough summers with her noble family to be perfectly at home in any society.

He had no qualms. He was confident he'd be able to fit in here as the heir to his long-dead father's eldest brother, his Uncle Martin Delacourte. He'd fit . . . but never belong.

His slight smile twisted. How bloody ironic. After years of being a poor relation, he was now to take his place here as the richest and most powerful man in the district. He was heir to a man whom he'd never met, a man who'd never even bothered to acknowledge his existence.

A shout interrupted his acid thoughts. "You there!" A square, ruddy-faced man on a big rawboned bay pointed in Adrian's direction. "Get down here and hold these horses."

Adrian was about to make a sharp retort, but stopped as if run aground under full sail. *God! What a beauty!*

A green-eyed woman regarded him calmly from the back of a chestnut mare that gleamed as red in the sun as did her own thick braid of hair. The emerald color of her velvet riding habit echoed and intensified the green of her eyes, and her silken skin was as white as

spindrift in moonlight. But it was her expression that
arrested him. The expression on her lovely face was
full of intelligence, curiosity . . . and something more.
Something infinitely more.

Mechanically, he walked toward her, his gaze
raking the grace of her slender figure, then returning,
bold-eyed, to her face. His wits as addled as if he'd
taken a blow from a belaying pin, he could no more
have looked away from her than he could fly.

Forgotten was the caustic comment he'd been about
to make to the man who'd addressed him. Adrian
reached for the stout squire's reins and then for hers
like a man in a dream. Golden flecks appeared to swim
in her eyes. He saw her breasts rise as she caught her
breath. Her delicate nostrils flared and her soft lips
parted.

Adrian smiled a slow, somnolent smile. He knew
she was as completely aware of him as he was of her,
and a heady elation rose in him.

"I say!" Another voice sounded plaintively from off
to his right. "The lout is staring very rudely at Lady
Elise."

Adrian laughed.

"I'll be damned!" A third man, tall, handsome, and
elegantly dressed, edged his horse forward. Leaning
from his saddle, he poked Adrian hard on the shoulder
with his whip.

Ashe spun around without letting go of the reins,
caught the whip, and pulled it out of its owner's hand.

Finally, he answered the squire, "Hold your own
horses!" He tossed the reins away, sending the man's
horse rearing back and skittering off. He saw to it that

the woman had her reins safely in hand, looking deeply, intimately, into her eyes as he did.

After a long moment, during which he could feel the outrage building in the group of men like thunderclouds, he turned and stalked back up onto the porch.

Before he picked up his tankard of ale, he stared pointedly into the flushed face of the man to whom the heavy hunting whip belonged. He tossed it to him. To underscore the point he was making, he slowly, deliberately lifted his tankard toward the glorious woman on the chestnut mare and silently toasted her.

A tall, dark man sitting his horse easily at the back of the group called out, "You there! If you're looking for work, apply to the Malfont Mine. I'll see to it that you work off some of that temper swinging a pickax for me."

"Really, Sir James! You can't be serious!" It was the man who had prodded Ashe with his whip. "We don't want this ruffian hanging about!"

Adrian leaned his broad shoulders against the wall of the inn, and pointedly ignored them all.

The man who'd offered the job laughed.

Adrian made careful note of it.

Malfont's laughter wasn't a pretty sound.

Elise felt her breath catch again. She looked from one man to the other. Malfont, resplendent in a superbly tailored riding coat, radiated superiority. The stranger, somehow magnificent in cheap gray cloth and a simple linen stock, simmered with rebellion.

Malfont and the stranger had locked gazes. The tension between the two men was a palpable thing.

Sir James was the first to look away. With an impatient toss of his head, he dismounted and turned toward Elise.

Admiration for the commoner rose in her. She hadn't met many men who could face down Sir James Malfont. Fighting an overwhelming desire to look boldly at the man on the porch, Elise leaned down from her saddle and placed her hands on Sir James's shoulders. She smiled broadly at him, determined to ignore the stranger whose regal bearing was so at odds with his cheap clothes. But she was acutely aware of him as he stood leaning against the wall of the inn, his brooding eyes fixed on her. By a mighty act of her will, she kept herself smiling down at Sir James. In her mind's eye, she still saw the man who'd so insolently saluted her with his tankard of ale.

She could see again the strong movement of his throat as he'd quaffed his ale insultingly in her honor, and his eyes . . . his deep, gray, smoldering eyes . . .

Outwardly, Elise knew she appeared cool and detached, a woman ready to enjoy a rustic luncheon with five of her male friends. Inwardly, her senses were reeling. Who was this man? Why did he affect her so? Careful not to look beyond the faces of her friends, she allowed them to escort her, laughing, into the inn.

Sir James whispered maliciously, "Well done, my dear."

Elise merely smiled.

It was better once they were inside. Much better.

It was as if the thick stone walls of the inn acted as a shield to insulate her from the sheer masculinity that seemed to flow out from the stranger. She sighed with relief.

Malfont chuckled, his eyes knowing.

Blast Sir James! Irritated, Elise frowned, then caught herself. Malfont wouldn't betray her, because having the others know would take away from his own enjoyment.

She made certain that her frown was gone by the time her companions' eyes were no longer blinded by their transition from the bright day to the dimness of the inn. It would never do to let them see her scowl. They'd tease her mercilessly if they guessed she'd taken even momentary notice of some wanderer. Well, he'd be gone by the time they left the inn. He'd be gone and she'd be able to draw a normal breath. Why then did she feel as if she would have lost something of inestimable importance?

Deverill moved to her side. He was a good friend who had stood by her from the first. All of the men except he and her late husband had been annoyed by her intellect and by what they saw as her unfeminine attempt at interference in their business. Deverill had been the only one among them who enjoyed her company as an intellectual equal and had taken her seriously when she indicated she wanted to carry on with her husband's work.

She supposed, to be fair, she should say the same about Sir James Malfont. But Sir James, even though he respected her intelligence, found her concern for the miners no more than amusing. Tate, Effers, and Squire Jepson simply could not understand why she cared about lowly workers.

"What would you like, Lady Elise?" Squire Jepson was pounding the bar for the innkeeper, his face still flushed from their ride.

"A little less noise, probably, Jepson," Deverill drawled.

Elise smiled and said, "A little ale . . ." She ignored the disapproving hoots of the men. Ale was the best for quenching thirst. Let *them* drink ratafia. "And one of Mrs. Brown's lovely meat pasties, please. Fruit and cheese."

"My dear, you'll eat enough for us all!"

Laughing at Deverill's words, they moved to their regular large round table near the window. Three of the five men vied for the privilege of seating Lady Elise. Deverill let the squire have the honor so that he could grab the chair beside hers, grinning.

Malfont chose to sit opposite her, distancing himself from the scramble with cold dignity. The squire settled on her other side by virtue of superior bulk, and Tate and Lord Effers were left to complete the table.

"Comfortable, Lady Elise?" Squire Jepson always asked.

She nodded and gifted him with her smile.

Mrs. Brown came in, her plump cheeks rosy from the kitchen fires, with a platter of meat pasties and a bowl of fruit. She was followed by her husband, the innkeeper, bearing tankards of ale, three in each hand. Beaming, he set them down and told his wife, "I'll get that round of Stilton, Missus."

"Bring the cheese knife, Husband." She turned her full attention eagerly to the Quality and asked as she rushed around the table placing the tankards of ale, "Have you heard? We've a new master coming!" Mrs. Brown was aglow with the news, her curiosity overcoming her reticence about bothering the Quality. "Would you be knowing anything of him?"

Deverill murmured, "Impertinence," under his breath and was rewarded with a swift kick in the shins by Elise.

"No." Elise smiled at the innkeeper's wife. "None of us has heard who he is or when he's coming. And I assure you, I am as curious as you are."

"Is that so?" The query came from the soberly dressed Tate, the one cit tolerated in their little group because Elise had insisted on it. To have excluded him would have been to condemn him to a solitary existence, surrounded as his property was by their estates. He had fit in so well that even Malfont was glad to have Tate's company.

Tate put his tankard down. "With almost all of Haverford's kin having drowned with him, no one seems to be able to guess who will succeed him as earl." With serious brown eyes he regarded each of the men around the table in turn. "I would have thought one of you would have sent to London to find out who the blighter is."

"Perhaps I shall do so if he doesn't turn up in a week or two." Malfont seemed almost to be talking to himself. "We've need of a magistrate."

Elise heard him and challenged, "To investigate Ethan Frost's death, Sir James?" She leveled her gaze at him as she said it.

Malfont returned her look with a cold smile and a

lifted eyebrow, accepting her challenge even as he declined to answer.

Effers stepped into the breach and answered her, though, exasperated. "No, Elise, m'dear. No one doubts that Frost died as a result of injuries sustained in a brawl." He shook a finger at her. "People"—he emphasized the word in a way that told her clearly he meant her—"must give up this odd notion that he was murdered." He sent a brief smile toward Sir James, of whom he seemed perpetually in awe. "Malfont means we need a magistrate to keep these miners from thinking they can gather to demonstrate and behave as they did when Ethan Frost was alive to lead them in their disobedience."

He shook his finger at her again; the large ruby ring on his hand flashed as it caught the light. "Even though you had a great deal to do with Frost and his impudent ideas, it's past time you admitted that we can't have miners making demands. Can't have them thinking they can tell mine owners how to run the mines, can we now?"

"How fascinating," Deverill murmured, "that Effers can speak with such confidence for all of us. Particularly our Malfont." His gaze rested lazily on the handsome man across from Elise.

Malfont returned his regard with a chilling smile.

Elise, impatient with Deverill's continuing animosity toward Malfont, said coolly, "I should imagine that the *miners* would be the best ones to know how to make the mines safe. They are, after all, the ones who risk their lives in them daily."

Effers was offended. His cheeks took on a hectic

tint that echoed the peach coat he wore. "Come, come now, Elise. Why do you bother your pretty little head about the lot of a few miserable, complaining coal miners?"

Deverill broke in with a grin. "Have a care. You're trespassing on our ladyship's finer feelings. Walk warily, or you'll find yourself in deep going."

"Deverill!" Elise turned his way. "*You* go carefully. Take care *you* don't antagonize me with your lack of concern."

She let her gaze travel the circle of faces. Deverill wasn't alone. Not one of them was the least bit concerned about the death of a mere miner. They didn't care that he was as fine a man as any of them. Didn't admire the fact that he had stood up for his fellow colliers manfully. To them he was beneath their regard by virtue of the job he did—almost a slave by the law of the land, forbidden under pain of death to speak out against his employers.

With a mighty effort she reined in her anger. "England desperately needs coal to fuel all the industries that are growing so quickly now that we have steam engines capable of driving so many wonderful inventions." She felt her teeth grate as she noticed Effers and Tate exchange bored glances. "Why," she dared to add, "production in my mine will increase twofold as soon as I put in the new steam-driven pump to keep it clear of water."

Deverill shoved his knee against hers in warning.

Right. He was right. If she continued to show that she was more familiar with technical innovations than they, she'd lose her neighbors' attention entirely.

Quickly, she shifted back to her main concern. Her voice deepened and warmed with feeling. "You just don't seem to be aware of the conditions under which your mine workers have to labor. Lately there have been so many accidents—"

"Ah." With a finger held out toward her again in admonition, Effers interrupted her. "Elise, my dear, my so very charming young friend, you can't mean to ruin our outing with one of your little lectures."

For a moment, Elise had an absurd urge to leap up and bite his pointing finger. *You'd think he'd have learned not to thrust things at people after the tall, dark-browed stranger pulled the whip from his hands.* She wished with all her heart that she could drag Effers down into his mine so he'd be forced to acknowledge the deplorable conditions under which his badly paid employees worked.

Instead, she took a deep, calming breath and forced her body to relax in her chair. With an effort, she put a charming smile on her face, and said sweetly, "I wouldn't dream of giving you a lecture, my friend."

Outside in the lengthening shadows of the day, Adrian Ashe finished his tankard of ale thoughtfully. Leaning, as he was, near the window, he'd heard the conversation of those inside. His dark brows drew down in a frown.

So there was something amiss at the mines belonging to these people, was there? Interesting. If that were the case, there was probably something amiss with the mine he'd inherited from his uncle as well. He was hardly surprised. Didn't he know from his own bitter experience how little the gentry cared for those who served?

Perhaps he would look into this situation. There might be something he could do for the families of these miners of which the redhead had spoken. Doing for them what he'd been powerless to do for his own loved ones might help to expiate some of the crushing guilt he felt.

This Ethan Frost must have been their spokesman. Obviously the man had been silenced. He'd reserve judgment on whether or not it had been by murder until he was in the possession of more of the facts.

And he'd never get those facts as a mine *owner*.

Besides, he wasn't ready, on such short acquaintance, to join this charming circle of men he'd just encountered. He thought he'd wait awhile. The plight of the miners was surely a cause he could espouse. Their lowly station tugged at him. He felt a kinship with them. God knew he'd learned enough about living as little more than a slave in His Majesty's navy.

Perhaps he'd replace this Ethan Frost whose death was under debate by his new neighbors. It sounded to him as if the man might have been something of a thorn in the side of the local gentry. The idea of becoming a similar irritant appealed to him . . . greatly.

Adrian had learned long ago how to irritate those in authority over him. He bore whip marks on his back to attest to it. *Surely*, he thought with heavy sarcasm, *it would be a shame to neglect such a hard-won skill!* He smiled sardonically.

A part of his mind warned him he should reconsider. It whispered that he'd have no chance at all to discover the banked passions he sensed in Lady Elise Whoever, if he were no more than a common laborer from a mine. She was a gentlewoman who would never look twice at a common laborer.

Possibly.

Interest lit his features. At any rate, it was a challenge. Could he seduce her if he appeared to her as a commoner? The mere question brought a reckless grin to his face.

Adrian Ashe had always welcomed a challenge.

Like a duelist snatching up a thrown gauntlet, he decided to try it.

Malfont *had* offered him a job in his mine, after all. The high-handed nobleman could share the responsibility for any . . . rash acts.

He quaffed the last of his ale, put the tankard on the windowsill beside him, and pushed away from the wall on which he'd been leaning. It was time for him to go, he decided, obeying the devil that drove him. Time for him to find the mine of the man called Malfont.

Malfont. His eyes narrowed as he recalled the image of the man. He was the handsome one with the eyes of steel and the chilling smile.

Ashe grinned again. His spirits lifted.

Suddenly, he was possessed of a sharp determination to be the man who wiped the smile off the face of that particular mine owner—and put a smile on the face of that breathtakingly beautiful Lady Elise.

Chapter Two

ↄⅤↄ

Elise arrived back in her room like a whirlwind. The moment she did, she hurled her hat toward the bed—where it promptly bounced off the white damask cover onto the floor—and threw her riding crop and gloves after it. "Nothing! I accomplished absolutely nothing today."

Frustrated enough to throw other things, too, but sensible enough not to break the treasures with which Lawrence had surrounded her, she began pacing the deeply carpeted floor and viciously kicking the train of her riding habit out of her way as she made her turns.

"Here, here, now." Agnes bustled into the room on her heels and headed for the hat and gloves Elise had thrown. "What's got you in such a pet?" She picked up the tall-crowned beaver and brushed it lovingly back into shape.

"The men! My blessed neighbors." She seated herself at the dressing table with a plop and regarded her abigail in the mirror.

"Ah." Agnes looked back at her mistress sharply, instantly attuned to her mood. "Yes. I see."

19

She'd served Elise almost all her life—since her own girlhood. Her very first position had been as a nursery maid to the great house of Heatherington. There, she'd been the youngest and least important of the nursery maids, but the tiny, squalling Lady Elise Gail Heatherington had taken to her, the poor little motherless tyke, and her position had been secure.

Agnes had gone on through the years that followed, moving up the ladder of service. After being maid to the girl child—a position in which she'd honorably earned every gray hair in her light brown tresses—she'd been lady's maid to the debutante and to the bride, and now she was abigail and informal companion to the Widow Danforth.

She placed calming hands on Elise's shoulders. The gesture was a familiar one to them both.

How many times through the turbulent years since her lady's infancy had Agnes soothed her like this? She had been such a passionate, impetuous child, feeling things so keenly. Elise had grown into a lovely woman, but some things had never changed.

Gently kneading the tightness she felt in Elise's velvet-clad shoulders, Agnes said quietly, "Blessed you may indeed call them, Lady Elise, whether or not you meant it exactly that way. For all in all, they do treat you kindly." Her eyes looked into Elise's reflected ones, and she nodded gravely. "Not one of them has tried to cheat you out of what's rightfully yours . . . nor has one attempted to force himself on you"—she held Elise's startled gaze with a level one of her own—"as happens to many a widow, my dear."

Elise stared at her, shocked.

"Oh, yes." Agnes gazed back with affection, reaching for Elise's bright auburn braid.

"That's often the way of things in this sinful world, milady," she told her softly, "when there's no man on hand to protect you. Never mind that you're livin' in the eighteen hundreds. So I say, blessed indeed be those you call your neighbors for being better than to do any such to you." She undid the black ribbon at the braid's end and began to loosen her employer's hair.

Elise closed her mouth, her eyes grave, her spirit calmer. Agnes's words gave her food for thought. Her neighbors were, for all that they wouldn't listen to her about the mines, indeed, her friends. Sitting there, she admitted that all Agnes had said was perfectly true.

Deverill might tease her for a kiss, but he'd never force one from her.

James Malfont might have unclothed her occasionally with his eyes, but his hands never followed their path.

Effers and Tate, at opposite ends of the social scale, were nevertheless always perfect gentlemen in their behavior toward her, the crude Tate no less so than the elegant Effers.

Bluff and hearty Squire Jepson never failed to see to her safety and comfort when the group of them were out on one of their jaunts. And he and his wonderful wife, Betsy, treated her as if she were in reality the daughter they'd never had.

All of them always included her in their entertainments, when they could have ignored her altogether, leaving her sitting at home alone. So Agnes was right, she concluded, with a penitent sigh. They were her friends, and she was wrong to be so angry with them.

Squaring her shoulders, she accepted it. "Very well, Agnes. Undoubtedly you have a point." She wasn't going to surrender docilely, however. A hint of sarcasm crept into her voice. "My neighbors are paragons of virtue all."

"Och, now. I didn't say that!"

"Very well," Elise finally capitulated, her cheerful disposition reasserting itself. "You are right, of course. I'll agree that just because I'm frustrated doesn't mean I have to be angry with my friends." She smiled wickedly. "*Nor* does my having forgiven them mean I'm going to leave them in peace." Her gaze met that of her abigail. "I've absolutely no intention of doing *that* until I've made them see things my way. I may have accomplished nothing today, but there's always tomorrow." Her voice took on bold assurance. "I'll make them change their views, you'll see."

Agnes threw up her hands and muttered, "When pigs fly." She picked up a silver-backed brush and began to brush Elise's hair.

Elise chose to disregard Agnes's remark. It was hard enough to keep a positive outlook.

Staring into the mirror, she touched her cheek to remove the speck of mud she'd no doubt picked up from some flying hoof as the small party of riders had raced her home from the inn. Unbidden, the image of the stranger came to mind.

The strength of the man's personality struck her afresh. He had dominated every man in the group of

her friends—except possibly Malfont—with the sheer
force of his will. It had been fascinating to watch.

She glossed over the fact that he had certainly
dominated her as well. She felt a little thrill as she remembered, and shook it off irritably. She would only
go so far as to admit that she *had* stared at him like a
mindless ninny. But suddenly she had the oddest feeling that he was meant to be a part of her . . . her mind
stumbled over the word "life," and she quickly substi-
tuted "plans."

"Agnes," she murmured.

"Yes, milady." Agnes, alerted by something in her
mistress's tone of voice, was all curiosity.

"There was a man today." Elise spoke slowly, her
eyes shadowed with serious thought. "At the inn. A
stranger."

Agnes stopped dead, hairbrush in midstroke, a re-
ceptive expression on her face. "A stranger, milady?"

"*Hmmmm.* A tall, dark man in a common suit."

Agnes noted with interest that it was the suit Lady
Elise called common, not the man.

"He was drinking ale on the porch of the inn." She
smiled over her shoulder. "Squire Jepson ordered
him to hold our horses." She laughed, emerald eyes
sparkling. "For a moment I thought I was going to
hear language unfit for a lady's ears."

"And did you?"

"No. He contented himself with throwing our reins
back at us and telling us to 'hold your own horses.' "

"*Tsk, tsk.* Well, that was certainly not very courteous." She watched sharply to see if her mistress

would let that comment pass uncorrected. *Would* only the suit remain common?

A thoughtful expression replaced Elise's smile. She concentrated hard for a moment. Her eyes narrowed. Finally, she said very slowly, "You know, Agnes, I'm rather certain he was neither courteous nor a gentleman."

Back in the village, the man who was neither courteous nor a gentleman reentered the inn. He turned left into the spacious, low-ceilinged public room. Hesitating an instant, he stood, his shoulders almost filling the doorway. The approaching innkeeper, Mr. Brown, looked a bit apprehensive. It didn't trouble Adrian. Men frequently were intimidated when he wore a serious expression.

He didn't bother to smile the man to his ease, but merely said, "Supper, landlord, and a bed for the night."

The innkeeper looked at him only a moment before asking, "Will you require a private parlor?" There was something about the stranger that put him strongly in mind of the Quality, for all that he wore cheap clothes. Hard put to know just how to treat him, the innkeeper was decidedly uncomfortable.

Adrian considered. As it had earlier on the porch, desire for the luxury of solitude pulled strongly at him, but, since he'd come here incognito to learn more about the place, he resisted the temptation to indulge himself.

"No. A table in your common room will do."

Mr. Brown nodded and led the way. A group of

men clustered at the bar on the back wall fell silent as they passed.

Adrian ignored them and followed the innkeeper to one of the scarred and well-scrubbed tables that stood along the window side of the room opposite the bar. It amused him to think that it was possibly even the one the glorious redhead had graced earlier.

Thinking about the beautiful Lady Elise wasn't his reason for being here, however, and he forced himself to think about matters at hand. He was here to learn about this place, his place—his responsibility—not to dream about some woman.

As he eased his length into the chair Mr. Brown had pulled out for him, his gaze raked the group of men standing at the bar. They'd finished looking him over and had returned to their conversation. He was free to study them at his leisure.

Gaunt and grimy, they were solemn-eyed men with no hope in their faces. They seemed almost to huddle under the blue gray cloud of their pipe smoke. Coal dust ground into their skin gave them a grayish pallor that even the flush that their ale and eager conversation had brought to their faces couldn't dispel.

Adrian had never seen a sorrier lot. Their appearance shocked him. Some seamen might be gaunt and hopeless, but they were tanned by the sun. Yes, and ruddy-faced from the fresh air and the wind over the sea.

"Aye, Malfont could do somethin' about the water iffen he'd a mind to," said one of the men who seemed the oldest, the most ill, least long for this earth.

"What could he be doing, George Grant? Tell me

that. We already have the horse gin"—the speaker ignored the rude sound Grant made—"but that's not going to take care of it if the tunnels go farther out under the sea, I can tell ye."

"An' I'll tell you what he could do about it!" The ancient stabbed at him with his pipe stem. "He could be putting in steam pumps like her ladyship talks about, that's what he could be doing. Why, didn't that there Thomas Newcomen, that there ironmonger over to Dartmouth, see the need of it back in the early 1700s? Built a steam-powered pump for a coal mine over to Dudley Castle way back in 1712, he did. That's over a hunnert years ago."

"Iffen *he* could pump the water out of a mine way back then, seems to me like Malfont could do the same now. That old horse gin don' bring up more'n a few gallons at a turn, going 'round and 'round the whole day long."

"Aye. You've the right of that. But who's going to be asking Malfont to spend his money on seeing to it that *we're* safer down in the mine"—the man's voice hushed respectfully—"now that Ethan Frost's gone?"

A chorus echoed the question. "Aye, who?"

The graybeard hung his head. "Are ye saying there's nary a soul left to stand up to the owners?"

One of the men slammed his tankard down on the bar. "Aye. That's exactly what we be saying." His expression was truculent, daring anyone to call him craven. "We be simple men. We haven't a way with talking. With Ethan out of it, who's to say a word for us? Always excepting the Lady Elise, o' course." He snatched up his ale again, lifting the tankard high. "God bless her!"

"God bless her!" They toasted in unison.

One of them, bursting with reflected importance, broke the good news, adding, "Aye! And bless the steam engine that she's ordered to pump out Danforth Mine!"

There was a babble of excitement at that news, and the man who'd made the announcement, a slim, sandy-haired man with an honest face, was identified as Hal Lime in the general hubbub. Adrian filed his name away.

Listening attentively, he digested all he heard. He was deeply disappointed when the miners had quaffed the last of their ale in honor of the redheaded beauty, for the discussion seemed to have ended then by unspoken mutual consent. With muttered comments that it was time to get home to supper, the men filed out.

"Would you care to hear what's available for your meal, sir?"

Adrian turned to the innkeeper, surprised the man had come upon him unawares. Instead of answering, he demanded, "Do those men meet here like that every night?"

"Lord, no, sir!" The innkeeper was clearly astonished. "They haven't the money to spare for a pint of ale any more than one night or two in a month. They're colliers," he said as if it explained the matter. "Miners, don't ye know."

"I see." Adrian let the matter drop as he'd no desire to have his interest noted. He promptly ordered his supper. When it came, he ate in pensive silence.

The last of the very good meal finished, he startled and delighted the landlord by sending his compliments to the cook. Then he asked for a pipe.

Settling back in his chair, he let his gaze travel the comfortable room, lingering here and there on the shining brass and glowing copper, taking in the hunt prints on the whitewashed walls. This inn was more than a cut above those he'd known as a simple seaman. This one, of course, catered to the local gentry as well as the common folk hereabout—a vastly different society from that of a seaport.

The idea of going to the mines as a common laborer began to take a real hold on him. Obviously there was something going on, some sort of conflict between the workers and their employers. Some sort of conflict in which the redhead had embroiled herself. Some sort of conflict in which a man had died.

He wanted to know more about it. And about the death of the man called Ethan Frost. *Had* the man been murdered? Was the conflict so serious that a human life had been deliberately taken?

When he took his rightful place as the Earl of Haverford, he promised himself that investigating the death of the miner would be his first order of business. After all, he was expected to take over as the district's magistrate, as his London solicitors had informed him and as he'd heard one of Lady Elise's party remark when he'd eavesdropped earlier.

A log shifted and dropped in the huge fireplace. A shower of sparks flew out onto the well-scrubbed floor. His ruminations interrupted, Adrian rose, kicked the larger embers back onto the hearth, and tapped out the pipe against the heel of his boot, letting the contents fall into the fireplace.

As if the cleaning of the rented pipe had signaled him, Brown appeared. "Will ye be wanting yer bed now, sir?"

"Yes, thank you." Adrian handed the innkeeper the long white clay pipe.

Brown took it and snapped off the inch that had formed the mouthpiece Adrian had used. Then he replaced the pipe in a rack of others just like it to be rented to the next patron who wanted to smoke but didn't carry his own pipe.

Leading the way, he headed up the winding wooden stairs to the bedchambers.

Halfway up the stairs, Adrian paused and asked Brown, "Are there many mines hereabouts?"

"Aye. All told, there be seven in these parts, and a few more farther up to the north of us."

"Oh?"

"Yes, sir. Here there be Tate's, Effers's, Jepson's little pit, and Malfont's." He gestured roughly northeast. "Then there be Haverford's—though no man knows what'll become of it now the old lord's gone and the new one's not yet here—and Lady Elise Danforth's mine. They be the two best. Haverford be the biggest, and Danforth the safest. Then Deverill's be south of us, inland from the coast a bit."

Stopping with his hand on the knob of the door to one of the bedchambers, he looked at Ashe with obvious interest. When the tall man offered no comment, Brown opened the door to his second-best bedchamber and stood aside.

"Thank you." Adrian passed into the neat room, giving the man nothing with which to assuage his curiosity.

By the time he'd finished preparing for bed, Adrian's decision was firm. He'd decided not to work in his own coal mine. He'd made up his mind to accept Malfont's cavalier offer of a job.

Since fate had seen fit to make him a mine owner now, he was bloody damn well going to find out why the blazes honest workers were kept so poor that they could buy good English ale only once or twice in a month's time.

Chapter Three

❧

The late afternoon sun was beginning to peek under the awning Elise's estate manager had had rigged for her near the mouth of Danforth Mine. A rising breeze ruffled and snapped it, and the plans for the steam engine were in danger of blowing away.

"I think we should call it a day, Mr. Rodney." Elise looked to where the men toiled, resolutely denying fatigue in their eagerness to finish assembling the steam engine and pump.

She smiled at her estate manager and straightened up from the large square table over which the two of them had been working all day. Plans for the steam engine that had been shipped to them in parts lay scattered over its surface, weighted down by pieces of coal and large chunks of golden-hued limestone.

"Yes." Her estate manager watched the weary men, smiling, too. "They're eager to see if the water will really gush out of the mine. Whether the pump will work." His long, earnest face wore a deeply satisfied expression. "The men have lost so many friends to flooding mines that we'll have to order them to stop work."

Pressing her hand to the small of her back, Elise told him, "Do so, please."

"Very well, milady." Elias Rodney walked off to where the men worked with the huge parts and heavy gears.

Elise began gathering up the various sheets of plans, amazed that she'd been so absorbed, she hadn't noticed how stiff her back had become.

Her estate manager returned and took over the job of putting the plans in proper order for her. "It went well today, milady. The men say they'll be able to finish setting her up before noon tomorrow."

Elise was amused. Somewhere in the long afternoon, the steam engine had become "her." She nodded, then hurried to untether her mare.

Mr. Rodney rushed after her. "Permit me." He offered his clasped hands. Elise smiled her thanks as she placed her booted foot in them, and he threw her up into her saddle.

She could take the road that wound toward the double row of stone cottages James Malfont's grandfather had built for the men who worked in his mines, but Columbine liked going cross country, and so did she. Soon she was cantering across lush meadow.

She was eager to visit Hal and Lettie Lime to see how little Megan Frost was faring. Since Hal Lime worked in Malfont's mine, and thus lived in one of his cottages, she had a nice distance to ride to reach his home.

She'd be glad to talk to Hal Lime, too. Maybe he'd have a suggestion about a replacement for Ethan Frost.

Even though they'd been unable to interest the miners farther up the coast, Ethan Frost and she *had* been able to get most of the miners in their own district to rally 'round them. That hadn't been an easy task, with weary men and oppressive laws. It would be a shame to lose their momentum.

She saw the smoke from the cottage chimneys. It rose, twisted and thinned, transparent against the deep blue of the evening sky, then disappeared on the wind that swept briskly in from the nearby sea.

She put her mare at the low stone wall that separated the pasture they'd crossed from the almost ditch-like narrow road. Columbine cleared it like a bird.

Elise was patting the mare's neck and telling her, "Good girl!" when three men stepped into the road.

Columbine slid to a halt and reared, screaming her fright and flailing the air in front of her. The men jumped back to avoid the iron-shod hooves. Columbine, thoroughly unnerved by their sudden appearance, snatched the bit, bogged her head down, and started running away.

"Sorry!" Elise called back over her shoulder, then muttered, "Drat," as she fought to control her horse. She wished she could have stopped to be sure that the man who'd reached for Columbine's bridle was all right. He'd narrowly escaped being hit by her mare's hooves!

Behind her in the road the largest of the three men snarled, "Why'n hell didja have to step out like that? Ye knows bloody well he said we was jes' to take a good look at 'er!"

"So? Who asked you to step out with me?" He

glared his companions down. "No harm done. And none of us got hurt!"

His scowl kept the others from disagreeing. An instant later, with a mercurial change of mood, the man who'd led them out into the road grinned. "She was worth it, wasn't she?"

" 'Ere, now. None o' that." The first man leaned down and pushed his face into that of the man who'd just spoken. " *'E* said we warn't to touch her." His gaze intent, he thrust a finger against the other man's chest and tapped out his words. "And iffen I was you, I'd remember that."

"I'm not afraid of him."

The man who'd hitherto been silent whispered hoarsely, his words slightly spaced, "Then, more fool you."

The words hung ominously in the air as the three men slunk off the road.

Elise urged her mare along the narrow, cobble-stoned street. She was as eager to see how little Megan was doing as she was to consult with Hal Lime. She hadn't seen the child since Ethan's funeral. She halted a now fully cooperative Columbine in front of the cottage in which the Limes lived.

The horse whickered.

Instantly, the door of the simple stone cottage burst open.

Smiling, Elise tossed her reins to the gangly boy who ran out to greet her. "Thank you, Willem." She slid from the saddle. "Would you walk her, please?"

"Yes, milady." Even more eager to please Lady

Elise than he was to earn the much-needed coin she always gave him, he took the mare off. Columbine went with the boy happily, nuzzling his shoulder, and Elise turned to the thin woman standing in the doorway.

"How are you, Lettie?" She touched the rosy cheek of the baby the woman held on her hip, and her voice softened. "And how are you, Bobby?"

Bobby chortled, waving his chubby fists, and his mother said, "We all be fine, Your Ladyship." She smiled warmly and stood aside, inviting Elise into her home. "Can I offer you some tea?"

Mindful of the cost of tea and the poverty in which the other woman lived, Elise said, "No, thank you. I shan't be staying that long." She stripped off her riding gloves and removed her hat, placing them beside a cheap vase full of bright wildflowers on a small table near the door.

No sooner had she seated herself in the single armchair the room boasted than, with a delighted whoop, a six-year-old girl ran in from the cottage's other room and flung herself into Elise's lap. "You've come! I knowed you'd come." She kissed Elise soundly on the cheek and reared back, her hands firmly locked behind Elise's neck, to demand, "Why have you taken so long? It feels like it's been forever and ever, My Lovely."

"Megan! Leave her ladyship be."

"No, no." Elise laughingly put Lettie at ease. "Don't scold her." She gave the tiny girl a tight squeeze and felt a rush of longing as the wiry little arms returned her hug with all their strength.

God hadn't seen fit to bless Lawrence and her with the children for which she yearned, and this dear little orphan held a special place in her heart.

She was Ethan's only child. Ethan and Megan had had no one but each other, just as she'd had only Lawrence. The bond she felt with the bereft child was strong. Smiling down at her, Elise said, "It does seem a very long time, doesn't it? But I've brought you something by way of apology. Would you like some sweets?"

Megan's eyes grew round and eager.

"Meggie." Elise's hostess reminded the child of her manners.

"Oh, yes, please, My Lovely. I truly would, thank you."

Lettie made a small sound, but didn't interrupt.

"Then would you mind going out to Willem, quietly, so that you don't startle Columbine, and ask him to give you the bag tied to my saddle?"

"Oh, no, My Lovely, I wouldn't mind at all. I should very much like to do that. And I'll be very careful, because," she assured her friend solemnly, "I wouldn't want to be kicked by Columbine." With that she slipped down and was out the door in a flash.

Elise brought her hands back to her lap trying to deny the way they'd clung to the child, trying to tell herself that a child of her own might yet be somewhere in her future. She smiled at her hostess and said softly, "She is very dear."

"Yes."

"She is doing well?"

"Yes. Sometimes she cries at night."

"I can imagine. Her father was all she had." Elise reached out and touched the other woman's threadbare sleeve. "We must never let such a thing happen again."

For an instant, anger flared in Lettie's eyes. "As if we could have stopped it."

Elise paled and looked away. "No." Her voice was low, husky with sorrow. "We certainly failed to prevent the tragedy." She gazed again at Lettie. "I meant that whomever I get now to help me with our crusade must be a man without a wife and children."

Lettie's face shone with relief. "Ye mean ye've not come to ask my Hal to . . ."

Elise shook her head slowly, suddenly realizing the torment her visit must have brought this woman. "No, Lettie. I came only to ask his advice. I'm so sorry I've caused you disquiet."

Lettie had tears in her eyes. "Oh, Your Ladyship. I do be that glad, and no lie about it."

"I want Hal's advice. Since he was closest to Ethan, he probably has information that I'll need before I can continue." She smiled apologetically. "I *am* sorry I frightened you."

Lettie's answering smile was radiant.

Elise glanced at the door. "You've done wonders with Megan. I hope she hasn't proved to be too much trouble."

"None at all. She do be fine. Except for her bad dreams, Your Ladyship. And that's only to be expected, I suppose. But they do be terrible bad." Her face cleared and she offered, "She's happy enough here with my four, though."

"She's a charming child." Her brow was clouded with the thought of Megan's suffering nightmares. It was, as Lettie said, only natural, however.

"Yes. She talks about you all the time, and we've tried to teach her to say 'Your Ladyship,' but she do insist on calling you 'My Lovely.' It's like she thinks she owns you, and feels that Hal and me are the ones addressing you wrongly." She sighed. "I do be that sorry."

"Oh, never be sorry for that, Lettie." Elise's smile was wistful. "In truth, she does own a part of my heart." She looked down and smoothed out the wrinkles that holding the child had put in the lap of her riding habit. When she lifted her head again, she spoke briskly. "Is the money I sent you enough to defray her expenses?"

Lettie refused to pretend. "You know it is, milady. That and a lot more."

Elise asked quickly, before the proud woman could try to reduce the sum Elise had set, "Now then, where is your good husband, Lettie? I would speak with him."

Lettie looked surprised, then frowned. "Why, Hal be at the mine, Your Ladyship. He be working through the night now. All night."

"All night!"

"Yes, milady. Lots of the men be working at night. Sir James says there's no reason the mine can't be worked around the clock." Her voice was full of resignation.

"But why?"

"Sir James says working the mine night and day

will double production. Lord knows he isn't the first to do it.

"At least them that works at night sees a bit o' the sun unlike them miners that never sees the light o' day." Lettie sighed. "I reckon it don't make no difference. Once you leave the surface, it's surely no darker down there at night than 'tis in the daytime."

Elise fought down the shudder that always accompanied the mere thought of going down into the blackness of a mine. Her tone guarded, she asked, "But Hal doesn't work both night *and* day, does he?"

"Oh, no, milady."

Elise relaxed. At least Sir James wasn't driving his men altogether like slaves. That was a relief. She didn't need yet another complaint to add to the list of those she had against her friend.

"If you want me to, I can tell Hal to come to you when he gets home."

"No, Lettie. Of course not. It's far easier for me to ride over here than for Hal to walk all that way just to answer questions for me. If you tell me when he gets out of the mine, I can meet him and walk back here with him. That way I can have the answers to my questions without taking time from you and the children."

Lettie beamed. "You be so thoughtful of all of us, Your Ladyship. We all feel—"

"Look!" Megan rushed in, heaven-sent, to save Elise embarrassment. "Look, Lettie! Just *see* how many sweets there are." She held up a sizable bag, her eyes shining. "Why, I can give some to all the children in all the cottages!"

"Which is no doubt what her ladyship had in mind, Meggie," Lettie Lime said softly.

Elise laughed. "Why, no. But what a generous thing you are planning to do, Megan. Next time, I shall bring even more."

Megan, suddenly shy, said, "It's really enough if you just come yourself, My Lovely." Her voice dropped to a whisper. "Please come again soon."

Elise stood abruptly. "I must go." Her voice was husky, her eyes suspiciously bright. Her gaze locked on the tiny girl.

Lettie put an arm around the child. Megan leaned back against her and smiled up at Elise, the bag of sweets clutched in her arms.

Elise reached out and touched Megan's blond hair. "Truly, I shall come again soon. I shall see you tomorrow." She lightened her tone and teased, "But I doubt that I'll have time to go get more sweets."

"Just you come, please, My Lovely."

Elise and Lettie laughed. "Yes, I shall, I promise."

"I'll go get Willem and Columbine for you," Megan said, barely touching the cobblestones as she ran.

Elise turned back to Lettie, feeling oddly bereft.

Lettie watched her with eyes that saw too much, her expression sympathetic. She said quietly, "The men get out of the mine at six in the morning, Your Ladyship."

"Thank you, Lettie." Elise drew her gloves on. "I'll be sure to bring Hal straight home."

As Elise disappeared out of the cobblestoned alley, Lettie sighed, sure that she should have shared with

Lady Elise the extent of her worries over Megan's nightmares.

Night after night the child cried out such troubling things, but could never recall the bad dream well enough to answer questions about it. Surely the dear mite ought to be able to recall something of what frightened her so?

She sighed again, this time deeply enough that little Bobby clung all the harder, and, finally, nuzzled his face into her neck.

Lettie hugged him tight. She wished with all her heart that she'd told her ladyship all about Megan's dreams.

Chapter Four

❧

Well before six, Elise was waiting a short distance from the mine entrance. Columbine shifted under her now and again, but on the whole was being amazingly patient for a thoroughbred. Elise smoothed her gloved hand down the mare's satiny neck to calm her and watched for the men to come up out of the mine.

The cavelike entrance to the shaft was lit on either side by huge torches. Their flames, never quite able to alleviate the blackness just inside the entrance, were beginning to pale in the strengthening light of dawn.

Near the mouth of the mine, the pair of horses that turned the gin—the huge horizontal wheel that wound and unwound the ropes running to the pulleys in the roof of the mine shaft—were asleep in their harness, shaggy heads hanging. A man in colorless, tattered clothing was even now approaching the weary animals to prod them round and round to lift the first of the miners who had worked the night shift up out of the dark maw of the mine.

At last the horses powering the gin began plodding their patient circle. The thick rope by which the men were lifted from the lower galleries of the mine creaked in the pulleys. Finally the men, closely grouped, came into sight. For all the world like bunches of grapes, Elise thought.

The men sitting in the loops of the coal-blackened rope were almost as black themselves. Rivulets of sweat from the heat in the lower levels of the mine made bizarre patterns through the thick dust on their faces.

Suddenly, without warning, a tingle shot through Elise. Startled, she looked sharply at the men. *He* was there. Taller, straighter, more commanding than any of the men around him, the stranger from that day at the inn walked confidently out of the mine.

She was too far away to truly identify him, even if he hadn't been as disguised as the others by a night's work in the stifling filth of the coal mine—but she knew him. She knew him by some sharp, inner awareness she'd never felt before.

His face was turned toward her. Though she couldn't see his eyes at such a distance, she knew from the sensations that flooded her that his gaze was fixed on her. As the distance between them closed, his steady regard never wavered.

She could still feel the tingling. The strength of her own response to the man—a man whose very name was unknown to her—frightened her. For the first time in her life, Lady Elise Heatherington Danforth had to fight the urge to turn tail and run.

And fight it she did. She sat quietly on her mare and met his gaze, her chin imperiously lifted. Centuries of breeding gave her the control she needed at the moment when her heart was pounding so strongly she was afraid her chest heaved.

She was aware of no one but him. Steadily he came toward her, covering the ground in long easy strides.

She forced herself to look away from him with an effort. As she did, she gave her attention to the man at his side and cold common sense reasserted itself. She'd come to speak with Hal Lime, and there he was—leading the stranger toward her.

She fastened her gaze on Hal's face and forced a casual smile she was far from feeling. Every sense was alive with awareness of the tall, silent stranger. She had to strive not to look at him.

"Hal, how are you?" She smiled down at her friend.

"I'm well, milady." He touched his cap. "I hope you be the same." His eyes clearly told her that he knew she wanted to talk with him. No doubt Lettie had given him her message. They also said that the stranger's presence was a hindrance.

"I'm fine, thank you." She glanced toward the stranger, then returned her regard to Hal. Her own eyes asked a question. Hal shrugged slightly, and she realized he wasn't sure the man at his side could be trusted.

Elise felt a sharp pang of disappointment. The broad-shouldered man with the commanding air could have been the perfect replacement for Ethan Frost. Until this moment, she hadn't known that was in the back of her mind. Now that she knew, she still hoped he'd prove trustworthy, and that she and Hal could persuade him to replace Frost.

Heaven knew he was *arrogant* enough to stand up

to the mine owners. With startling clarity she recalled how he'd tossed Squire Jepson's reins at him that day in front of the inn . . . how he'd handled Lord Effers's whip. What a spokesman he would make! Nothing could come of that idea, though, if Hal weren't sure he could be fully trusted.

She offered the excuse she had neatly planned for just such a situation. Lightly touching the large wicker hamper that hung from her saddle, she said, "I've brought pasties for your family's breakfast, and I promised your wife I'd see to it that you didn't loiter on your way home."

Hal understood immediately and grinned. Lady Elise intended to talk to him at his house now that Ashe was in the way.

Both men walked along beside her mare. Hal at Columbine's shoulder, the stranger on the other side. She had to work at ignoring the stranger's stare.

"Megan is very special, isn't she, Hal?" The tenderness she always felt when she thought of the child touched her and her face softened. For just an instant, she forgot the stranger.

"Ah, she do be a cunning little thing." Hal laughed.

Adrian hadn't expected Viscountess Danforth to be soft on a child who lived at Hal Lime's house. Most ladies of Quality were indifferent to the children of the poor. For that matter, none of them conversed this easily with their inferiors, either.

His cool gaze rested speculatively on Lady Elise for a long moment. He let it linger on the alabaster skin of her face and idly wondered if it were as soft as the silk it resembled. He forgot his cynical observations as his fingers itched to touch her face.

Elise felt his regard. It was almost like a hand caressing her cheek. Startled by the sensation, she shot him a reproving glance.

The stranger laughed briefly, his strong white teeth flashing in the coal-dust-marred tan of his face. He regarded her with mocking eyes.

Elise felt her hand tighten on her whip. The man was insolent. No man had the right to look at her as boldly as this one was looking, not even the men of her own class. Her mind supplied, unbidden, *much less a miner*. At that piece of snobbery, she felt a hot flush of contrition.

Hal Lime, sensing the tension between his new friend and Lady Elise offered uncomfortably, "This here is Adrian Ashe, Your Ladyship. He started work in the mine yesterday. Sir James asked me to get him settled in the house"—his gaze became intent, carrying a special meaning—"two doors down from my own."

Elise paled as the significance of Hal's pause hit her. The house two doors down from his was the house in which the widower Ethan Frost had lived with his daughter, Megan. She was all but overwhelmed by an unreasonable resistance to the idea of this insolent man taking over kindly Ethan Frost's house. She turned toward him for the second time and acknowledged Hal's introduction stiffly, "How do you do, Ashe."

Adrian felt a prickle of annoyance as he noted the

absence of even a polite "mister." "Fine, thank you, *Lady* Elise."

She was startled at the emphasis he placed on her title. Whatever did he mean by doing it? But why should she care? She had more important things on her mind.

Ignoring him—or at least pretending to—she went on to talk with Hal. She hoped Ashe *would* feel left out, bad manners on her part or not, as she said to Hal, "We must find someone to take Ethan's place, Hal."

Hal hesitated a fraction of a second, his eyes deeply troubled. The next instant he took a deep, steadying breath and said, "I could."

"No!" She said it more sharply than she'd intended to, then smiled apologetically. "No," she said softly, "not you, Hal."

"But . . ."

"You have your family to think of."

He started to say something, but Elise cut him off. "No. There is never going to be another Megan Frost if I can help it. Never." Her face was stark with the thought of what her crusade had cost the child. "I must insist that the man we find have no family." She pressed her lips firmly together to still their trembling and turned huge green eyes to him. "I couldn't bear it any other way."

Adrian saw the strain in Elise's face. Immediately he wondered what Frost had meant to her. Had she had a *tendre* for the miner?

He permitted himself a half smile. If she had been intimate with the deceased Frost, she wouldn't be the

first highborn lady who'd amused herself by dally-
ing with her social inferiors. He had cynical personal
memories on that score. Hadn't half the gentlewomen
he'd found it so easy to seduce told him that his
being a common seaman had added greatly to their
excitement?

At that remembrance, his eyes narrowed and became hard, but his gaze never left the mounted
woman's face. Inattentive to the twists in the path, he
stumbled. He recovered himself with easy grace and
went on, his jaw set in annoyance.

Elise, her pulses quickened by his scrutiny in spite
of her best efforts to remain indifferent, laughed an
abrupt, nervous laugh. Then, irritated that she'd let
laughter be startled from her, Elise told Ashe in a
scathing tone, "Perhaps you would fare better if from
now on you watched where you were putting your
feet, Ashe."

Shocked, Hal Lime looked from one to the other.
He'd never heard Lady Elise waspish before.

Stung, Adrian did watch where he was walking
from then on. His teeth felt as if they would shatter if
he stumbled again, he had them clenched so hard.

Elise settled back in the Limes' only chair and
sighed. "Another living in Ethan's house so soon. It
doesn't seem right, somehow." Her voice was soft
with memories of her friend.

"It do be hard, milady." Hal's voice was troubled.
"Though he seems a right sort, it still be hard." If
she'd been of his class, he would have touched her

shoulder to comfort her, but she wasn't. He slipped his arm around his wife instead.

Lettie slid a few inches down the bench they shared to be even closer to Hal and said, "Ethan was a fine man, milady. We all know that you set great store by him."

"Yes. He *was* a fine man, Lettie. We became good friends while we decided what to do about conditions in the mines. I shall miss him as dreadfully as all of *you* do."

Lettie rose and went over to the curtained area that was her kitchen. She changed the subject. "Ye've brought so much to eat, Lady Elise." She smiled at the stuffed basket. "Even Willem will be full for once."

"*Hmmm,* Cook always does well by us, doesn't she? Columbine complained all the way over." Elise sent a glance toward the other room of the cottage, then one toward the twisting stairs. "Where are the children?"

Lettie saw the wistful expression in her guest's eyes. "She'll be back for breakfast, never fear. She promised. Wild horses couldn't keep her away. She knows you're coming." Chuckling, she added, "Besides, I sent my girls with her to make sure."

"Speaking of wild horses, Willem must eat before he walks Columbine."

Hal laughed. "That'll put him in a twist, milady. That mare is the one thing that interests him as much as food."

As if brought home by their talking about them, the Limes' daughters threw open the door and clattered into the room. The girls ran over and stopped dead in front of Elise. Quickly they made their curtsies. Sally sniffed the air. "Oooh. Pasties. May I go tell Willem and Megan so's they'll hurry along?"

"Aye," Hal told them. "That do be a good idea. Better get 'em before I eat all the pasties myself."

The two girls squealed, turned and ran from their father's teasing threat. The door slammed behind them.

"They do look forward to the treats you bring, Your Ladyship. I hope you don't mind their manners."

"Not at all. And Hal, you surely know that Cook packed enough pasties for an army." She was still smiling when the door opened again.

Her breath caught in her throat. Silhouetted against the light from the wide alley outside, Elise saw the broad shouldered, slim hipped figure of the stranger.

Megan held tightly to his hand. The child said softly, "Oh." And delight lit her face. "Oh, I'm so glad you're here, My Lovely."

Elise reached out for the tiny girl, but her gaze locked on the stranger's face. The air between them became charged with some odd magic that made her powerless to look away.

Adrian entered the house reluctantly. He was sorry he'd come, sorry he'd let the elfin Megan bring him. With half an ear, he heard the child say, "There was nuffin' in his cupboards, don't you see. I had to bring him home to eat with us. You don't mind, do you, My Lovely?"

The sight of Adrian Ashe standing there in clean work clothes, his ruggedly handsome face scrubbed rosy and drops of water sparkling like diamonds in his thick dark hair, sent a shiver through Elise. As if from far away, she listened to her own gracious reply.

Megan hugged her fiercely around the waist. "I knew you wouldn't mind. You never mind sharing."

With an effort, Elise pulled herself back from the edge of fantasy and looked down. At the sight of the child's shining face, she was herself again, anchored in reality by Megan's adoration. "Of course, dearest. We'll be happy to share breakfast with your new friend."

She wasn't, of course. She had absolutely no wish to welcome Ashe. His presence was going to keep her from talking to Hal. *How very irritating!*

The man across the room seemed to recover from some momentary lapse also. Moving further into the room with a grace curiously inconsistent with his size, he mockingly touched his fingers to his brow—like a servant pulling his forelock to his mistress, Elise thought—and said, "You are most kind, Your Lady-ship. I'm honored."

Elise frowned at the falseness of his humble gesture. His manner and speech were out of place in this simple dwelling. That bothered her enough, but the thing that disturbed her even more was the faint hostility she sensed behind his words.

Hal heard it, too. His expression was puzzled as he told them all, "Very well. Gather 'round. Unless I miss my guess that's the tea her ladyship brought that my missus is brewing, and I, for one, am gonna have mine hot."

"Permit me to move your chair closer, milady," Ashe offered.

Elise nodded and stepped aside for him. She watched his hands, long-fingered and fine, as they clasped the arms of the chair she'd just vacated. She saw the muscles in his shoulders bunch slightly under the rough linen of his shirt as he lifted the heavy chair and placed it effortlessly at the head of the table . . . and chided herself for the helpless interest she was taking in the man.

She seated herself and patted her lap for Megan to sit there. As the child snuggled comfortably, Elise took a deep breath, hugging Megan to her.

Adrian was far from feeling comfortable as the meal progressed. Watching Hal's Lettie, at the moment unencumbered while the youngest of her children napped, was easy. Doing so merely created for him a homey atmosphere that made him glad he'd yielded to Megan's sweet childish insistence that he come. Watching Lady Elise Danforth, though, was a different matter.

One minute he was coolly registering the picture she made, her pale skin luminous in the dimness of the cottage, her hair glowing like banked embers, and the next, he found himself reacting achingly to the way she reminded him of his mother.

His mother had presided like this over *their* table, in circumstances only a little more comfortable than those in which he found himself here and now. Sweetly she had poured tea and graciously offered far less appealing fare than this to those at her table.

Just for a moment in his mind, Elise's graceful hands, pouring the tea she'd so thoughtfully provided, were his mother's hands. Megan was his little sister,

Beth. Then, with a wrench of pain so violent he had to close his eyes against it, he regretted once more that he'd never see his mother or Beth at tea again.

He turned his head away—as much to hide the agony in his eyes as to avoid the faint curiosity in Elise's.

"Are you all right, Mr. Ashe?" It was the child, Megan Frost, who asked, but when he looked up it was the eyes of the woman in whose lap she sat that caught and held his own. Green as emeralds, they pierced to his very soul with their combination of compassion and curiosity.

He was startled by the strength of the resentment that gaze brought him. He wasn't an object about which she could be curious, and he sure as blazes didn't need her pity. Forcing a smile, he told the child, "I'm fine, little one."

She bristled instantly. "I'm not a little one. I am almost seven."

"My most abject apologies." He rose for an instant in a half bow. "Please say you will forgive me."

That sent her off into gales of laughter, and she slipped down off Elise's lap to run to him and throw her arms around his neck. "You're so silly. You make me laugh."

"Do I, Princess?" He heard his own voice, and it was breathless. Breathless with the pain she brought him because, laughing, she was so like his beloved little sister.

At the edge of his vision, he saw Elise look his way again. Again something passed between them, something with the strength of a tidal surge.

With an almost superhuman effort, Adrian called up all the barriers he'd built to hide his feelings for the past six years. He looked directly into her glorious eyes from behind those barriers. The icy disdain he offered her in return for her concern had the effect he desired.

Elise, oddly saddened, turned away.

Chapter Five

໑

Elise tried not to think of him on her way home, but the memory of his stormy gray eyes was strong in her. Over and over she saw them, mocking, taunting, challenging her.

Irritably, she wondered why. What had she done, or what did he know of her that made him look at her as if she were an adversary?

The puzzle fascinated her. So, she admitted, did the man. And she had neither the time for nor the intention of being distracted by a man. Shaking her head as if the physical abruptness of doing so would toss Adrian Ashe out of her thoughts, she turned her mind to other things.

Deverill and Sir James were coming for dinner.

She wanted to try once more to get them to share her plans. They were the only two for whom she had any hope. Deverill for all his devil-may-care airs was a thoughtful person, and Sir James . . . well, Sir James was blazingly intelligent. Surely she could at least get them to understand her concerns.

The matter of the condition of the timbers shoring up the lower galleries of Deverill's mine was, to her, the gravest. Then there was the knee-deep water, still rising in the lower galleries of the Tate mine, that men stood in to harvest the coal. In addition, one of the men from Effers's mine had reported that, in some of the galleries in which the veins of black riches had disappeared they'd been ordered to take the coal out of the support pillars. The pillars that were previously mined around and left to hold up the roof.

Dearest God! Her concern was as a prayer. Didn't Effers realize that if the pillars were reduced drastically in size, the ceiling of the room could collapse, burying the men who worked there under tons of rock and coal? He'd never listen to her, but if she could convince one of her dinner guests to speak to him, then perhaps . . .

She put all that out of her head—time enough to fret about that tonight—and got back to her most pressing problem. She still had no one to speak up for the miners. Even if Dev or Sir James would do it for her this one time, she was almost certain they'd refuse in the future. Perhaps the stranger . . . No, she could no longer think of him that way, she knew his name now. Ashe, Adrian Ashe.

Adrian Ashe. It almost had the ring of a gentleman about it. Could that be the reason he'd learned so well to ape the manners of his betters? For he certainly had. Even in the brief time she'd spent at the Limes' table with him, she'd been acutely aware that he was curiously well mannered.

In her mind's eye she saw him there again, broad shouldered and handsome, totally confident, his smile easy. No, she corrected. His smile was easy for the Limes and their children, but strangely tight when he

smiled at Megan—for all that she had been the one
who'd invited him into their group—and nonexistent
for her.

"Oh, botheration!" Impatiently, she sent her mare
into a gallop. The sooner she was at home in her bath
the sooner she'd stop this foolish speculating about
Adrian Ashe.

Back at the Limes' Adrian offered his tobacco
pouch to Hal. "A smoke seems in order before a man
tries to sleep through the daylight hours, don't you
agree?"

Hal eyed the smooth leather pouch avidly. Smiling,
he said, "It's been long weeks since I've had a pull at
me pipe. I'll be thanking you as soon as I find my old
faithful."

Before he could rise, Lettie brought it to him and
pressed it into his hand, her eyes gentle. "Here be your
'old faithful,' Husband." She turned to Ashe. "Thankee,
Mr. Ashe. 'Tis kind of you to share with my Hal, tobacco being so dear an' all."

Adrian understood. The memory of forgoing every
luxury to feed his little family had never gone from his
mind. "I'm happy to do so, Mrs. Lime."

"Lettie." She blushed a little and added, "It's Lettie
to our friends."

Warmed to be included as a friend, Adrian told her,
"And I'm Adrian to mine."

Hal grinned. "She'll never manage it." He knew his
Lettie, and he knew this man would never hear her call
him by his first name. It was as plain as the nose on his
face that Ashe was a cut or two above them. His Lettie

wasn't blind. He looked over at her fondly. She could see it clear as day. Adrian Ashe, miner or no, was Quality. The wonder of it was that Lady Elise didn't seem to see it as well.

Hal thought about that as he tamped and drew on his pipe, finally puffing a fragrant cloud of smoke around his head. He was more than a little uneasy about the way the air downright crackled between Lady Elise and the big man beside him.

It had been a long while since the viscount had been killed. On cold nights after they'd made love, Lettie and him often lay in each other's arms and wondered how such a kind, warm-natured woman as Lady Elise did without the comforts of the marriage bed. But they knew she did.

None of the five men with whom she ran about the countryside had ever shared her bed. They were certain, for there wasn't a move she made that the servants at her place or the inn or the homes of her neighbors didn't gibble-gabble about every evening. Even on those rare evenings when he and the other miners went to the pub, no one had the slightest thing to tell about Lady Elise Danforth that wasn't to her credit.

Now, though, there was Adrian Ashe. Adrian Ashe, with the mocking eyes that smoldered at her ladyship whenever she looked away from him. Thinking back on the time they'd just spent together, Hal stirred uneasily on the hard wooden bench he shared with Ashe.

He'd seen Lady Elise look away from Ashe many a time, as well. He'd seen because she'd looked *at* Ashe many a time. That made him right uneasy, too, the way she couldn't seem to keep her eyes off the man.

Lady Elise's interest, coupled with the hungering look he saw in Ashe's eyes—well, it just looked like trouble on the way to him, was all. Trouble, and maybe heartbreak.

And him powerless to do a thing about it. Hal sighed a great sigh. He chased it around in his weary brain for another minute before giving it over to prayer. Then he followed Ashe's example and leaned his shoulders back against the rough-plastered wall and closed his eyes to fully enjoy this respite.

Neither man, exhausted by a night of hard labor in the mine, heard Megan, her little nose wrinkled in distaste, whisper to Lettie, "If Hal likes to do that, why doesn't he get his own tobacco?"

Lettie bent down to the child and whispered back very gently, reluctant to share the burden of it, "Because, Meggie dear, we've just not enough pennies in this house to stretch to such as the buying of tobacco."

Her baby chose that moment to awaken and set up a howl, so Lettie didn't notice the thoughtful expression on the child's face. Turning away from Megan, she hurried to the cradle in a corner of the only other downstairs room.

None of them heard Megan, smiling and pensive, whisper brightly to herself, "Willem said they pay *children* pennies to work at the mine."

Dinner at Danforth House was something of a disappointment. Elise sat back in her chair with a heavy sigh.

Sir James and Deverill sat appreciating the picture

she made with her heavy crown of bright auburn hair spilling errant curls down the back of her neck and the emerald silk of her elegant gown seeming to make her pale skin glow above its fashionable décolletage. Both found her a fitting ornament for the opulently furnished dining room.

Appreciation of their hostess was the one thing upon which the two men agreed. Right now, even that agreement wasn't sufficient to keep the evening peaceful.

"Come, come, my dear," Sir James said, "surely you don't expect us to share your passion for mine improvements?" Raising his wineglass to his lips he sipped appreciatively. "Very nice wine, my dear."

"Thank you," Elise said impatiently. Her only desire was to talk about the things that needed to be done to make the mines safer. James knew that. Why wouldn't he cooperate?

Deverill was no better. He'd kept a fulminating glare aimed at Sir James the whole evening. What was the matter between them *this* time?

Finally matters came to a head between the two. Malfont twirled the stem of his wineglass idly in his long fingers, his gaze fixed on Deverill. His words were to Elise, but his attention was all on Deverill.

When finally he spoke, it was in his laziest drawl. "Mine improvements are expensive, m'dear." He shot a heavy-lidded glance at Deverill. "After all, for what you spent on your steam engine, Deverill could have bought six or seven high perch phaetons"—his expression was malicious—"instead of just the one."

"Oh, Dev! You didn't!"

Deverill left off cursing Malfont with his eyes and turned his full attention back to Elise. He was boyishly charming. "Afraid I did, m'dear." Dev's eyes twinkled with mischief. "Man doesn't live by duty alone, you know. Have to have a little fun sometimes."

Malfont, having successfully set the cat among the pigeons, settled back against the ivory brocade of his chair to enjoy the result.

"But, Dev, you promised!" Elise didn't know when she'd been so disappointed. "You *know* the dreadful condition of your mine. Why, you could have bought new shoring timbers and begun—"

"Elise, my love." Deverill spread his hands helplessly. "You see before you a completely perfidious wretch." He grinned disarmingly. "Selfishness continually motivates me, alas." He hung his head.

Malfont snorted.

Elise shot him a quelling look.

Deverill drew her attention. "Will you forgive me if I promise to try to do better?"

"Oh, Dev." Elise shook her head helplessly.

"For God's sake!" Malfont rose and slammed his napkin down beside his plate.

"James!" Elise was shocked.

"Damn it, Elise—" Suddenly he shut his mouth with a snap on whatever he'd been about to say, bowed stiffly, and ground out, "Please forgive my outburst, Lady Elise."

Nothing improved from that point until the two men left.

Chapter Six

❧

Adrian awakened slowly, yawned, and stretched mightily. He'd slept like one of the dead, and he felt as if every muscle in his body was tied in a knot. Exhaustion still reached out to touch the edges of his strength.

Labor in the dark bowels of the earth had none of the invigorating properties of working aloft on a wind-blown sea. As he shook his head to clear the cobwebs, he smiled wryly. "No doubt in your mind as to which you prefer is there, Ashe?" He spoke around another yawn.

Hearing himself speak aloud caused him to smile. Six years in a stinking forecastle with the rest of the crew of whatever ship he'd been forced to serve on had given him this strange desire to talk to himself. He laughed at the urge, recognizing it as ridiculous, then promptly indulged it again, just because he could, shouting, "Hallo, Ashe, you great fool!"

He stretched again then, tightening and relaxing the muscles of his lithe body until he'd got the last of the kinks out. With a scowl, he noticed the darkness of a fleck of coal dust under the thumbnail of his right hand.

"Damn and blast. I thought you'd scrubbed well, Ashe."

No doubt this was going to be a continuing problem. His fastidious soul rebelled. His practical nature told him he'd better get used to it.

He grinned. "I wonder how the glorious Lady Elise would react to a prospective lover with coal dust under his fingernails?" With an even wider grin he leaned back and folded his arms behind his head. Lazily he recalled her image. He saw again how the firelight from the Limes' hearth had struck an echoing flame in her heavy mane of hair. Saw again the light in her magnificent green eyes when she'd looked up and seen the child in the doorway. He took wry pleasure in remembering how those eyes had registered shock, not mere surprise, at seeing him there beside the little girl. She had—

A hammering sounded through the house. His wool-gathering went flying. Someone shouted, "Ashe!" There was more frantic pounding on his door. "Ashe! Wake up!" The voice was Hal Lime's.

"What the devil?" It was too damn early to go to the mine; it was still bright out. Adrian leapt from the bed, thoughts of Elise Danforth scattering like spume in a nor'easter. He yanked on his pants. Thrusting his feet into his heavy work shoes, he clattered down the stairs. At their foot, he ripped open the door and demanded, "What's amiss?"

"It's the child, Megan! No one's seen her since dawn. Lettie's frantic. We need your help."

Megan! The child who reminded him so painfully

of his little Beth. Megan was missing. His jaws clenched against the unexpected stab of pain.

"The sea?" His thoughts shot to the danger he knew best. "Could she have gone down to the sea?" Adrian's heart pounded as if he'd climbed, double time, from the deck to the crow's nest.

He let his breath go in an explosion of relief when Lime answered, "No. No chance of that. The fishermen were there on the beach mending nets today. They'd have seen her, and they didn't."

"Has anyone checked the mines?"

"The mines?" Lime was clearly startled.

"Well," Adrian's voice was savage with impatience, "if she's nowhere else, why the hell haven't you checked the bloody mines?"

Hal Lime wasted no time being offended. "I'll check Effers's. Willem can get into Malfont's; all the men there know him. You take Tate's. You move faster than I do and it's farthest. That ought to do it."

"There are four other mines." Adrian's voice was grim.

"Aye, but Haverford's is guarded, and Deverill's too far away. Her ladyship would sack anybody who let children into her mine, so the tyke can't be there. So would Squire Jepson. His wife would kill him if he used children."

"Very well. How do I get to Tate's?"

"It's half a mile beyond Malfont's. The road's clear to see."

Adrian had thrown on the rest of his clothes as they talked. Urgency driving him like a ship running before a gale, he spun Hal around and growled, "Let's go!"

Running and walking alternately they arrived at Malfont's mine in record time. Shoving the panting Hal toward the short road to Effers's mine entrance, Adrian broke into a run again, going on further to Tate's operation.

He wasted precious breath cursing his lack of a horse, and doubled his speed. The mere thought that the tiny girl might have hired herself out to work in a filthy mine gave him wings.

Arriving at the entrance to Tate's mine, he leaned one hand on a timber brace, and slammed the other hand to the searing stitch in his side. He gasped his question at a man coming out of the darkness. "A girl. A little six-year-old. Have you seen her?"

"Might be I have, mate. We've a few down below."

Biting back curses at the miner's casual attitude, Adrian shouldered past the man and walked on into the mine.

"Hear, now. Ye don't belong in Tate's. Ye be Malfont's man." Now the man cared who went into the mine. He skittered after and around Adrian to attempt to block his way.

Adrian snarled, "I'm my *own* man. And if you know what's good for you, you'll get the hell out of my way." Shoving the man aside, he went deeper into the mine.

"Aye," the miner told the space the stranger had occupied a moment before, "I can see the sense of that. No skin off my nose who goes down this damned hole." He'd raised his voice to try to reach the tall, well-built man, but the stranger was already darting into the right-hand gallery.

Giving it up for a bad job, the miner exited the mine, shaking his head. Outside, he was surprised by the sight of a bright chestnut horse stepping out from behind a shed, its reins trailing along the coal-dust-covered ground.

"Gorblimey," he muttered. "This do be the day for odd things, don't it?" Odd or not, he was too weary to give the matter further thought. He trudged off homeward.

Deep in the mine, Elise held her candle in trembling fingers and contemplated the tunnel that joined the gallery in which she stood with the next one lower down from it. They called these tiny slanting tunnels winzes, she remembered inanely, stalling.

A rough-looking little man wearing nothing but his trousers and boots had stopped his work only long enough to point to this opening when she'd asked if he'd seen a small blond girl. Her unexpected appearance there in the mine had clearly startled him.

Now, he was still throwing uneasy glances her way as he worked, obviously torn by indecision. She knew instinctively she'd better go on before he decided to escort her up out of the mine.

Elise stepped into the entrance of the tunnel he'd indicated. As she did, she took great gulps of air, ignoring the sting of the coal dust that tingled at the back of her throat. She didn't care what she was breathing into her lungs. Megan was in that hole.

Megan of the winsome smile and delighted eyes, her Megan, was somewhere in the bowels of the earth in this tunnel that looked to Elise no bigger than the burrows she sometimes found in her garden. When her gardener had complained about the moles that made them, she'd only felt pity for the poor half-blind things doomed to spend their lives tunneling underground. Now she had a new and frightful appreciation of their existence.

Never had she wanted to go anywhere less than she wanted to go into this winze, but Megan was in there; she knew it. She had to find her. Find her and bring her up out of this terrible heat and darkness. She had to bring her up to the sun and the light and the air.

She was terrified that she would prove unequal to the task.

Before she lost the last ounce of her courage, she began walking into the winze, careful of its downward slope. Before she'd gone a yard, the faint light of her candle showed her a hole a foot or two above the tunneled floor of the winze. Dear God! It was even smaller!

Elise had no choice. She had to investigate it. Megan might be there. With a trembling hand, she hiked up her heavy riding skirt and put a knee up into the opening.

As she shifted her weight to that knee to bring the other up into the mouth of the tunnel, the hair on the back of her head felt as if it stood straight up. Tingling rivulets of sheer terror ran down her spine.

Clenching her teeth so hard she thought she could hear her jaw crack, she inched forward a little. Now she was all the way into the opening. She was committed to searching the tight little tunnel.

Instantly, the full weight of the mine above pressed down on her shoulders, draining every vestige of strength from her limbs.

Closing her eyes, she held herself utterly still. Biting back the whimper that threatened to escape her throat, Elise told herself that her strength was returning.

After a moment, it was true, and she could move again. Forcing herself forward, she crawled down the rock tunnel.

The flame of her candle diminished as she continued along. Diminished as if the walls of this place were *draining* the light away. She refused to think that the flame itself was growing smaller, that lack of sufficient air on which to feed was causing it to die. She told herself that it was an illusion, a trick of the mind.

"Because you are a coward, Elise Danforth." She sought words with which to flagellate herself. Words to strengthen her spirit. Words with which to drive herself onward . . . and to quell the panic rising in her. But after that first accusation, none came. She told herself that she was silent because she hated the way her voice sounded in this confined space.

She refused to believe she was too afraid even to speak.

The scraping of the toes of her fine leather riding boots along the rough rock floor became the only sound in the world. The tapping of the miners' picks in the gallery behind her had ceased as she made her way around a turning.

She was alone at the center of the earth.

Terror swelled in her throat, then closed it. She

gasped for air. Despising the tears that overflowed and coursed down her cheeks, she fought to stop them . . . and failed, loathing herself for her failure.

How she hated this darkness! It was a live thing. An enemy.

It was a malignant force just like the darkness she had felt as a child. That awful darkness that had flooded in from the corners of her nursery when her beloved nanny had gone from her room. Black velvet. Tangible. Cloying.

She could feel the blackness pressing against her face. It whispered against her cheek. It stifled her breath.

She fought to keep herself from thinking of the things that were frightening her. She tried to think of the sunlight and the sea air above. It was no use. If she didn't find Megan soon, she would go mad!

"Megan!" She'd meant to shout, but the word was a quivering whisper. Even so, it reverberated around her here in the womb of the world. Reverberated and confirmed her worst fear—that the tunnel was getting smaller even as she moved forward.

Panic clawed at her, mocking her puny effort to locate the lost child.

Suppose the man who'd told her Megan had gone this way had been wrong? Suppose Megan was not in this tight little tunnel at all?

Suppose when she tried to turn around she got stuck . . . Suppose she . . .

Then, just ahead, she heard a faint sound.

* * *

Far above Elise in the mine, Adrian stopped the first man he saw. Reaching into his pocket, he offered him a coin. "Here. Sell me your lamp."

The man took one look at the gold gleaming dully in Adrian's hand and grinned widely. "Aye. To be sure I will, sir. Have ye no need of me boots?"

Adrian didn't give a damn if the man thought he was daft. His whole being was focused on searching the mine for little Megan. He couldn't bring himself to believe the child could be here, but as long as there was even the slightest chance . . .

Gallery after gallery he searched, plunging through them, questioning men, descending lower and lower. The heat was becoming oppressive. He passed men who worked stripped to the waist, sweat pouring in runnels through the coal dust that begrimed them. He knew that there would be others at lower levels who worked naked in even greater heat, their clothes piled neatly at the entrance to the gallery in which they toiled.

Plunging down a winze that joined this gallery to another below it, he was brought up short. "What?" The word was startled out of him by the sound he heard as he was slithering down past the small mouth of an obscure tunnel. Bending almost double, he strained to see into its darkness. The sound came again. It was like the whimper of a small animal.

What or whoever had made it, they were too far from the entrance at which he stood for him to be able to make them out. They were well out of the range of the candle lamp he wore.

There was nothing else to do; he'd have to crawl in

to check to see what—or who—had made the tiny noise . . . if he could fit! Forcing his shoulders into the hole, he started toward the sound.

After he'd crawled only a few yards into the narrow opening, he heard it again. It *was* a whimper, faintly suppressed as if its source wanted to keep its distress a secret.

Could it be the child? His heart leapt. The very thought caused him to crawl more quickly. His back and shoulders scraped the sides and ceiling of the low tunnel.

Then he heard the whisper. It stopped him dead in his tracks. As he crouched there on his knees, incredulous, it came again, quivering with fear. "Hold tight to my skirt, dearest. I'll get you out, I promise."

Then he heard the breathless little answer, "I know you will, My Lovely." And more faintly, as if she were hanging on to the promise with the last of her courage, "I know you will."

Adrian threw himself forward, lacerating his knees against the unforgiving rock floor, tearing the skin from his hands as he fought to get his large frame through to them.

Them! Them, by all that was holy! He was going after the two of them, and his mind was spinning with the knowledge that one of those voices in the suffocatingly small tunnel before him was that of Lady Elise Danforth.

At last, around a sharp bend in the tunnel, he saw a pale gleam.

"Ah, thank God. A light!" Her voice was barely

recognizable, no more than a fear-filled thread of sound.

Elise, her eyes so large they seemed to fill her face, struggled toward him out of stygian blackness. Her hair had escaped its bindings and fell around her in a welter of unruly curls. The rich gleam of them was dimly visible even here in the dark depths of the earth.

Her voice shook as she asked him, "Are we far from the end?" Her tone was that of a pleading child, the hand she held out toward him had a tremor. "Have we a very long distance left to go?"

He could see that her eyes glittered with tears of fright. She was hanging on to her courage for all she was worth. If she hadn't had the child, he had no doubt that she would have broken down before now. He'd have gone to her, but the tunnel had gotten too small for him to move any farther forward.

His voice rough with raw concern he growled, "Why the devil haven't you a light?"

"Oh! It's you." Recognizing his voice seemed to strengthen her own.

The fact that she had known him, even without being able to discern his face, filled him with an odd elation. Still he demanded, "Your light. Don't tell me you came here without a light."

"Of course, I didn't." The frantic pounding of her heart slowed a little. The relief evident in her voice a moment ago gave way to irritation. "No one but a fool would come down here without a lamp."

"And yours?" he goaded her. He was enjoying the way her eyes glinted now with anger at him. By the feeble light of his candle, he could see the terror draining from their emerald depths. Seeing her spirit returning thrilled him. Damn it, he had to admit it, he was relieved.

Elise was relieved, too. She was more than happy to have him here with her. His large, competent presence gave her a feeling of security that she had lost aeons ago down here in the mine.

She felt as if she had been crawling through the tunnel for years with staring eyes that could not see. The knowledge that she had a precious child to get to safety had been all that had kept her going.

Just minutes ago she'd been afraid she would lose her grasp on reality. Fantasy had reached for her. Horrible fantasy like that of the nightmares children had of running up and up unending flights of stairs with something unspeakable in pursuit. This horror, though, had been of the rock walls around her ... growing closer and closer ... of the end of the passage sealing itself off, and the rock invading her very flesh.

She shuddered.

Now that Ashe was here, she could think again, admit terrors again.

It had taken almost all her courage to hide her mare and slip unnoticed into the Tate mine. She'd known she'd had to do it. She was driven by the hope that she would find Megan before something awful happened to her.

Since the death of her husband and the men who'd accompanied him on his inspection tour of their own mine, it was beyond her power not to fear the worst from any of them. Only her dear Megan could have lured her into one. Her thoughts, kept at bay until now, tumbled chaotically through her mind.

The most bitter enemy she'd had to face was the fear that she could be leading Megan deeper and deeper into the mine. Fear that she might be taking the child she'd come to rescue farther and farther away from the entrance with every tortuous inch she crawled had almost overwhelmed her.

She'd even come to mistrust the fact that she knew she was going back the way she had come, the fact that there was no other way *to* go. She'd been grateful that she'd been able to find the child. Now, she thanked God even more fervently that someone had found *her*!

Elise was quite beyond pretending to any more bravery. Her nerve had all but broken under the terrible weight of the dark and the tons and tons of earth and rock pressing down on her. Pressing down with incalculable strength on her shoulders. Seeking to crush her into oblivion.

If she hadn't had to be brave for Megan, she would have given up and stopped. Stopped and curled up into a ball and lain where she was, sobbing.

Megan had been her reason for descending into this fearful hole in the ground. Megan was her reason for trying to stay sane enough to get out of it, but her jaws ached with the strain of holding back the fear-filled cries that clogged her throat.

She was grateful beyond words for the large stranger crawling backward in front of her, lighting her way. After her seemingly endless sojourn in pitch-blackness, his candle looked as bright and as welcome as the beacon of a lighthouse. It was infinitely precious.

"Can't you hurry?" She tried hard to sound calm but her words were so strained she sounded peevish. That almost pushed her over the brink into hysteria.

How in heaven's name could she sound peevish? Inside she was ravingly elated that he was there. That he had come. He was a god to her. A kindly, merciful god who'd come down into her personal hell to grant her one more chance at life. At light and air.

Out, she only wanted to get out of this living, underground hell. Out to the light and the sun and the breeze that swept in from the clean, clean shining sea.

Completely unaware of her state, her rescuer was answering her. "I probably could go faster," he told her steely-eyed, "if I were able to turn around." With deliberate cruelty he asked, "Would you like me to try?"

Instantly he regretted his evil impulse. His heart twisted to see terror leap to her eyes.

"No! No! Don't try to turn. Oh, please don't. You might get stuck—" Fear stopped her voice as abruptly as if someone had slapped a hand over her mouth.

Adrian felt like a beast. Silently he cursed himself. Who was he to let his bitterness for her class, his own class, bring him to so frighten a helpless woman? A woman who'd come down into this hellhole in search of a wayward child?

When he spoke again his voice was gentle. "We haven't far to go," he told her. "You're safe with me. I shall get you both out of here." His voice deepened with sincerity as he swore to her, "I give you my word."

Elise was unable to answer. Her throat closed and her eyes filled with tears. Still, after a moment, she managed to whisper to the child behind her, "There, Megan. You see. We are quite safe. Your Mr. Ashe has come for us."

Then she cried out, "Oh!" Having taken her concentration off the task of watching how she crawled on her heavy riding skirt, she tripped herself as its tough folds pulled tight between one knee and the other. She pitched violently forward.

Adrian reached out to steady her. At his touch, something leapt between them. Something like St. Elmo's fire running from mast to spar at sea. Startled, he pulled back. When he did, he slammed his head against the ceiling.

The candle lamp he wore was knocked askew by the force with which his head struck the solid rock above them. He heard Elise gasp in fear.

Dizzy from his own stupidity, but vividly aware of her panic, he reached up a hand to steady the light. He managed to burn his fingers for his trouble. "Damn it!"

But he had saved the light.

"That's not a very nice thing to say in front of My Lovely, you know, Mr. Ashe." Megan's voice was small and muffled slightly by her position behind Elise, but Adrian got the message and was amused. Even down here, with her beautiful, self-appointed guardian falling to pieces as she rescued her, the child was still completely herself.

He answered her without a pause in his backward

scraping along the tunnel. "Quite right, Mistress Megan." Then, to please the child more than to pacify the noblewoman, "I do apologize, Lady Elise."

Elise made a small sound that told him she was barely aware of the exchange, and he looked at her closely. Tears ran down her cheeks. Her breath was coming in tight, short gasps. It was obvious to him that she was very close to hysteria.

Instantly, he dropped flat and began to push himself backward up the slight incline as quickly as he could. This way, he knew he would be less threatening to her. With him flat on his belly, the tunnel wouldn't seem so filled with his bulk. He watched her in the dim radiance of his candle and saw that he had guessed correctly. Lady Elise's eyes lost some of the wildness he'd seen in them.

An instant later, he felt the toe of his work boot drop and knew they were at the end of the tunnel. They'd reached the winze that joined the gallery he'd left to the lower gallery he'd been about to search when he'd heard Elise whimper.

Shooting out into the taller passage, he stood and reached back into the tunnel for the woman. He had to pull her out by one hand, for, while her strength had deserted her to the point that she could no longer help herself, she still kept her death grip on the child she'd come to find.

Pulling her tightly up against him, he held her there, quivering, in the circle of one arm while he reached back into the tunnel for Megan. As he did, he became acutely aware of Elise's softness. And the scent of her. A strange tenderness flooded him.

Elise melted against him, burying her face against his shirt. She closed her eyes as tightly as she could, willing herself to believe they were already on the surface, already out of this horrible tomb. She clung to him more tightly than she'd ever embraced another living being, not caring what he thought, not caring what *anybody* might think, only knowing that without him, something in her would have died down in that utter darkness.

A part of her mind cried out for her to move away from this stranger, to stand on her own two feet—that she was safe now. But she'd been too long in this place that fashioned her nightmares. She wasn't strong enough yet. Had Adrian Ashe been the devil himself, she wouldn't have let go of him.

Adrian's breath caught at the sensations that shot through him to feel Elise cling trustingly in his embrace. His senses reeled as her body fitted itself flawlessly into the contours of his own.

The purely masculine urge to give her the ultimate comfort surged through him so strongly that he was lightheaded. If the child hadn't been there, no power on earth could have stopped him from taking Elise. There. Right there on the rough tunnel floor. Nothing would have stopped him from comforting her with his body until she forgot her fears, forgot everything but him, and the passion he knew would take them to the stars . . . no matter where they lay in reality.

Hoarsely, he spoke to the child, fighting with all his strength merely to hold her friend safely in his embrace. "Are you all right, Megan?"

"Yes, thank you. My Lovely was taking very good care of me."

Adrian tightened his arm around Elise and scooped Megan up in the other. "I think it's time I got you both out of here, don't you?"

"Yes," Megan assured him gravely, her expression solemn. "I think My Lovely is all wore out. We need to get her home to her bed."

Under other circumstances, he might have laughed, might even, in his rough disguise, have whooped with laughter, but not now. Elise was clinging to him like a child, and the tenderness he felt for her at this moment outweighed all the bitterness that had grown in him the past few years.

His need to keep her safe almost overwhelmed him. All he could think of was getting her out of the mine. To the surface. She needed fresh air. But most of all, he sensed, she needed light . . . and freedom.

He threw Megan onto his back where she held on like a little monkey and scooped Elise up into his arms. Only the child noticed the startled looks thrown their way as Adrian carried them through and out of the mine.

Chapter Seven

✧

Outside in the air, in the blessed sweet clean breeze that blew in from the sea, Elise clung to Adrian and drew great breaths into her lungs.

Adrian held her close and braced himself against the urge to bury his face in her hair as it took fire and flamed in the clear light of the westering sun.

Megan squirmed down and told him matter-of-factly, "I have to go to Lettie and Hal. They'll be worried. Will you please take My Lovely home?"

He nodded, not trusting himself to speak.

With that Megan was satisfied. She walked away, her determined little strides taking her quickly out of the secluded, sheltered cove to which he'd brought them.

Adrian watched her go and wondered at the strength of the feelings that held him motionless, cradling Elise in his arms and letting the child go.

Elise stirred as if beginning to awake from a dream, and looked up at him with eyes still shadowed by the remnants of the terror she'd felt in the mine. Her voice was tremulous. "Will she be safe?"

"She's safe. Half the countryside is out looking for her." *Dear God.* An odd tenderness flooded him. He was overcome by wonder. *In spite of her terrible ordeal, she could still think of the child.* Admiration for her blossomed in him.

Elise shuddered, and he knew she was remembering the mine. He pressed his lips to her forehead, consoling her, and his body tightened. "Tell me about it. Talking about it will help."

She didn't question his firm command of the moment, she was just grateful he had it. She spoke. Haltingly, and with her eyes widening as she remembered, she told him, "As I came back from the village, one of the miners told me Megan was missing. That she"—she shuddered hard—"that she was probably down in one of the mines."

Adrian stroked her hair. Quiet. Waiting.

"I . . . I hate the mines. They frighten me so badly I can hardly function when I'm in one." She looked up at him, willing him to understand. Her lovely eyes clouded. "My husband died in our mine. He was killed in a cave-in."

Tears came. She buried her face against his chest again as if to hide them from him. Her words were muffled. "And mines are . . . so dark."

He felt the tremors that racked her as she remembered and tightened his embrace. His pulse quickened.

Elise's arms went around his neck, and she clutched him closer. There was no question of man and woman in her mind, she was a child again—a frightened child—who needed desperately to hold on to the strength of him. To the strength that had carried her from her nightmare, out of hell to this lovely place beside the sea.

Adrian's blood began to sing through his veins. As she pressed herself against him, his body flamed into aching desire. He smoothed a hand down her back, drawing her closer, inadvertently easing his own need while he kissed her hair and sought to meet her need for comfort. "Yes. Mines are dark."

Elise rubbed her cheek against his shirt, liking the way his deep voice rumbled in his chest. She was taking comfort from his strength, finding her way back to life by it. Shivering uncontrollably, she whispered, "I felt *entombed* down there."

He made an inarticulate sound of sympathy and lifted her in his arms. Easily he carried her to a grassy spot against the foot of a low cliff. There the warmth the living rock had stolen from the sun all day could help him restore Elise. He sat with her still in his arms, his back against the rock wall and Elise in his lap, engulfed in his embrace, sheltered by the sun-warmed cliff face.

She remained lost in her nightmare, wanting nothing more than to hang on his strength and talk out her fears. Her head rested on his shoulder now, as she was taller in his lap. With her face turned up to his, her breath feathered his throat lightly. Combined with the wonderful scent of her hair, it nearly drove him over the edge.

He reminded himself that he'd brought her here to help her through this. To help her to regain her usual confidence. To enable her to return to her home, to her own world.

Commanding his body to behave, he prompted her, "So you went to Tate's mine to look for her."

"Yes." Another tremor passed through her.

The slight movement sent him into torment.

"I still had Columbine, my mare, under me, and she was still fresh. So there was no need to delay." She looked up at him again, her emerald eyes as wide and trusting as a child's. "Tate's was farthest. I thought it best to start there and work my way back home as I was certain my courage would desert me more and more as I went from mine to mine."

Fear surged to the back of her eyes. They filled with tears. "Only . . . I . . . I would never have made it to another mine." Her slender hands grabbed the collar of his shirt. "Megan might have been lost forever if I'd failed her, if I'd not found her in the first mine. I'd never have been able to go on to another. My courage deserted me long before I found her at Tate's." Panic welled up in her. "I'd have lost her!"

"No," he soothed. "No, don't think about it, you did find her." Admiration for her pluck grew in him. "With or without your courage, you went on to find her. You brought her out."

"But . . ."

"No." Now wasn't the time to remind the shaking girl that others would surely have found the child if she hadn't. This was her triumph, her own incredible triumph over her fear, and he wanted her to know that.

He kissed her forehead again and told her firmly, staying her self-recriminations, "You did find her." He pressed his cheek to the glory of her hair, inhaling its sweet fragrance. "And if you hadn't found her at Tate's, you would have gone on until you did."

She shook her head wildly, denying.

Her hair fell in a shining mantle down to her waist and tossed around him like a wave. The sun caught it in a million flaming fingers.

Adrian's chest hurt with the effort to draw air into his lungs.

"You would have found her," he told her breathlessly. "And if you hadn't, someone else would have." He said it in an effort to restore his own objectivity, not thinking beyond that.

"Ah!" It was a cry of fear.

His arms spasmed tighter in response to it.

"Then *I* would have been left down there," she cried, and threw her arms around his neck. Her lips were mere inches from his own as she poured out her terror. "I would be there still searching. Searching in the dark."

Panic made her emerald eyes the green of a forest at twilight. "I . . . I dropped my c-candle, you know. And Megan didn't have one. Ah, God! They told her she didn't need a candle. She said they told her to f-feel her way from gallery to gallery down that dark, airless tunnel."

Her hands dug into his shoulders, lifting her frightened face even nearer his. Their lips were a scant inch apart. "I was so afraid." She breathed against him.

It was too much for him. With a groan, he lowered his head and claimed her mouth.

She responded with a desperation that clearly told him how near she thought she'd come to losing her life. Clinging, pressing, she reached out for the warmth and wonder of him, the warmth and wonder that one human could draw from another. She snatched at the comfort offered by this man who had been a god to her in the bowels of the earth.

Ravenously, hunger for her stole the last vestiges of Adrian's control. His mind filled with his need to comfort her, to possess her. He'd wanted her from the first moment he'd seen her, a veritable goddess sitting coolly on her horse there in the dusty village street. And the wanting had grown steadily each time he saw her, until, now, it overwhelmed his control. His blood sang, hot, through his veins and the clamor of his need drowned out everything else.

He was glad he'd brought her here to recover. This cove was the one he'd found to use daily for bathing, to swim away the coal dust and grit from the mine in privacy. He knew no one could see them here, no one would come to interrupt.

Wild elation swept through him as he felt her respond to his kiss. Something in her seemed to give way, and she turned more fully toward him. Her breath quickening, she slipped her hands under his shirt to feel the vital warmth of him. Her lips parted under the insistence of his kiss as she surrendered to him. Her arms going tightly around to his back, she pressed her breasts against his chest. Her mouth opened under his kiss, and she moaned softly into his mouth.

The movement of her turning in his lap drew a response from his body that was wonderfully painful. He groaned and deepened the kiss, his hands clutching her closer.

Elise felt her fears evaporate in the heat of his embrace. Passion awakened in her and sent her head spinning. His mouth was delicious. Demanding, firm, his lips plundered her own, taking her breath, stealing her very soul.

Comfort enfolded her, she was safe. She was here in his arms, far from the blackness of the mine, out in the sun and the fresh air from the sea. She was wanton with the relief of it.

Her breasts ached, and she pressed them harder into his chest. Desire rose in her. Hunger long denied stole away all thought. Returning his kisses, answering the urgency of his tongue with her own, she could hear herself moaning with the desire that was raging through her.

Adrian felt as if he were losing all control. As if he'd become a creature with but one thought, one purpose. He must possess this flame-haired goddess or die.

Twisting his body, he turned so that she lay on the soft grass under him. His mouth never left hers. His body roared its need as he felt her arms tighten while they moved, holding him close, seeking from him the very thing he most wanted to give her. He went up in flames.

She moaned softly as his hand moved up to rest lightly on her hip . . . then her thigh. She made an involuntary little move toward him, lifting to meet him where he lay across her.

He felt the fullness of her breasts against his chest, and knew he'd die if he never touched them. Removing his hand from the curve of her thigh, he unbuttoned her riding jacket, one slow button at a time. While he did, he opened his eyes to see her face.

Somehow she sensed it, and opened her own. Passion-glazed gazes locked and held as he slipped his hand into her shirt. He skimmed his fingers lightly down her alabaster skin to touch the silken swell of her breast. His fingers reached for and found the rose-tinted peak.

Elise's glorious eyes closed in ecstasy as he lowered his mouth . . .

Velvet softness caressed the back of his neck, warm breath flowed around it. Lost in his passion, he—

A piercing whinny shattered the stillness, ending the moment. With a surprised curse, Adrian leapt to his feet to stare at the chestnut mare that had picked her way down to the cove by following the scent of her mistress . . . and nuzzled the back of his neck!

Columbine stared back. Curious. Cautious. She didn't recognize this man. He didn't smell deliciously of the stable, anyway. Immediately she lost interest in him.

She gave another demanding whinny. It was late. It was time for her rider to get up and take her back to the stable for her oats. She shouldered past the man and dropped her head to nudge her mistress.

Elise regarded her mount with dazed eyes. "Wha-what in the world? Columbine?"

Adrian's heart soared as he saw that she was reluctant to register the mare's presence. Reluctant to leave the wonderful shelter of their shared passion. He smiled.

Elise looked vaguely around her. Slowly she registered that she had been lost in the delightful pleasures

so long denied . . . and it had been so long, and he was
so . . .

With a shock, she returned to reality instantly. What
was she doing? What in heaven's name had she been
about to do?

Fiercely embarrassed, she glanced down at herself.
Her unbuttoned jacket and blouse caused her to blush
to the tips of her exposed breasts. Humiliated, she
struggled to her feet, clutching the front of her jacket
together in spite of her need to manage her skirts so
she could rise.

When he saw that she was tripping over her skirts
and about to fall, Adrian reached for her.

"No!" She gasped, recoiling from him, shrinking
back against the limestone face of the cliff. "Don't
touch me!"

Stung, he stopped smiling and told her, icy eyed,
"You weren't saying that a moment ago."

She blanched and lifted her chin at him. Anger
replaced the bewilderment in her eyes. Hurriedly, with
fingers that shook, she began buttoning her jacket,
her unbuttoned blouse and her rosy, silken skin disappearing as she did.

He watched, feeling a sharp sense of loss. With her
every movement, she repudiated all that had happened
between them. Bitterness welled up in him. He understood. His jaw locked. Then, ignoring the clamor of
his body, he reached out in anger and grasped Elise by
her waist.

When she cried out in protest, he ignored her.
Yanking her roughly against him, he held her there for
one more instant of exquisite torture. Then, his face

full of scorn, he lifted her and effortlessly sat her on her horse.

Backing away from her, he stood mutely while she looked down at him. He saw the shock in her eyes as she registered the marks of her fingernails on his shoulders. Saw her horror when she realized she'd torn his shirt half off.

And suddenly he was amused. Vastly amused.

He appreciated the irony of the situation. He might have gallantly rescued her from her deepest fear, but class distinction had reared its regal head. Obviously, a knight errant's reward was not to be his—even if Elise had wanted it to happen as much as he before the blasted mare's interruption.

He could see that now she was only horrified that she'd been about to accept the comfort she needed from a lowly stranger. Throwing his head back, he laughed. It was a full-throated laugh of derision, and he saw Elise scowl, her temper rising.

Something deep inside him rejoiced at this sign of her recovery. Something else growled in frustration. His own reaction fell somewhere between the two, and he said, "Good! Now that you're yourself again, *Lady* Elise. Go home." He bowed mockingly.

With a slap on the rump of her horse, he sent her back to her world. The world he despised.

Chapter Eight

❧

Columbine galloped over the deep green meadows, driven by her rider's spur. Elise was headed for home as fast as her mare could run. Panicked by her passionate response to Adrian Ashe, she rode heedlessly. Her head still swimming with the strength of the desire he'd so easily aroused in her, she didn't even take proper care when she negotiated the stone walls and fences that separated her from the sanctuary of her bedchamber.

Shock and shame warred in her as she rode. Aghast at what she was thinking, she rode only by instinct. She'd wanted him. She'd wanted Adrian Ashe to make love to her.

How could she? How could she have so forgotten herself as to behave as she had? She could feel heat burning in her cheeks and knew that even now, more than a mile from the little cove in which she'd almost surrendered to Adrian Ashe, they still flew the flags of her humiliation.

A miner. A lowly coal-mine laborer. Dearest Lord, she must have been out of her mind!

Thankfully, Elise seized on that. She had been, of

course. She *had* been out of her mind. She'd been temporarily driven out of her senses by the awful fear she'd experienced in the mine. Ashe had seen that and had taken his chance to . . . She refused to put the . . . *episode* into words.

He'd had no right to take such advantage! How dared he? He knew who she was. He was no fool. Surely he knew *his* place.

She turned her humiliation to anger. Anger that a man so far beneath her in status had presumed to lay hands on her, had kissed her . . . had . . . She refused to let her mind recall the liberties Adrian Ashe had taken with her person!

Elise tasted blood. She was biting her own lower lip.

Tears of frustration filled her eyes. This wouldn't do. In an agony of spirit, she knew she couldn't go on like this. She, who would hate lying to anyone else, was flagrantly lying to herself.

Another sort of shame assailed her. A deeper, darker shame than the shame of admitting she'd so wanted to surrender to his sweet seduction. It was the shame of dishonor. She was being totally dishonest. How could she have thought, even for a moment, to lay all the blame at his door?

That her emotions were in turmoil was not reason enough for such perfidy. Her conscience ripped at her and she flinched physically at the strength of its accusation. With lacerated sensibilities, she faced the truth. She was as much to blame as he. Having been a married woman, she understood about men. She knew how very easily they were aroused.

Worse, she'd been drawn to Adrian Ashe from the moment she had first laid eyes on him. She'd felt an exciting response to him surge through her from the first glance they'd shared. How could she blame him?

Ah, no. Painfully she faced the fact that the fault was hers more than his. No matter how much she might wish to rail at him for laying hands on her, she was more guilty than he. There was no way she could, in good conscience, shift the responsibility for what had almost happened—for what *would* have happened—if it hadn't been for Columbine. She had behaved like an outraged virgin when her pride was piqued. Oh, no. She'd lashed out at Adrian Ashe as if he, and he alone, were the person to blame. "Oh, Lord," she murmured miserably. "What have I done?"

There was no answer from the Almighty, only a quick backward flick of her mare's ears.

Then, cold and implacable, another truth came. One she was even more loath to face. It was the one she'd been desperately repressing all along—perhaps all her life. Now it had surfaced and she was forced to admit to it. She possessed the dreadful social prejudice of her class. Though she'd always prided herself that she was above such pettiness, she knew now that she was not.

Elise's spirits plummeted. She rode on with her face white and strained as she sought to come to grips with this unwanted piece of self-knowledge.

In the little cove Adrian Ashe waded to shore, his magnificent body dripping cold salt water, his passion-heated blood cooled by his swim. Standing over his clothes, he stretched long and hard, then combed his fingers through his thick, dark hair. He toweled himself dry with what Elise Danforth had left of his shirt.

Smiling widely at the memory of her shocked face when she'd seen how she'd ripped it, he pulled on his trousers and tossed the tattered shirt over one shoulder. He wanted it to look as if he merely disdained to wear it. Striding briskly, he started for home.

As soon as he was again decently clad, he stopped in at the Limes'. He wanted to check on the brave child for whom Elise Danforth had dared so much.

"How is Megan?"

Hal Lime answered the door. "Come in, come in."

Lettie was all smiles. "She's fine, Mr. Ashe, just fine."

Meg came running to him. "Did you take My Lovely to bed, Mr. Ashe?"

Hal made a strangled sound and struggled to hide his grin.

Adrian looked down into the clear innocence of the child's face and told her, "I tried." How true that was, a fact of which Hal was well aware. "But she wanted to ride her horse home instead, you see, so I could only watch her go."

"Oh. Then she was really all right if she could ride home, wasn't she?"

"Yes, I think she must have been."

Megan came over and hugged him around the waist. "Thank you. Thank you for everything."

He swung her up into his arms and took her over to the room's single armchair. Sitting, he put her on his knee so that their gazes met at eye level. "Tell me, Meggie, what were you doing in the mine?"

"Aye," Hal broke in. "We've been so busy loving and scolding that neither Lettie or me have had the sense to ask her!"

Meggie looked at him solemnly. "I was earning pennies."

Adrian asked quietly, "Pennies for what?"

"For tobacco," she told him impatiently, as if he should have known. "For Hal."

A sob escaped Lettie. She lifted trembling fingers to her lips.

Hal slipped an arm around his wife and drew her close. He shook his head at her to keep silent. Tightening his embrace, he kissed her forehead.

Lettie shoved the hem of her apron against her lips and let the tears roll unhindered down her cheeks.

Adrian's voice was soothing. "You went to work at the mine so that you could earn pennies to buy Hal tobacco?"

"Yes." She nodded vigorously. "He seemed to like yours a lot." She wrinkled her little nose. "I think it's awful stuff, but you and Hal seemed to like it, so I asked Lettie why Hal didn't buy his own and she said because there weren't enough *pennies* in the house to do that." She cocked her head at him and told him brightly, "And I remembered that Willem said that they paid children *pennies* to work in the mines, and so . . ." She beamed at him, waiting for him to understand.

Lettie was all but wailing. She was certain now,

where she'd only feared it was so before, that it was all her fault. Hal shushed her with gentle kisses.

Adrian's voice was grave as he asked the child, "So you went to work for the pennies to buy Hal tobacco?" He smoothed her hair. A long moment passed, then he said, "That was very nice of you on one hand, Meggie." He paused before saying, "But it was very bad of you on the other. Do you know why?"

"Weellll." She drew the word out for the space of two heartbeats. "I suppose I have been very naughty because I didn't ask if I could go to the mine." She shot a glance toward Lettie and Hal. "And because I caused everybody to worry . . ." She paused to frown. "Please don't cry, Lettie."

Lettie gulped and tried to smile.

Meg returned it with a glowing one of her own, then turned back to Adrian and finished her sentence. ". . . and to go search for me." She took a deep breath and added in a rush, "And because I caused My Lovely to come and look for me when she is so afraid of the mines." For the first time, she looked as if she was going to cry.

Adrian pulled her close and hugged her tight. "Good girl." After a moment, he released her and looked deep into her eyes. "I have to ask you something, you know."

The child regarded him with great, solemn eyes. "What?" she asked tremulously.

"I must ask you to promise never to do such a thing again. Not only are the mines no place for children, but you really upset"—there was only a slight hesitation— "Your Lovely."

He watched her absorb that before he added in a lighter tone of voice, "Besides, I have plenty of pipe tobacco, and I pledge to you that I will make it a point to share it with Hal. Always."

"Then I promise that I will never ever go back down in a mine!" Meg gave him a smacking kiss on the lips to seal her vow.

After a startled moment, Adrian laughed.

Hal gave a gusty sigh of relief and teased Lettie. "There. You see." He grinned broadly. "Now I get half of Ashe's pipe tobacco. Something good comes of everything."

Lettie shoved him hard.

Scrambling to regain his balance after being pushed off the bench beside her, Hal stumbled into the center of the room. Staggering, he fell over the footstool, and they all dissolved into the merciful release of laughter.

Elise was far from laughter as she sat in the semi-darkness of her room. Her chaotic emotions were giving her the very devil. What was she to make of them?

What was she going to *permit* herself to make of them?

She got up from the window seat where she'd been watching twilight steal across the gently rolling hills and moved to the rosewood-framed pier glass. She touched her fingers to her bruised lips, and, with a thrill she'd give half her life to deny, remembered his kisses. She watched her eyes grow large in the mirror's reflection, then she looked away, unable to meet her own accusing gaze.

Her unrelenting honesty compelled her to admit it.

She'd committed the unpardonable sin of her society. She'd allowed herself to develop a passion for a man who was so much her social inferior that nothing could ever come of it.

That wasn't what was tearing her apart, however. The force that tore at her was the shame she felt. The shame she felt at her horror of this passion for someone who could never, ever, share her life—a man who would never be accepted by those in her circle. The circle in which she lived and *belonged*.

She threw up her hands to rub her temples with shaking fingers, then dropped them to her sides and began pacing. She hated this feeling! Her emotions were running riot, and she seemed unable to calm herself. Never had this happened before. Her stomach felt as if it was tied in a knot.

On top of it all, there was no doubt in her mind that Adrian Ashe knew she'd responded willingly to his caresses. Worse, the handsome stranger knew that she considered a relationship between them hopeless. Shame flared again as she realized how unfairly she had acted. She'd let him see how ashamed she was of what she had done.

He'd seen the shocked withdrawal in her eyes. He'd read it in her face. There was no chance of denying it. She hadn't the slightest doubt about that, either.

And she'd seen the quick hurt in his eyes. Then the scorn that had instantly masked it, leaving her uncertain that she'd seen the hurt at all.

And indeed, had she? Or was that the fond wish of her own lacerated pride? That he'd been hurt at her shock was infinitely preferable to believing that he'd only been taking cold advantage of her vulnerability.

She put her hands up to cool her flaming cheeks.

Stopping in front of the pier glass again, she told herself sharply, "You can't go on like this, Elise."

Then just how in heaven's name *was* she to go on?

Why did she keep wishing it could be? She was usually more sensible. What an utter fool she was being.

Did she think she was some Cinderella of fairy-tale fame? "Well, you're not!" She scowled at her reflection. "And you have no Fairy Godmother whose magic wand could turn your coal miner into a prince!"

Her coal miner? That made her gasp! She watched her eyes widen. "Oh, dearest Lord!" She groaned aloud. It was even worse than she'd feared.

She whirled away from the mirror, unable to face herself.

Compelled to be honest, she had to acknowledge that she had wanted, with every fiber of her being, Adrian Ashe to make love to her.

She forced herself to look at the mirror again, to look herself in the eye. Oh, yes, she'd wanted him. She met her own gaze steadily in the reflection. "Yes, admit it." Her expression was almost truculent. "You *wanted* him."

There. She'd said it aloud, and there was no recalling it.

She lifted a hand to push back her wind-tousled hair and her arm brushed her breast. Sharp awareness shot through her. Still, hours after she had lain in his arms, her body was so sensitive . . .

No, that was false, too. There was no way she could

tell herself that she'd merely lain in his arms. That she had merely rested there quiescent under his passionate assault because she'd been held in thrall by the terror of her experience in the mine.

She *had* been terrified in the mine. Yes, and she *had* been in some sort of stupor of fear when he'd first brought her and Megan out.

But by his second kiss . . . ah, by that second kiss . . . she had been herself again, a self she hadn't been for two long years . . . a self that she thought had died with her beloved Lawrence.

That passionate self had sprung up and vibrantly sought for life and comforting . . . yes, and for relief from the long, aching loneliness she'd experienced since her young husband had died.

Adrian Ashe had only held and comforted her. *She* had reached for and clutched at him.

Her cheeks flamed once more, but she lifted her chin and looked herself straight in the eye. Adrian Ashe had done no more than hold her gently and smooth her hair soothingly. He hadn't kissed her until after she had clung to and pressed herself against his strong, hard body like a shameless wanton.

She closed her eyes as she remembered. Closed her eyes as if reluctant to meet her own in the mirror. But instead of fighting down the burning shame she knew she ought to feel, she savored the memory. She thought of nothing but the wonderful, steadying strength of him. Nothing but the clean taste of his mouth with its faint hint of pipe tobacco, the gentleness of his touch. The lean, lithe hardness of his body against her own.

For the first time in two long years, she'd felt like a woman again.

Her eyes flew open. Wave after wave of intense feeling washed over her. A part of her mind cried out again that he was far beneath her station. The thought was like a physical blow. Ashe was far beneath her. A miner. He was only a lowly miner.

But, God help her, that didn't matter to her emotions. She was already halfway in love with him.

She was hurtling out of control down a path her pride would never let her take.

"Halfway, Elise?" Her voice was very soft, then became caustic as she said, "I think not."

Chapter Nine

❧

Things were no better in the morning, but at least Elise was back in charge of her emotions and ready to get on with her responsibilities. Ready, but far from comfortable.

She paced the vast, deep Oriental rug in her spacious, book-lined study, her sapphire blue slippers silent on its silken surface. Whether or not she felt all kinds of a fool for her behavior yesterday, it was time to get on with her plans.

She'd sent for Adrian Ashe to ask him to take over where Ethan Frost had left off. Although she and Ethan had fought so hard, efforts to make improvements to conditions in the mines had ceased with his death, and Elise feared a mining catastrophe was imminent. That was the problem that should be foremost in her mind, not whether or not she could face the man over whom she'd made such a fool of herself. Taking a deep breath, she refused to let one incident, no matter how embarrassing, interfere with more important considerations.

She needed Adrian Ashe to head up the miners. He was bold and brave—cocky, Deverill called him—and his arrogance made him the perfect choice to stand up for the men who were unable to speak for themselves. They needed him. Therefore, she needed him. And she intended to have him. Now, she had only to hope that she'd found an answer to how she was to face him, with absolute calm, over this desk in this very room after she had behaved so inexcusably yesterday.

Just then, from the hallway, she heard the boom of the great brass knocker on the front door. "Oh, thank heaven!" Relief surged through her. Her "answer" had arrived. She wasn't going to have to face Ashe alone.

She was glad she'd thought to invite her two friends even if it was a bit awkward. She was truly grateful Deverill and Sir James had come as she'd asked.

She met them in the sunny, wood-paneled foyer with a broad smile, a hand extended to each. "Thank you. Thank you both for coming."

"Delighted, m'dear." Dev kissed the hand she'd given him with enthusiasm. "Always delighted to see you, and don't you look charming? So good to see you in something other than black. Save for your riding habits, you've looked like a crow."

"Dear Dev," she said, eyes twinkling.

Sir James let go of the hand he'd held briefly and snorted. "What are you up to, Elise? What do you want with us?"

"Great Scott, Malfont. Bit blunt, ain't you?"

Elise linked arms with them and led them toward the study. Their bantering continued as they sauntered along.

"She's up to something. She'd never summon us here in the morning otherwise."

Elise had the good grace to blush lightly even as she laughed. "Yes, James. I admit it. I do have an ulterior motive. I've invited you to give me moral support."

Malfont drew his brows down over his piercing blue eyes. "Moral support for what?"

Deverill turned to face him. "Lord Malfont, isn't that obvious? She wants support when she asks that lout to help her by heading up her miners."

"Is that it, Elise?" Malfont scowled at her. "You *really* called me here for that? You want me to lend you a hand in recruiting a man you fully intend to encourage to be a thorn in my side?" He looked incredulous. "You must be daft."

Deverill pulled out his handkerchief and flapped it at Malfont as if he were shooing off flies. "James, James. Gently if you please. You know that Elise has a cause."

"Yes." Malfont snapped at him. "And that's annoying enough in itself. Why does it have to include that particular upstart?"

"Now, James." Deverill made his voice that of a prim spinster to amuse Elise. "Don't upset our fair Elise."

Ignoring his companion's feeble attempt at humor, Sir James got on with his particular dissatisfaction. "Irritating brute. Arrogant."

Elise laughed, emerald eyes sparkling. "To which do you refer, Sir James? Adrian Ashe or Deverill?" She paused. "Or me?"

Malfont chuckled as if he couldn't help himself, his angular face softening.

"Elise!" Deverill's soprano yelp of outrage forced all of them to laugh.

"Very well, my dear." Malfont lightly touched the impressive sapphire stickpin in his stock, shot his cuffs, and fought his smile until he was again his sober self. "If I can be of service, I shan't mind having to suffer this rogue's company." He nodded toward Deverill.

While Dev pretended to sputter objections, Elise laid a hand on her other friend's sleeve. "Seriously, though," she began. Her expression apologetic, she paused regretfully to quell Dev's merriment with a glance. "Seriously, though," she repeated, "dear Sir James. That's exactly it. You see, the qualities you've just ascribed to Ashe—irritating and arrogant—are the very ones that make him valuable to me. Without them, how can I expect him to stand up to all you mine owners when you refuse to listen to the problems of the men you employ?" She smiled disarmingly. "Especially you, James." Her eyes twinkled. "You know you are quite forbidding."

Malfont shook her hand off. "Plague take it, Elise. Why must you involve yourself in such things? It's devilish awkward! Why can't you just remarry and busy yourself with a woman's concerns?"

Deverill stepped toward him. "If that's a proposal, Malfont, it's a damn shabby one." He insinuated himself between Elise and Malfont, thrusting his chest out like a bantam cock, willing to play the fool to ease Elise's tenseness about the coming meeting with the ruffian. "In any case, I must remind you that you are in line after me. If Elise is to marry either of us, I can assure you, it will be me." He smoothed his dark curls and threw the solemn Malfont an arch look. "My Irish charm will easily win out over your sardonic English personality." He shuddered delicately. "So taciturn, my friend. So devilish *serious*." He grinned impishly. "Far better Elise marry me and mend my—"

Malfont's brow was thunderous, he loathed light-mindedness. "Your fortune?"

"I was going to say my manners, you wretched miser."

"Wastrel!"

Elise interrupted. "That will be enough, you two!" Laughing, she told them, "If you're not careful, you'll have people believing you're not the best of friends."

Deverill burst out, "Best of friends. Ha! If the company weren't so thin around here, we wouldn't be friends at all."

Malfont raised a disdainful eyebrow. "Whatever makes you think we are?"

At that moment, Elise's butler, Helmsley, appeared in the doorway of the study and announced in icy tones, "Milady, there is a *person* to see you."

Elise was already struggling not to laugh at the verbal antics of her two friends. Helmsley's obvious disapproval of her caller was the last straw. Laughter spilled into her voice as she said, "Show Mr. Ashe in, please, Helmsley."

She looked away from Dev and Sir James to Helmsley, and her heart leapt up in her throat. *He* was there.

Obviously, Ashe had refused to wait in the ante-room for Helmsley to return with her permission to come to the study. She felt a faint annoyance at that, but it was, after all, just that sort of impertinence that she wanted in him. He'd never accomplish all she planned for him if he were the sort who stood, hat in hand, waiting to be told what to do. Fortunately for her cause, she couldn't even imagine him ever doing so.

Making every effort to behave normally, she lifted her gaze to his face to find him staring insolently at her. She raised her chin slightly and took a deep breath. She refused to blush—refused to let him know by a single sign that she even remembered what had passed between them yesterday afternoon. She'd die before she let him guess how deeply it had affected her.

To guard against that possibility—to keep from giving herself away—she got right to the point. "Ashe, I've asked you here to request you consider taking a post that has . . ." She couldn't help the pause. Memories flooded her of a gentle, caring man. The earnest Ethan Frost had worked tirelessly for the miners. Her tiny pause was the least tribute she could pay to her late friend. ". . . recently become vacant."

"So I've heard." Ashe's voice was solemn. His eyes unreadable. When he shifted his gaze from her face to the two nobles, she thought they became accusing. With all her heart, she wished she knew what he was thinking.

Adrian Ashe stood, feet wide apart and legs braced, like a man on a quarterdeck in a heavy sea. He'd taken in the occupants of the room at a glance, and his mouth had tightened.

Elise Danforth, imperiously slim and erect, looking

every inch a lady of the ton, stood bracketed by the two most elegant gentlemen of the district. Obviously she meant to put the lowly miner in his place.

The line was drawn, and he had no doubt to which side of it she'd consigned *him*. The message was perfectly, painfully clear. If she'd flown a banner that read "This is where I belong, these are the men of *my* world," she couldn't have made a more emphatic statement.

It was a slap in the face. Then she added to it by neglecting to introduce him to the two nobles. They probably would have resented such an introduction to one of the lower class anyway.

Very well. He could deal with it.

A burning started in the pit of his stomach. His nostrils flared. She'd sent him two messages—neither of them very subtle. He could send his own. Narrowing his eyes he did.

"So," he told her without speaking, *"you can't face me alone."* His smile twisted. *"Yesterday haunts you, does it, milady?"*

But Elise wasn't the only one struggling to maintain equilibrium against the remembered emotions that had run between them the day before. Emotions that still leapt between them like summer lightning. Adrian knew himself to be awash with them as well.

Wryly, he decided that in all fairness, he should have sent her the thought, *"Yesterday haunts you, too,"* because the memory of her soft body in his arms rose like a sudden spring mist to cloud his senses. Desire coursed through him in waves, numbing his mind.

As his eyes traced the soft, full bow of her lips and

he remembered the honey of her mouth, passion as strong as it had been when he held her cradled to him in the cove, stirred his body. A possessiveness so savage that it shocked him seized Adrian in its crushing grip. The sight of her standing there so coolly with men on either side brought him a cold and purposeful anger.

His blunt, square nails bit into his palms. Attacking the noble pair hardly figured in his plans at present.

The effort he had to make not to rush over to the little group and forcibly remove Elise from it amazed him. Never before had he felt so damn primitive.

Stop being a bloody fool, he snarled in his mind, *she's gentry.* Then, denying all he'd discovered about her when he'd found her valiantly attempting to rescue a child in a mine that sent her into a living nightmare, he told himself, *She's not worth the trouble.*

But telling himself to stop being a fool was easier than controlling the fierce possessiveness he felt toward Elise Danforth. Watching her standing there, so regal and perfectly poised while his own conflicting emotions writhed through him like poisonous snakes took a toll. It raised in him an anger in proportion to his passion.

His anger was a double-edged sword. It cut *at* him because he knew she'd sent for him to persuade him to take Ethan Frost's place. The place of a man all the miners believed had been murdered because he'd done Lady Elise's bidding.

Now she was willing to put *him* at risk to gain her own objectives. Damn her. She would sacrifice him for her blasted cause without a care for what that might do to the magic there was between them.

A thought hit him like a cannonball. Perhaps she was willing to sacrifice him *because* of the attraction she felt for him. Wasn't she standing there arm in arm with the two most supercilious jackanapes he'd seen lately? She certainly wasn't standing at his side, expressing her gratitude for his having hauled her out of Tate's foul mine.

At her clearly stated preference for *gentlemen of the gentry* over honest men, his anger rose higher.

Elise Danforth was his! Every delectable, silken inch of her. Every sigh and soft surrender was his, blast her! And she damn well knew it! There was no way he could have misread the agony in her eyes as she realized it. The desperation to deny it had been written all over her face as her mare had plunged away from the cove yesterday.

She knew. Elise Danforth knew she was his. No matter how she might wish to deny it, she knew. Knowing that, and knowing as well that she was fighting to deny it with all the strength of her will maddened him further.

She faltered noticeably before the blaze of scorn in his eyes. "I-I've sent for you to ask if you will take over the committee that Ethan Frost headed." When he only stared at her, she took a deep breath and added, "It's very important that his work continue."

When Elise spoke, it turned his anger to ice. For she spoke in a composed voice that denied she'd ever lain in his arms clutching him to her with a strength born of desperation—that forgot she'd left his shirt in shreds and the marks of her fingernails in his shoulders and back.

"The committee is one that takes the grievances of the miners to the mine owners."

When still he didn't respond, she spoke as if she were hoping he would grasp how important the project was to her without her having to address him as someone she thought of as an equal.

Her hypocrisy sickened him. . . . So did his own. Still he wanted her.

Suddenly, desire crossed over into frustration and he despised her for being *able* to speak to him as if they'd not both been struck by the same lightning less than twenty-four hours before. He made his own voice as impersonal as hers when he spoke. "Yes," he said in a voice that matched hers tone for tone for calm . . . for distance, "I know all about what Ethan Frost was striving to accomplish."

He tore his gaze away from Elise and focused it on Malfont. With a self-deriding smile he told himself that if Elise's indifference hadn't cooled his blood, the chilling expression on Sir James Malfont's face should do it.

Looking from Malfont to the man beside him, he noted that while they were each of a very different stamp, the eyes of both men watched him with the same wariness. Only their expressions differed in that the handsome dandy's was as heated as Malfont's was cold. The eyes, and the watchful wariness in them, were the same.

Interesting.

Taking the post Elise Danforth offered might be

interesting, too, but he'd be damned if he'd do it and thus oblige the cold, exquisite marble statue that just yesterday had been his all too flesh-and-blood woman. Deliberately, he looked her directly in the eye.

He wanted to see the quick disappointment there as he told her no. He made his voice that of a gentleman talking to a lady of no more than equal rank. "No thank you, Lady Elise." His voice took on a hint of derision when he saw Malfont was piqued at hearing an upper-class drawl issuing from the lips of his lowly mine worker.

He was smiling sardonically as he added, "While I'm sensible of the honor you seek to do me, I've no intention of ending *my* days with a beating intended to murder me."

He looked straight at his employer, Malfont.

Malfont colored with anger and almost stepped forward. At the last instant he recollected himself and stood his ground.

Elise gasped at Adrian Ashe's effrontery. He'd as good as accused Sir James of having Ethan Frost set on by the thugs who'd killed him.

Deverill spoke up for his friend. "Now, see here, Ashe. The men who fought with Frost weren't from around here. And if he staggered over the cliff after the fight because he had blood in his eyes, then it wasn't their fault he died, anyway." He thrust a finger at Ashe. "You can't stand there, glaring, and accuse Malfont."

One eyebrow lifted imperiously, Ashe gave the man opposite him the coup de grace. "As I understand it, it's only a capital offense if I *voice* accusations while in my present employment as a miner. But, certainly, I may glare, if I please, mayn't I?"

Deverill looked as if he were about to explode. The angry red of his face contrasted sharply with the cool bottle green of his expensive riding coat.

Malfont had gone deadly quiet.

Suddenly Elise was afraid of what might happen.

Malfont's face drained of color.

The other man's flamed.

Adrian couldn't resist the childish temptation to pour salt into their wounds. With an elegant bow designed to further infuriate them, he said in perfect French, *"Alors, je m'excuse."* His gaze caught and held Elise's. *"Au revoir, madame."* Then he turned regally to taunt the men, *"Messieurs."*

He straightened, spun on his heel, and was gone.

A long moment of silence followed his exit. "Impertinent bastard!" Deverill's mood was savage.

"Be still," Malfont said softly, his attitude more dangerous than Deverill's curses. "You're in a lady's presence." But Malfont wasn't looking at the man he corrected. His concern was all for the slender woman at his side. "Are you all right, my dear?"

Elise, white as chalk, turned to her friends. Spreading her hands in a helpless gesture, she said, "I tried."

Malfont saw that she was focused inward—and that there was a great deal more going on in her mind than the simple acquisition of a man to champion her cause. He saw . . . and he left it alone.

She had never confided in him, in spite of the fact that he had been her husband's closest friend. Dev had taken the post of confidant when Lawrence was killed and held it still. Knowing that, he realized he'd have to wait. Gently he said, "You look fatigued, my dear. May I suggest that you go and rest?"

She shot him a grateful look. "Yes. Yes I am a little tired, thank you." She permitted her shoulders to sag. "I had so hoped . . ."

"We know." Then, in a tone designed to make Deverill seethe he said, "Come along, Deverill. Elise has no further need of our company."

On their separate ways home from Danforth Manor, one of the men who'd answered Elise's summons vowed that he'd do more—much more—than accept the insolence of the blasted miner. Well, he would take care of that and a good deal else. Hadn't he removed Danforth when he became too troublesome? And hadn't he been able to block most of Elise's meddling improvements? Finally, hadn't he disposed of Ethan Frost when the man had had the temerity to agitate on behalf of the miners?

No, things were going too smoothly for him to tolerate any interference from the insolent Ashe. In fact, he found, he resented the man's mere existence. Impertinent, insufferable bastard!

His decision made, he turned the head of his big bay mount toward home, and sent him into a comfortable, ground-eating canter. It was just as well he met no one on his way. The smile on his face would have chilled them.

Chapter Ten

❧

Elise slept late, reluctant to begin the day. When Agnes came in again at ten o'clock, the morning's bright promise was fast fading as storm clouds gathered to the east. It was going to be a dark day. Elise rubbed her arms, suddenly chilled.

Agnes picked up her lacy wrapper and held it for Elise to slip into.

A brisk knock sounded on the bedchamber door. Elise was struck by its urgency. Her gaze shot to Agnes, then to the white-painted, paneled surface.

Agnes nodded and hurried to the door.

Elise's butler, Helmsley, his face grim, stood just outside in the hall. His manner was hesitant.

Throwing the door wide, Agnes stepped back into the room for him to enter.

Instead of coming in, Helmsley signaled her to come out.

Mystified, she did so. "I'm just helping the mistress get dressed, Mr. Helmsley. What is it?"

The butler shot a troubled glance to where his mistress stood beside the huge, white damask-draped bed.

Drawing a long, ragged breath, he bent down and whispered to Agnes.

Agnes's face blanched. She nodded comprehension, though her stunned face seemed devoid of it, and stepped back into Elise's bedchamber. Quietly closing the door, she leaned weakly against it.

"Agnes!" Dread filling her, Elise leapt across the room to her, ribbons flying. She slipped her arm around Agnes, giving her support. What was the matter? What had Helmsley said? Panic raced through her. "What is it, Agnes? What's happened?"

Agnes raised tragic eyes to her. In a voice that shook, she told Elise, "There's been another cave-in, milady."

"A cave-in?" Terror flooded through her. Her voice was a strained whisper. "Where?"

It seemed an eternity before Agnes answered, "At Malfont Mine!"

Elise's blood ran cold. The world stopped spinning with a jolt. *He* worked at Malfont. Adrian! Oh, dear God, what if he were . . . She'd never told him . . . She'd treated him so badly!

She pulled herself up sharply. Hal worked at Malfont, too. Hal who had children. Hal who was Megan's new father. Hal who had been her good friend for over a year. She was appalled that she had thought first of the stranger Adrian Ashe—more than appalled at the significance of her having done so.

She spun away and rushed across the room. She threw herself into the low-backed chair at her dressing table and began struggling with her hair. "Tell Helmsley to get every man and every carriage and wagon over to the mine. Tell him to take all the shovels and hoes." She pressed her fingers to her forehead. "Oh, and all the buckets, too. Perhaps they will be needed to move debris. And tell him . . ." She ripped the last of her hair from its braid and tossed the great shining mass back over her shoulder. "Oh, tell him to do everything sensible he can think of as quickly as he can."

As she pulled her night rail over her head, Elise added in a voice muffled by fine linen and lace, "And tell him I'll be right down."

At Malfont Mine, Elise hauled the lathered carriage horses to a sliding halt. Every other vehicle she owned arrived almost instantly behind hers. Coachmen, footmen, her farmers, all piled down off them to await her orders.

Leaping from the box, she stumbled over her skirts on landing, and went sprawling. Ignoring Agnes's yelp of dismay, she picked herself up and ran up the slight rise to the mouth of the mine before any one of her men could help her.

She was horrified by the scene she found there.

Dust was rising from the main shaft like thin smoke. It curled back on itself of its own weight and settled on the wreckage of the whim machinery. The ropes by which the men entered and left the mine were hanging slack—tangled and useless.

Family members of the miners trapped below clustered in a knot, grim faced. Mutely they stared at the place where the mine opening had been—waiting to learn how bad it was.

Off to one side, a low keening rose from a small group of women wrapped in black shawls. Elise's quick sympathy for them was tinged with irritation that they'd already given their men up for dead.

In spite of all the people there, still nothing was being done to help the miners trapped below.

Elise accosted a man sitting on the ground surrounded by people. His face was black with coal dust. There was an abrasion on the side of his head as big as her hand. "What happened?" She didn't recognize her own voice.

" 'Twere a collapse of the main shaft, milady. We'd no warning, just a mighty puff of air. Like getting your ears boxed, it was. And then everything started to go." His face was pale under the coal dust, his eyes frightened at the remembrance.

Taking a blanket from some helpful soul who'd brought it but didn't seem to know what to do with it, Elise threw it around the man's shoulders. "Try to tell me more," she said gently.

The miner burrowed into the blanket gratefully. His teeth began to chatter. "I was one of the lucky ones. I was already on my way up. Already at the top o' the lift." He turned and looked at the mouth of the mine. "Thank the Lord there weren't no one behind me on it."

He shuddered to think what would have happened to them, had there been other miners in the loops of the lift rope. Mournfully he stated, "Nobody'll be coming up that way anymore."

"Not for a while anyway." A deep, positive voice, a firm tread, and *he* was there.

Elise spun around to face him, weak with relief. She saw his face above the crowd, stern, purposeful. He was alive! Ah, thank God! She quivered with the strength of her relief.

Adrian Ashe pushed through the last of the people surrounding the survivor. Down on one knee, he rested a forearm on the other and leaned toward the blanket-wrapped man on the ground. "How many men are down there?"

The man was eager to talk to someone who might be able to help his buried friends. "Most of the men on this shift had already got out, Mr. Adrian. There're maybe twelve or so men left down there." His eyes rolled toward the ruined main shaft.

"What are their chances?"

"I can't say, sir. I don' know how much of the mine went."

"Oh, Lord," a woman quavered, "don' let 'em *all* be gone."

Adrian kept his attention on the man he was questioning. "What level were the men working on?"

The man answered, and Adrian asked him several other questions. Then he rose lithely from where he knelt beside the survivor and said, "I'm going to try to go down the draft chimney and see what I can find out."

Elise's heart stopped. She pressed her hand to her chest and took a gulp of air. Frantically, she wondered whether it was to steady herself or to give her the breath to cry out a protest.

The survivor voiced her fear for her. "Down the draft chimney? Are you daft? Ye'll cook!" His eyes took on a wild look. "That fire down at shaft bottom is a monster!"

Adrian looked at the man, his gaze level. "It has to be to draw the air through a mine as big as Malfont." His deep voice was perfectly calm. "I understand the risks."

"No, ye don't! For God's sake! Don't be a fool. Ye can't go down that way. The smoke'll choke ye so bad, ye'll fall the rest of the way into the fire." He turned to Elise. "Don't let him, Lady Elise. He'll be killed!"

Elise was stunned. It was true. Elise knew. That fire was kept ferociously hot, flaming as high as the keepers could get it in order to draw noxious gases from the mine while drawing fresh air in through the main shaft. The fire was the most important thing in the mine. It was the reason winzes connected tunnels and galleries—to provide the circulation of air for the men to breathe. For the men to live.

The whole mine depended on the draft from that blaze, and it was always kept well stoked. There was simply no chance that it had gone out. And no chance that a man could survive a descent into its chimney shaft.

The thought of any man trying to go down into the mine through its heat and smoke was mind-boggling. The thought that that man might be Adrian Ashe sent her heart plummeting!

Elise felt her head spin with the enormity of it. She was afraid she was going to faint. She could feel the skin of her face tingle as the blood drained from it. He couldn't. He mustn't!

But he was going to, of course! He stalked off without a backward glance. Purpose filled every line of his athletic body, and Elise knew there was no way she could stop him. Oh, God, there was no way she could stop him!

Her mind in agony, she realized that there was no way she *should* stop him. Adrian Ashe was the only chance they had for the recovery of the men trapped below. The only chance for the families that loved them.

She watched him helplessly for a moment, her heart in her throat. The tearing pain she felt at the very real possibility that she would lose him held her momentarily transfixed.

An instant later, she gathered her skirts as well as her senses, and ran after him.

Chapter Eleven

✦

In spite of the urgency that drove him, Adrian finally turned, drawn irresistibly to her presence. Over the heads of the milling, anxious crowd, his gaze sought out Elise. Acutely aware of her, he found himself equally aware of her deep distress . . . distress that was mostly for him.

The bright blue of her riding habit stood out like a signal flag against a storm cloud among the drab grays and blacks of the people surrounding her. A single glance discerned her sense of alarm. She was chalk white, as white as the shirt and stock she wore, and looked as if a breeze would blow her off her feet. Her emerald eyes, glistening with tears, were full of apprehension. And they were fastened on him.

Fear. With a wild burst of wonder, Adrian knew that she was frightened for him. Obviously she felt deep concern for the poor unfortunates trapped below in the mine, but the awful fear he saw in her face was for him! Elation flooded him, washing away all caution. The aloof Lady Elise was inadvertently giving him proof that she wasn't indifferent to him after all. His heart soared.

He knew better than to let her see he'd noticed her unguarded expression. He relegated it to cherished memory instead. His own expression carefully guarded, he pushed his way to her side.

An old man with a panicked face rushed through the crowd seemingly going nowhere, moving only because he couldn't bear to be still. He accidentally jostled Elise and Adrian reached out to steady her. Ignoring the electricity that leapt to his hand at the touch, he asked, "How many men did you bring?"

"All of them." He saw she was having trouble with her own jolt of sensation.

His fingers bit into her arm. "Steady." His voice softened and he told her, "I need you."

Elise drew a deep, quivering breath and her head cleared. "I've brought twenty-three—all the men in my employ except my butler. They have brought all the carts, wagons, and carriages from Danforth to take the injured to their homes."

"What to dig with, milady?" He was certain she'd have thought of that. His gaze was intent, waiting.

"All the shovels, hoes, and even all the buckets. Blankets for warmth, sheets to be torn into bandages. Brandy for ... for whatever they're always giving injured people brandy for," she finished her catalog lamely.

"Dear God, woman." His grin flashed white. "You're a paragon."

Any other time, Elise would've felt the obligation to pretend to take offense at his familiarity, at his speaking to and of her as if he were her equal. But men were dead and perhaps still dying below in the mine. Instead she asked briskly, hoping for any answer but the one she knew was coming, "What are you going to do?"

"The only thing I can think of." He half turned to walk away, throwing back over his shoulder, "Come. Have your men bring blankets and buckets. Buckets full of water."

There was no time to question; she knew as well as he did that, with the main shaft blocked, the fire below was devouring the air in the mine at an astonishing rate. The few other, pitifully small down draft shafts would never keep up. If they didn't work quickly, the men trapped below would suffocate!

Elise called, "Mudge, Rafferty, get as many of the men as you can to fill buckets with water and follow me!"

She darted to the carriage she'd driven to the mine herself, pulled three blankets out of its interior, and told Agnes, "Bring more!" Then she whirled, snatched up her skirts, and dashed after Adrian Ashe.

Over the heads of the people between them, she spotted him. He was racing to the opening of a shaft several hundred yards away. A shaft from which white smoke streamed—a tattered banner smeared across a storm-dark sky.

She stopped, staring, unable to make her feet move. Her mind still refused to consider what she knew he was going to do. Fear rose in her again and she fought it like a tiger. He was heading straight to the chimney shaft of the huge underground bonfire that made working in the mine possible.

She'd always thought of the blaze as a friend. Stoked

by attendants night and day, it roared and danced, carrying away on its fearsome breath the mine damp that caused explosions and the fumes that choked men to death.

Now it was no longer a friend! Now, ravenously, it consumed the fuels that enabled it, and waited, a crouching, voracious monster, to singe and sear anyone foolhardy enough to approach it from above. And all the while, with its main source of fresh air blocked, it sucked the remaining air in the mine from the very lungs of the men trapped below.

As Elise approached the shaft, she could see Adrian Ashe shielding his face against the rising heat with an upthrown hand, bending forward at the very edge, peering down into the chimney shaft. He was utterly intent on the rescue of the men trapped below. In the smoke he was a shadow, a wraith, and, as he stood there—sometimes clearly visible, sometimes enveloped by smoke—something of a god.

Elise stood stock-still, her hand pressed to her heart, staring.

Then Adrian Ashe leapt back away from a shower of heavy sparks, said, "Blast and damn!" and the spell was broken.

The next half hour was a scene straight out of hell! Elise watched her men, driven by a tireless Ashe, toiling to bring bucketful after bucketful of cold, salt water from the sea only to see it turn to steam as they poured it down the chimney shaft. Their efforts to extinguish the mighty blaze seemed futile.

On and on they worked, passing bucket after bucket

up the steep slope from the sea. "Good men," Ashe would say now and again as he took a bucket from the man stationed last in line and leaned out over the steaming maw of the chimney shaft to pour the water down it.

Suddenly, there was a commotion at the edge of the group. Men scattered. Looking toward the disturbance, Elise saw her friend, Sir James. His usually calm face was distorted with rage. She heard him shouting.

"What the devil do you think you're doing?" Fighting to keep his horse from spinning around and plunging away from the heat and the hiss of steam, he materialized out of the fog Adrian's work was creating. "Damn you, Ashe! You'll put out the draft fire!"

Ashe turned a sweat-streaked face toward the mine owner. "That's the idea, Malfont. How the hell else do you think we can get down to the men?"

"Dig out the main shaft, curse you!"

Ashe walked over to Malfont's dancing horse, took hold of the reins under the bit, and quieted the animal with a firm hand on its neck. "That would take days."

"So what if it takes days! It'll take days to get the draft fire hot again if you continue with this insanity."

"The draft fire, damn you, Malfont," Ashe spoke through clenched teeth, "isn't as important as the lives we'll save by getting downpit as quickly as possible." He lowered his voice to keep his words from the families. "And that fire is depleting the air in the mine!"

Frustration warred with understanding in Malfont's eyes. He'd be damned if this lowly stranger was going to dictate to him about his own property! He raised his whip.

"At your peril!" Ashe growled the words, stepping forward to meet the intended blow.

Elise broke out of her stupor and ran forward. "James!" She couldn't believe her eyes. Hadn't been able to believe her own ears. "What can you be thinking?"

Ashe answered, his lips drawn back from his teeth in a snarl. "About falling production levels, no doubt, Elise." His tone was scathing. "After all, the mine will be unworkable for several days." He spun away, then, shouted, "Back to work, men! Let's get that blasted blaze out!"

Malfont looked down at Elise as if he were seeing a ghost. "Elise! What are you doing here?"

"The same thing I hope you are doing here." Her eyes were accusing. "Trying to save the lives of the men trapped below in your mine. Your men."

"Oh, for God's sake, Elise." Malfont's shoulders slumped. The anger he'd directed at Ashe drained out of him. "Put out the damned draft fire if that's all that will content you." He straightened and became himself again. "Just don't expect *me* to be a participant in your little drama!"

He shot a last glare at Ashe, gave rein to his nervous mount, and was gone. His horse's frantic hoofbeats quickly faded as it raced home.

Elise put her terrible sadness over Malfont's ugly behavior out of her mind and turned back to the men at the head of the shaft. She was just in time to see them wrapping one last wet blanket around the tall shadow that was Adrian Ashe. "No!" It was a cry torn from her heart. She ran toward the little group shouting, "No. You can't do that. The fire's not out yet!"

She threw herself on Ashe, clutching at him as desperately as she had that day in the cove by the sea. But this time it wasn't *her* life she sought to preserve, it was his. He mustn't try to go down into that shaft until they had subdued the last of the monster fire. He *mustn't*!

Adrian looked down at her, and one corner of his mouth curled upward. He felt something in the center of his chest soften and seem to give way. Her face was full of anxiety *for him*. He looked into her tear-drenched eyes, and his stomach knotted with desire. Still, he managed to say coolly, "Yes, milady?"

It took all his strength not to enfold her in his arms, hold her close, and tell her . . . His mind jolted with the realization of just what he wanted to tell this lovely member of the gentry he despised, then sheered away like a ship avoiding a collision at sea.

At his cool words, Elise jumped back from him as if she'd been burned. What could she be thinking? The tenseness of the present situation explained her lack of restraint, of course. And, of course, anyone would strive to stop a man bent on suicide! Nevertheless, she felt confused.

Adrian saw it and understood. The tenderness he felt for the woman standing with him at the very edge of Hades evaporated as if it had never been. Blast her! She was ashamed. Socially embarrassed for having run to him, a lowly miner . . . for having embraced

him, a stranger. For having even *touched* him in front
of onlookers.

He hardened his heart against her. What had he
expected? Bitterness scalded his thoughts. She was
gentry, after all. Her long, careful training in the snobbery of her class had made her regret the purely
natural act of a kind woman attempting to save a
fellow human from the probable consequences of a
dangerous act. Fiercely he denied that he was in any
way hurt by her attitude.

Then he took a deep breath and silently told himself, *So to hell with her!*

High on a nearby hill, the man who'd masterminded
the disastrous cave-in sat on his horse and watched the
drama below through eyes narrowed by hatred. "Go
on, Ashe. Go on. Play the hero." His patrician lip
curled. He expected the return of his well-paid
henchmen any day now. If the fire didn't get him . . .
or the cave-in, then his men would permanently settle
Mr. Adrian Ashe. He hissed at the distant Ashe, "You
haven't much longer to strut on *this* stage."

Chapter Twelve

∾

Having consigned the woman standing before him to the nether regions, Adrian turned away from her to the three men he'd chosen to hold his life in their hands. "Play out the rope steadily. If I jerk three times, it'll mean I can't take the heat. Haul me back up."

Three pairs of eyes stared at him gravely. Not one of the men trusted himself to speak.

His eyes on the men handling his rope, Adrian began his own descent into hell.

Elise stood helplessly, her heart in her throat and her emotions in a tangle. Wringing her hands wasn't going to do any good! There must be something she could do! Nothing. There was nothing. He'd thought of all that was needed. Clamping her teeth tight she gestured for two of her footmen to stand ready to take up the slack in the loose end of the rope in case more manpower might be needed.

Idle again, she wondered if she was going to be able to stop herself from crying out a protest as Ashe went over the now dangerously sodden side of the chimney shaft. The protest rose in her even as she watched his blanket-wrapped form disappear, watched his head—a mass of dark curls since it had been dampened to keep it from catching fire—sink from sight.

As if mesmerized, she watched the rope cut into the seawater-softened edge of the shaft. Even as she told herself not to be missish, she shoved the back of her hand against her mouth to prevent any outcry. Then, she saw that the men had stopped pouring water down the shaft as Ashe descended!

All thoughts of seeking relief in feminine vapors disappeared in a flash. "Rafferty!" she shrieked, her teeth meeting with a click at the end of the cry.

Rafferty, leaning over the edge of the yawning hole, was so startled, he would have fallen down on Ashe if Mudge, Elise's head stableboy, hadn't snatched him back. Wide-eyed the two gaped at the fury their usually calm mistress had become.

Elise didn't care how she appeared, how she sounded. "Get water! Get the buckets coming again! Pour it down on him! Do you want him to catch fire down there? Do you want to . . ." But the words, "kill him," stuck in her throat, caught there as if a giant fist had seized her neck.

Tears of frustration rushed to her eyes. These men didn't deserve her anger. They were her men, and they had worked hard. She was the one at fault. She should never have forgotten, in her concern over the man descending the rope, to give them their orders. In her distress, she'd been willing to take her fear and frustration out on her staff.

How could she do such a thing? This sort of behavior wasn't like her. Even under stress, she'd always prided herself on the fact that she could keep a level head, remain a lady. Now here she was acting like a fishwife!

Self-disgust reared its unwelcome head. Damn Adrian Ashe and the way he'd stormed into her life and torn it apart!

"More water, please," she managed huskily, her voice now the one her servants knew so well. "And hurry."

But they were already running to re-form their bucket brigade. Soon, water was cascading down on the man below in a steady stream of bucketfuls.

Halfway down the shaft on his rope, Adrian Ashe bit back the curses he longed to shout as the heat from what was left of the fire dried the salt water from the woolen blankets protecting him and made them steam. Where the hell were the men with the damn buckets?

Encased in an ever hotter cocoon of drying wool, he clenched his teeth against the cry of agony that filled him when a last flame soared upward from the dying fire and seared the edge of his forearm. Damn it! Why didn't they keep the water coming?

Then cascades of water fell again. Thank God! They'd re-formed the bucket brigade. The coolness of the water was salvation!

He thought he'd heard a woman shrieking at the men. Elise! He grinned there in the hellish red light of the narrow mine shaft. So. She was upset enough for him to forget to sound like the lady she was. His grin widened. His heart lifted as his mind pictured her there above him, exhorting the men to keep bringing water up the steep slope from the sea.

Elise was keeping him from being cooked alive!

Picturing her there, her flaming hair a defiant banner against the deep blue gray of the approaching storm, he ignored the pain in his fast-blistering left arm. Elise. Ah, God, she was a wonder.

This wasn't the place for daydreams, though. He could hear the sizzle of the water as it ran along the heavy beams that still glowed hellishly hot only feet below where he hung.

He'd have to drop onto and get the hell off those beams in the same split second if he didn't want to cook. His stomach knotted with more than the simple effort of holding himself on the rope.

Horror flooded him as an image flashed across his mind. He saw himself shriveling like a moth in a flame, his boot caught between two of the massive logs used to fuel the draft fire.

Fighting the crawling terror that raised the hair on the back of his neck, he sent a fervent prayer skyward. He didn't even give a damn if the men above heard him. "God! Don't let me get a foot caught!" Then he let go of the rope and dropped down onto the tangle of charred beams.

On the surface, Elise sent up a desperate prayer for Adrian's safety. As if to influence the deity, she asked silently, *Who but Adrian Ashe would attempt this rescue?*

It was an honest question. Who but Adrian Ashe would go down a rope into the fire of that hell? What man was there here in the mining community with both the courage and the compassion to go down over the still-living embers of a draft fire? Her mind quailed just thinking of it.

Though every man here might want to bring out the men trapped below, who of them would have even thought of attempting to do it this way?

She looked around at the earnest faces surrounding her. They were good men, all, and most of them would surely have tried a rescue. Hal might even have tried this one if it weren't for Lettie and the children.

Every other man there was so imbued with fear of the huge draft fire, that not one of them would have ventured down that shaft, even if they'd thought of it. They were kind and full of concern and compassion . . . but they were simple men.

And they were up here with her on the surface, safe. She felt resentment at the thought.

Only *he* had disappeared in the direction of the men who needed rescue. Only Adrian Ashe had been willing to risk his life for those of the men trapped below. Admiration rose up and all but overwhelmed her. Then came a deep respect for the man dangling many feet below.

After respect, something else pushed at her mind, but she fought hard to ignore it. She didn't want to acknowledge the next emotion—the one that so often followed respect and admiration. The one that never came, truly, without them.

She felt as if she were suffocating with the effort to deny that emotion that she knew so often followed admiration and respect. Followed, heedless of what one wanted.

A shout from the men jolted her out of her reverie. "More buckets, you lot! Shake a leg, there!"

The men at the edge of the shaft gestured for their companions to speed up the flow of water as they felt, from the length of the rope they'd played out, rather than saw, Ashe nearing the bottom of the shaft.

Elise, however, could see. She could see him in her mind's eye nearing a monster that was still dangerous even in its death throes.

Then the rope went suddenly slack. The men holding it staggered backward. He was down!

Rafferty leaned precariously over the edge. "Are you safe?" His shout would have reached the farthest corner of the mine.

It seemed as if an eternity passed. Elise was half mad with anxiety. An arm went around her waist. For the first time, she realized Agnes was beside her.

Then they heard, "Aye!"

The men began pounding each other on the back. Half of the men on the bucket brigade dropped down in their tracks with wide grins, too exhausted to join in the triumphant melee. The first part of the rescue was done!

Elise could breathe again. She was doing all she could do to help Adrian Ashe, now, by praying. She could hear that Agnes was doing the same.

Her head cleared. She was doing the only thing she could do to keep safe the man she ... Her eyes flew wide open, and she gasped. No!

She struggled manfully against the words, but they came anyway, surging against her fear-weakened will. She was struck motionless by the utter futility of denial. There was nothing she could do to protect herself against the secret she would guard from others to her grave.

Incredulously, she knew she wanted to savor the words for just this one mind-searing moment, even as she vowed never to indulge in them again. So she turned her face to the strengthening storm, tossed her hair back, and let the wind from the sea take it away from her face. Reveling in the strength of the wind, she gave herself over to the storm that filled her.

Her heart threatened to burst as she allowed herself, just this once, to admit that which she would never admit again. Her expression was exultant as she let the forbidden words flow through her. She was doing all she could to help . . . *the man she loved.*

Chapter Thirteen

✦

Elise felt as if she were living in one of her night-mares. The same awful sensations she'd experienced during those horrible moments after the fatal cave-in at Danforth Mine two years ago returned to assault her. She was reliving those moments in which she'd learned that the man she loved had been taken from her—taken from her by an impersonal fall of heavy earth and hard black coal.

Those around her rejoiced that Adrian Ashe had single-handedly tunneled to where he'd found their men alive. They rested in the certainty that a man who could do what he had done could bring them out safely as well. For Elise, however, the ordeal was still in progress. She was totally absorbed in praying for the safety of the man who was bringing the others up.

The fire was out, finally. It had been conquered by men toiling to the point of exhaustion. Working with a double line of buckets coming up from the sea, they'd lifted them from man to man up the steep incline from the water's edge. At last they'd extinguished the final spark. Now, restless and worried, they awaited word from below.

Suddenly, a shout rose from the depths. "Ahoy! Rafferty!"

Rafferty, the back of his belt grasped firmly by Mudge, slapped his hands on his knees and leaned out over the maw of the chimney shaft. His whole body was tense with anticipation as he called down, "What's the word?" His voice cracked with the strain they were all under.

"They're safe! Every man alive!"

A ragged cheer went up from the crowd surrounding the shaft entrance. Men pounded each other on the back and women collapsed into each other's arms, sobbing with relief.

Elise sagged against Agnes. It was almost over. Praise God! The trapped men would soon be returned to their anxious loved ones. *And he was safe as well!*

From below, men Ashe had assembled from all over the mine shouted a welcome chorus of messages up to those waiting above.

"Hazel." A lilting tenor carried up to them. "It's me, Alf. Are ye up there, luv?"

"Mary!" A deeper voice overran the first. "Mary Regan! I'm safe!"

"We all be safe. Somebody get word to my missus, please. She be near her time and I don't want her worrit."

"Never mind the message to his missus," called a rough voice full of humor this time. "Get us a keg o' ale an' stand aside. We'll be up in a minute."

"After me, Jemmy Mullins." Some of the men were laughing their release from the terrible tension they'd been under. "After me!"

When the exuberance the men felt at seeing the little patch of sky at the top of the chimney shaft had lessened a bit, the most important message came. "We'll have the others out soon, never fear."

"Aye! We'll have the hole Mr. Ashe dug big enough to get the lads out in jig time."

Their promise raised the spirits of those on the ground above them another notch. Once all were free and all together at the bottom of the chimney shaft, they'd begin their ascent.

Up on the surface, the wind was rising. Daylight was fast disappearing, sucked away by the approaching storm. The little plateau on which Elise and the others waited lacked even its habitual glow from underground. Now the draft chimney was dark, its monstrous fire defeated. It was safe to use it to bring up the survivors of the disaster.

The first of the men came up out of the ground, stretching forth his hand as his eyes cleared the edge. Mudge and another man grabbed that extended hand and heaved for all they were worth. An instant later he was out, clear of the shaft edge, gasping from his efforts and clutching the trampled grass as if it were a blessed lifeline.

When he could speak, he looked up and told Elise, " 'E sez to tell ye 'e needs some splints for young Rafe Egan's legs, milady. They do both be broke." His expression was apologetic, as if it were partially his fault. His voice was firm, however, as if there were only one "he" who could have made the request for splints—and as if he knew Elise would understand that.

"Agnes," Elise said, and the one word was all that was needed. Agnes turned and left her standing, wind whipped, at the edge of the chimney shaft. Elise shifted restlessly. Standing idle was about to drive her mad!

Agnes hurried back from the carriage with the splints.

Rafferty tied them to a light line and lowered them carefully. As he did, there was a low rumble and a section of the steam-softened walls of the shaft slithered downward.

When the splints came down, Adrian assessed this new threat quickly. The storm was almost on them. Even underground his sailor's sixth sense about the weather warned him. Heavy weather could further weaken the sodden, fire-slicked sides of the shaft.

Calmly he ordered the injured boy's legs set. Then he turned back to the problem of getting all the survivors out of the mine before more of it collapsed.

Knowing these men had little or no experience in dragging themselves up a rope, he climbed up behind every one of the escaping miners. His bruised and bleeding hands gave them purchase for their feet.

Above, Rafferty, Mudge, and the others valiantly tried to shorten the distance to the top by hauling the rope up as the men climbed it. Even with that help, Adrian knew, it was still a fearful effort for men who'd never gone aloft in ships' rigging.

Soon men shrouded in blankets lay on the ground like so much litter. They surrounded the life-saving shaft up which Adrian Ashe had helped them and gulped great draughts of fresh sea air into straining lungs. Their sweat- and coal-dust-smeared faces reflected the awe they felt at having reached the surface they'd thought never to see again.

Some cursed whatever had caused the cave-in. Most just lay thanking their Maker they were alive.

Elise stood, fervently giving thanks for the miracle. The men were safe. *All* the men were safe. Not one single man had died in the cave-in, and soon the last of them would be out of the mine.

Only one had been injured, and no doubt he would be brought up soon. Rafe Egan was the young, only son of a widow. When the accident happened, he'd been the man nearest the main shaft. He'd been caught and half buried by the weighty debris spewing out into the tunnel when the main shaft collapsed.

What would become of the little family now? The boy was the Widow Egan's only source of support. Both his legs had been broken. What would they do?

She supposed she would have to think of something. She'd have to do it later, though. Right now she had a more immediate concern.

How would Adrian get the boy out of the deep hole that was the only escape from Malfont Mine? Elise began casting about in her mind for a way to fashion a sling in which to bring Rafe safely up out of the mine.

At the edge of her awareness, she sensed that the storm was almost upon them. Gusts heralding its approach fingered her hair and tore bright strands of it from its bindings. A threatening darkness stole the light from around her.

Suddenly, there was a concerned murmur from Rafferty and Mudge who had dominated the situation at the top of the draft chimney since Ashe had disappeared down it. Eagerly, Elise rushed forward to the very edge. Screaming, "Lissie!" Agnes plunged after her and clutched desperately at the empty air just behind her.

Rafferty threw one arm up in a reflex, barring Elise from falling in, and peered down the shaft. "My God, man! Ye can't do that. 'Tis too far!"

There was a sound very like a snarl from below.

Rafferty glanced wildly about him. There had to be a way to keep Ashe from attempting to bring the injured miner up on his back. The man was worn to a thread! "Ashe! Wait!" Rafferty cast a harassed eye on the sky above and just behind him, and his face cleared. There was a way to make Ashe rest a bit. "Wait, man! We have a storm about to blow us away up here!"

Almost as if his words had brought it, the storm swooped down upon them.

It had been hanging low over the water while the men came up from the mine, waiting. Now it struck as if it had come to the end of its patience with this mighty effort of puny man. Heavy rain pelted them. It drenched them to the last anxious spectator as they waited around the shaft. Rivulets formed and ran down over the edges of the chimney shaft. Worried about the water cascading into the shaft, no one noticed his own discomfort.

Men who'd thought themselves too exhausted to rise from their blankets on the ground, got up off them, and wrapped them around themselves to keep off the rain. Wordlessly they came to stand watch at the shaft for their rescuer.

Agnes, ever watchful of her mistress, wrapped Elise in a voluminous cloak borrowed from the coachman and tried to lead her away. When Elise refused to go sit out the deluge in the carriage, Agnes huddled into the cloak's heavy folds with her rather than leave her alone there in the rain-whipped open.

Not one of them had any words to say. All of them just waited in numbed silence. Standing like sheep, they huddled together against the storm, staring down into the shaft. They waited for some further word from the brave man who'd descended into the shattered mine.

When finally the rain let up enough for them to see, they could barely make him out. Far below them with the injured lad, Ashe was reaching for the rope.

His voice a ragged combination of admiring exasperation and despair, Rafferty muttered, "The damn fool's going to try it." Then he remembered Elise, turned scarlet, and stiffened. "Begging your pardon, milady!"

Elise ignored his unnecessary apology. "What is it he's going to try to do?" Eager to know, she started to lean farther out. Agnes prevented her with a grip that clearly threatened to become painful if her charge moved any closer to the edge.

"Well, milady"—Rafferty squinted down into the mine shaft—"it looks as if he's tied the Egan boy's hands together and put them over his own head, like." His voice filled with horrified awe. "Looks like he's gonna try to climb that rope with the boy on his back."

Elise gasped. Before she could stop herself she'd blurted, "But he's too tired! He's worn out!"

There was a rumble and a muffled splash below them, and the ground shifted under her feet.

Agnes yanked her back from the edge of the pit.

Rafferty shouted, "He's coming up! Stand by!"

Mudge leapt forward. "Pray God he hasn't left it till too late!"

Three of Elise's footmen stepped determinedly to the edge of the shaft. They stood there clenching and unclenching their hands to be ready for whatever they might be called upon to do.

Agnes kept a firm hold around Elise's waist, as the younger woman strained forward. "Stay here, Lissie." She gave her a little shake. "You'll only get in the way!"

That sobered Elise, and she stood quietly beside Agnes, her gaze riveted on the edge of the chimney shaft.

After what seemed aeons, Rafferty's eyes widened, and he muttered, "Saints preserve us! His grip's weakening!" Then he gave a shout and threw himself flat and over the edge. "Hold me feet. For God's sake catch me feet."

Mudge slammed down on his belly with a wealth of language. His big hands closed around Rafferty's ankles in a death grip. Two of the footmen grabbed his feet in turn, and the third lay down flat next to Rafferty.

Rafferty grunted with the strain of holding on to the now completely exhausted Adrian Ashe. Sinews stood out on his neck like wires as he threw his head back. The footman beside him reached down into the shaft, and began to pull up mightily.

At a shout from Mudge, others of Elise's staff came crowding 'round. With many hands helping, Adrian Ashe, transformed by exhaustion from hero to burden, was soon dragged up out of the maw of the chimney shaft.

The ground shifted dangerously under their feet. They scuttled back from the crumbling edge. Adrian Ashe—an unconscious Rafe Egan hanging from his neck, cutting off his air—was firmly in their grasps.

Rafferty moved a safe distance from the shaft, flopped down, turned over on his back and drew great gasping breaths with swooshing sounds. Mudge and the footman who'd been the second man to help Ashe out of the shaft lifted the senseless Egan boy from around his rescuer's neck and laid him gently on a cloak someone had thrown down.

Tears running down her wrinkled cheeks, the boy's sobbing mother sank down beside him. Her trembling hands ran frantically over her son's face and chest. Again and again she touched him. It was as if she couldn't believe he was really with her. She was reassuring herself that he was truly there, truly safe. Then her gaze went to Adrian, and all the gratitude in the world shone from her eyes.

Adrian reached out and touched the mother's shoulder as he rose. His slight smile seemed to take the last of his strength. He turned wearily from the little group around the chimney shaft.

Straightening with an effort, he drew a single deep breath, and closed his eyes for an instant. Then he walked unsteadily away to sit alone, utterly spent.

While everyone around her congratulated the survivors of the mine disaster on their narrow escape, Elise had eyes only for the man who had saved them. It didn't seem right to her that Adrian should be apart from the general thanksgiving. Somehow, though, it seemed fitting. Suddenly, Elise knew that Adrian was the sort of man who'd always stood alone. In a flash of intuition, she knew he'd have been uncomfortable accepting thanks from those whom he'd saved. She looked at him with new insight.

Totally isolated from the hubbub of the others, he was leaning back against an outcropping of stone that reminded her of another rocky wall—one warm with sun and . . . kisses. Her heart accelerated its rhythm. Would he always affect her like this? How would she bear it?

The rain had let up. It was no longer pelting down on them. Now it fell with an impudent familiarity, its fingers tapping insistently at her shoulders. Adrian Ashe. Numbly, she thought, *Ah, dearest Lord, why does his name, just like the man, have to slip like silk into every recess of my mind?*

Everything about him tore at her heart. At intervals, tremors of exhaustion shook his frame. His head hung wearily, as if he were blindly contemplating the ground between his feet. His arms rested on his up-drawn knees, his hands dangling between them. They were torn and bleeding; his long slender fingers were so abraded by the soles of the miners' boots that they looked raw.

Elise's heart did odd things in her chest. She found herself moving toward him as if she had no volition.

She hardly noticed the heavy drag of her rain-weighted skirts.

Another tremor shuddered through Adrian Ashe's abused body.

Elise reached out to touch his shoulder in unspoken sympathy, but her hand went, instead, to his forehead, to caress the errant curl there back into the mass of his crisply waving hair.

His weary gaze lifted and locked with hers. Something came alive in the depths of his eyes.

Her fingers stilled.

Time stopped for a breathless instant while their souls met in that glance.

Then, as Elise gasped and stepped back from the intensity of his regard, Adrian's eyes quickly shuttered. The moment was gone.

Elise was left to stare at her outstretched hand as if it belonged to someone else and to stutter trite words of gratitude on behalf of the men he'd rescued. In her heart—the treacherous heart that seemed bent on betraying her—she knew very well that those stilted phrases weren't even akin to the things she longed to say. She felt false and empty as she spoke.

Adrian stared at her through her whole performance. It was as if he knew exactly how she truly felt and held her in weary contempt for not being honest.

His eyes burned at her as she coolly and politely thanked him. She thanked him—when all she wanted to do was to leave it to the men he'd saved to express gratitude while she threw herself into his arms and sobbed out her relief that he'd come back safely.

She wanted to cling to him—to touch him again and

again as Widow Egan had touched her son—and to tell him how she had feared, oh, so desperately feared, for him.

Something inside her wanted to cry out that her heart could beat again now that he was finally safe. Her obligation to her family and to her class stifled the natural inclinations of her heart and caught and held the impulse firmly in check.

Everything Elise Danforth was feeling showed plainly in her face. Adrian watched the changing emotions there and the way her trembling hand remained stretched out toward him. He knew her heart as surely as if she'd told him its longings. He also knew she was too much a creature of her upbringing, too much a member of her blasted class. There was no way Lady Elise Danforth could put her own happiness ahead of the pride of her family. There was no way she would.

In his weary mind, he cursed her and all the damned gentry. Stubbornly denying the tenderness he felt for her, he hoped she felt as if she were being torn in half!

Eyes narrowed with disdain, he vowed he'd make her admit her love for him. He'd refuse to give her any peace until she'd surrendered to her heart and conquered all the inbred snobbery of her class. To that end, knowing this promise would bring them together often, he told her, "I'll represent the miners, milady."

His voice was no more than a croak. His throat, bruised by the drag of the bound hands of the man he'd carried up out of Malfont Mine, could produce no better. But Elise heard it and smiled with relief. "Thank you. Thank you for everything."

He saw her catch her soft underlip in her teeth, as if

she were embarrassed by the depth of feeling she'd heard in her own voice. She turned away abruptly, then swung back toward him like a compass needle seeking north.

Helpless bewilderment showed briefly in her face as her attraction to him warred with her well-taught prejudices. Then she straightened her shoulders and took refuge in a lifetime of careful training. "Thank you, Ashe."

His stomach tightened in anger as he heard her again deny him a respectful term of address. Adrian felt his teeth grate as his jaw locked.

Elise ignored the muscle she saw jump in his jaw. Her tone was cool as she said, "I shall get in touch with you soon."

Elise took a deep breath. Her businesslike attitude gave her the strength she needed to walk away from him. She went before the weariness in his face lost out to the anger she sensed beneath it . . . or before her frail strength gave way to the frantic urging of her heart.

Ashe let his head fall back against the cool rock wall behind him. He watched her go out into the rain with burning eyes, hating the fact that she'd left him, rejoicing in the effort it took her to do so.

A resolve touched the edges of his mind. Fed by the bitterness of the last six years, it took root and grew. Only an uncharitable whim before, now it became a solemn vow. If it was the last thing he ever did, he swore savagely, he would make the glorious Lady Elise Danforth admit that she was hopelessly, passionately, in love with a lowly stranger.

Chapter Fourteen

❦

The next day dawned storm washed. Gulls wheeled and called in a bright blue sky. Underfoot, the grass was greener and softer in appearance than it had been for weeks, and even the tracks for the miniature railway that took the coal down for loading on boats looked clean, twin lines of silver leading toward the sea.

A gull dove down to skim along the waves and to rise again, a fish shining in its beak. Adrian glanced up at it. He noted the satisfied predator's graceful lack of concern and the frantic clumsiness of the struggling prey. He found an odd parallel to the situation in which he was about to embroil himself. The mine owners were powerful—blessed with the time and money to live in gracious ease. The miners frantically struggled to make ends meet, caught in the grip of the mine owners and totally at their seemingly nonexistent mercy.

Now he was about to step between the two. He'd agreed to represent the miners for Elise. Having been intimately involved in a mine disaster had filled him with a grim determination to stop any others from occurring. And, of course, there was Elise. Perhaps his motives weren't what they should have been when he'd made the commitment, but he was nevertheless ready now to do the job as well as he could for the men beside whom he toiled underground. The disaster at Malfont had decided him irrevocably. God knew the miners needed all the help he could get for them— and God knew they deserved it.

In addition, he was highly suspicious of the circumstances surrounding the collapse of the main shaft at Malfont. He'd been down the bloody thing too many times not to know that it was well shored and maintained. Malfont might not give a damn about his men, but he took excellent care of his property. There was no way that shaft had collapsed from natural causes.

He decided to send for old Foggerty, the gunner's mate he'd known on his first ship. The old man was living in Maidenhead with his son if he remembered correctly. Foggerty should be able to tell if explosives had played any part in the mine disaster. Unless he missed his guess, the old boy would be glad of a real job to do and a break from his retirement.

He hadn't had a chance to talk to Rafe Egan yet, but he'd heard from the man who'd been nearest the boy that Rafe had "shot up straight and looked quicklike" toward the main shaft just before all hell'd broken loose. He was more than interested to find out just what had startled the youth seconds before he'd been inundated by debris.

Those concerns would have to wait, however. The thing he had to do now was to arm himself with weapons powerful enough to accomplish his chosen

mission. It was time he went to Delacourte, the palatial home of his late uncle . . . his home now.

Turning the last bend in the road, he stopped dead
in his tracks. His first sight of Delacourte almost took
his breath away. Vast and golden in the sunshine, it
sprawled regally on its broad triple terraces, its extensive gardens spilling down to the far shore of the great
ornamental lake that reflected it. On the lake's wide
surface, swans, dozens of them, glided majestically,
their wakes arrowing behind them on the glassy water.

Something stirred deep inside Adrian. Generations
who had gone before reached out to him. A deep, cool
pride of ownership pervaded his senses, the strength
of it almost dizzying.

When he felt the spell tightening around him, he
shook his head angrily. The last thing he intended to
do was to tamely join the ranks of the landed lords he
blamed for the deaths of his family. Not anytime soon
anyway—and never tamely.

But Delacourte was his, and it was magnificent.
With one last glance of reluctant appreciation, he
straightened his shoulders and strode forward with
determination to cover the last half mile to the limestone mansion.

Heated by the long walk from the Malfont miners'
cottages to Delacourte, Adrian Ashe was in no mood
to suffer fools gladly when he finally reached his destination. He seized the huge brass sculpture of two
writhing sea monsters locked in eternal combat that
was the door knocker. With an iron grip he sent reverberations rocketing throughout the great manor house.

Almost immediately, a startled footman opened the

door. He took one look at the rough garb Adrian wore and tried to bar his way. Adrian shoved him rudely aside and strode into the great hall.

Pouring in through the high windows of the hall, a rosy golden light illuminated its back wall. Immense tapestries depicting great battles covered the spaces between impressive arrays of weapons. Flagpoles topped with golden finials jutted out at intervals. From them, stained and tattered battle flags and ensigns hung limply. Their faded colors were myriad in the pale shadows and the bright bars of sunlight.

Adrian wasn't interested in the glory of his ancestors, however. His mind was seething with plans. To get them into operation, he needed his secretary. And he wanted him *now*!

"I say!" The footman was a blur of scarlet-and-silver livery as he scurried around Adrian in a vain attempt to block his way again. "Now see 'ere!"

"Perkins!" Adrian's roar set up its own reverberations. They rivaled those he'd sent crashing through the solemn, silent dignity of Delacourte with the door knocker.

"Shush! Shush!" The footman pushed repeatedly at the taller man's chest. "You can't shout in 'ere like that."

The intruder walked on as if he didn't even notice. When finally he dropped his gaze to the determined face of the footman, he told the distraught minion, "I can do as I damn well please in here, thank you!" Then, only a little less irritably, "Where the hell is my butler?"

The footman paled and snatched his hands back as

if he'd been burned. "Your b-b-butler?" He added belatedly, "Sir?"

"Yes, blast you!" Adrian felt his temper rising again. He should have taken time for breakfast. "Go find Perkins."

A calm and unruffled voice announced, "Here I am, milord." Unperturbed, Perkins moved into view. He put Adrian in mind of a stately ship under full sail. "How may I serve, Your Lordship?" He drew the "how" out just a bit, and Adrian was reminded of a foghorn. He smiled, his bad temper forgotten.

The footman's eyes went round as saucers. His agitated gaze shifted rapidly between the other two men while the blood drained from his narrow face.

Reprieve came. "You may go, Parker." Perkins's tone left no room for loitering, and Parker wasted no time in removing himself from the overpowering presence of his new master. Grateful to escape and giddy with news, he could hardly wait to get belowstairs and spread the word that the new master was here at last. He'd let the others discover for themselves that the new earl was a man well made to scare the hell out of 'em.

"Perkins." Adrian's voice lost its anger now that his goal was within reach. "Get me some brandy and my secretary."

Untroubled by his employer's rough order, Perkins replied, "Will there be anything else, Your Lordship?" His eyebrow rose inquiringly in his carefully impassive face. "A bite to eat, perhaps?"

More of the tension went out of Adrian. He smiled. For the second time he was appreciative of the foresight his solicitors had shown in having Perkins present at their London meeting with him. His butler's ability to recognize him certainly simplified matters. "An excellent suggestion, Perkins. And tell my secretary . . . ?" He paused for Perkins to supply the man's name.

Perkins didn't miss a beat. "Mr. Lewis, milord."

Adrian continued his sentence, "that he's invited to join me at table—in the study, if you please."

"Very well, Your Lordship." Perkins led the way to the study. He was smugly satisfied that the splendid hot breakfast he'd commanded the moment he'd seen the new Earl of Haverford approaching the house would be just the thing.

"Plain paper, Your Lordship?" Adrian's secretary shuffled through the fine writing papers bearing the earl's crest as if he hoped to find something to suit his employer's purpose there. His handsome, fine-boned face reflected his confusion.

"Nothing I intend to do here tonight must be connected with me in any way, Mr. Lewis. Even this list we're going to make. Please keep that in mind."

"Yes, Your Lordship."

Adrian steepled his long, fine fingers and ignored his secretary's shocked notice of the scabs and bruises thus displayed. "I want you to spend the next week seeking out every mortgage, every gambling debt, every obligation of any sort that any of my neighbors have incurred. No matter what the cost, you are to buy all of them up for me. Is that understood?"

Alistair Lewis shook his fair hair back off his forehead and met Adrian's intent gaze with a bewildered one of his own. His light blue eyes were full of questions. The man in front of him had such presence, radiated such confidence and power in spite of his rough clothes, that he was too much in awe of him to ask them, however. Instead, he bowed and said, "Perfectly, Your Lordship." In spite of his best resolve, he blurted, "But—"

The bleak intensity of his employer's gaze stopped him in midutterance.

"Later, Lewis. I'll satisfy your curiosity later. For now, just do as I ask."

"Of course, Your Lordship."

Adrian ignored his secretary's slightly wounded expression. Plenty of time to smooth Lewis's ruffled feathers when he was certain the man could be trusted.

Lewis frowned. So this tall stranger with the brooding eyes was the new Earl of Haverford. Why then didn't he come to live here at Delacourte? Why was he dressed in the cheap clothing of a common laborer?

He was a handsome brute, he'd give him that. In the clothes of a gentleman—clothes he should by all rights be wearing—Haverford would be impressive. God, he was impressive now. Properly clothed, gentlemen would think him a Corinthian, muscled and coordinated as he was. As for the distaff side, he hadn't an instant's doubt that the poor man would be pursued by half the females of the ton.

The ladies would find him absolutely devastating. Not in those clothes, of course. No lady would risk bringing shame upon herself or her family by even *appearing* to notice him in his present garb.

He shifted uneasily, wondering again why the Earl of Haverford was going about disguised as a lowly miner. No answer was forthcoming he knew, so, though his curiosity was eating him alive, he gave it up. He suppressed a deep sigh. The earl looked up, and his secretary's thoughts went flying. He felt like a bug, impaled on that piercing glance.

Immediately aware of the feelings of the man across from him, Adrian smiled slightly. Calmly, he finished giving the slender secretary his list of orders. Then, his gaze level, he added one final duty. "One more thing, Lewis. There is a boy, Rafe Egan, who was injured at Malfont Mine yesterday. Find him something to do." His smile quirked. "Sitting down. Both his legs are broken."

"Both legs broken? But what good is he—"

"That is exactly what I require *you* to discover. Just do it. Put his mother to work in the kitchen as well. She's lame, but she should be able to sit and slice vegetables, at least. Winter's coming, I want her by the fire."

"But, Your Lordship, you already have a full staff of servants!"

Adrian's gaze sharpened. Very softly he said, "And I want two more." Without expression, he watched the man across the desk. "See to it."

The secretary pulled nervously at his spotless cravat. "Certainly, milord."

After a long moment Adrian asked, "Is the Haverford mine operating?"

"Umm . . . yes. After a fashion. Without your orders, it's been difficult."

Adrian scored one for his courage. "Hire the Malfont miners and bring Haverford up to speed. Make the arrangement so that Malfont knows he can have his men back as he needs them, but give them jobs to tide them over until Malfont Mine reopens."

"Very well, milord." Something bordering on admiration lit his eyes. He wasn't used to thoughtful employers. He shuffled papers to hide his momentary confusion.

Adrian dismissed the flustered man with a quiet, "Thank you, Mr. Lewis. That will be all."

After the door closed behind his employee, Adrian let his head rest against the ornately carved back of his chair. God willing, he had set in motion the first of his plans.

And he'd taken care of the Malfont miners, and Rafe Egan and his widowed mother so that they wouldn't suffer with the boy unemployable. What had he forgotten? He pressed a finger and thumb to the bridge of his nose and was annoyed to find them stiff.

His brain felt stiff, too. Weary to the point of inefficiency. "Damn," he murmured without much enthusiasm. He ached all over.

He wondered idly how Malfont was taking his loss.

He rested there a moment longer, then shoved himself away from the comfort of the great chair with an impatient thrust of his shoulders. Time to get on with it.

Sir James Malfont's secretary knocked at the door of his master's study. When he received no answer after a second knock, he entered the luxurious room. Just inside, he came to an abrupt, flustered stop.

Sir James Malfont sat sprawled in his chair staring into the low flames of the small fire on the study hearth, his eyes brooding. At his secretary's interruption, he looked up sharply. "What is it?" His voice was almost a snarl.

"I heard there was an accident at the mine yesterday, Sir James."

Malfont sighed mightily. "Yes. The main shaft"—he sought a word with great care—"collapsed."

"Then you will be wanting me to apply to Lloyd's for the insurance money, will you not, Sir James?"

Malfont looked at his secretary as if seeing him for the first time since he'd entered the study. "Yes. That would be an excellent idea. A most excellent idea."

Quietly, the secretary left the room.

Elise arose, amazed that she'd managed to get a good night's sleep.

"Agnes." Her voice was pensive. "I think I'd like to ride today."

"Of course, milady." Agnes went about the business of laying out one of Elise's new habits. She kept an eye on her mistress as she did so.

"Agnes?"

"Yes, milady?" Agnes turned her full attention on Elise. The girl looked dreamy. Agnes's lips pursed, her eyes narrowed.

"He was magnificent, wasn't he?" Elise's eyes were shining.

A thousand cautions rose in the abigail's mind. A hundred words of wisdom presented themselves.

One look at her mistress's face stilled them all.

She cringed inwardly as she saw with painful clarity the heartache that lay ahead for her dear young charge. There was only gentleness in her voice as she said, simply, "Yes, Lissie. He was."

With Malfont Mine closed, Hal Lime had no reason to be absent from his supper table. In a show of bravado against the capriciousness of a fate that had deprived him of his livelihood, he and Lettie asked Adrian to join them for the evening meal.

"That was the best stew I've ever tasted, Lettie. Thank you for inviting me." Adrian held up his pipe and raised an eyebrow, asking her permission as he always did, knowing it would be forthcoming.

Hal accepted the tobacco pouch his guest proffered with a grin. Adrian grinned in response, and the men settled back to tamp their pipes as Lettie cleared the table.

Before the first wreath of smoke encircled them, a terrified scream filled the night. Jolting upright, Adrian looked to Lettie, his eyes startled wide.

Lettie sighed and shook her head in resignation. She left the dishes to soak. Wiping her wet hands on her apron she turned toward the bedroom, offering an explanation. "It's Megan again, Mr. Adrian. She do have nightmares something awful."

Adrian sprang up to join her. Together they hurried to the child.

Arriving at the bedside, they found the other two girls sleeping determinedly, pillows clasped tightly over their ears. Obviously they were long accustomed to Megan's nightmares.

Lettie perched on the edge of the bed and gathered the sobbing child into her arms. Rocking her gently, she crooned, "There, there. It's all right. I'm here, little one. It's all right."

Megan grabbed her around the neck and hung on for dear life. "The cliff . . . oh, no! Not the cliff! Ooohhhh, Papa! Papa. You bad man! Don't!" She went rigid with horror. "No! Ah, no don't! Oh, Papa! Paaapaaa!" The word was a drawn-out wail. "How could you?" She was sobbing as if her little heart would break. "Oh, how could you do it? How . . . could . . . you?"

She hiccuped. She was slowly calming down as Lettie patted and rocked and soothed her. Finally, her eyes, screwed tightly shut as she lived through the terror of her dream, opened. They were dazed and frightened. "Oh, Lettie. It was that dream again. Thank you for coming."

Adrian reached for her and she went into his arms. Carrying her, he moved back into the warmly lit front room. "I came, too, Meggie. I came, too." He smoothed his hand in little circles on her back. Keeping her head pressed against his shoulder, he kept her from seeing how fiercely he scowled. "I want to make the dreams go away if I can." His voice was as soft as his expression was harsh. "Will you help me?"

She clung tightly 'round his neck for an instant. Finally, she responded to his gentle insistence, "Oh, yes, Mr. Adrian."

"It will be hard. Are you willing to try?"

She met his level gaze directly, her eyes solemn. "If it will make the dreams stop, I'll do anything."

Adrian sat with her curled in his lap, his arms strongly about her. "Can you remember the dream?"

Reluctance showed briefly in her face. She wasn't eager to recall the horror. Determination replaced it. "No, when I'm awake, I can't, but I'll try."

"I'm certain it was about the night your father died, Meggie." He hated that his words made her cringe against him. Gently he rubbed her back, his hand making more tiny circles. "Are you brave enough to try to think back to that night?"

Tears filled her eyes. "I've tried to, and *I can't*."

Adrian sat silent a moment. He'd seen sailors unable to recall moments of intense fear. He knew it was the mind's way of guarding itself from horror with which it wasn't able to deal. He weighed the wisdom of trying to get the child to remember. Would it help her? Or was it just that he wanted another piece to fit into the puzzle he was trying to solve?

He looked away from the tiny girl to find Lettie watching him intently. "She do need to be rid of these horrors, Mr. Ashe. Hardly a night goes by that they don't rob her of her sleep."

"And you of yours as well." His voice was rich with appreciation of her care of the child.

Lettie blushed and shrugged, downplaying with a simple gesture her unselfish care of the tyke, accepting it as part of her role as the mother of the family. Her concern, clear in her eyes, was all for the child Adrian held.

Looking down at Megan again he hugged her close. "You know the dream is of the night your father . . ." Deliberately he let his voice trail away. What word, if any, would the child supply?

"Was killed." Her lower lip trembled. "Yes, I know."

"Were you there?"

"No."

"Where were you, Meggie?"

"I was at my bedroom window."

"And you could see . . ." He cast his mind to the front window of the second story of his cottage—the cottage that had once been her home. Accurately, he recalled the winding path to the small plateau that overlooked the sea—and the foot of the cliff where Ethan Frost had died. ". . . the path and the edge of the cliff . . ." He tightened his arms as the child seemed to shrink to half her size against him. Hating himself, he pushed on, his voice barely a whisper. "And you saw?"

"I saw"—her voice was a fragile thread—"my papa coming up the path." She screwed her face up in awful concentration. Then she shook her head.

Adrian ignored her negative gesture. "And he was all alone? Or was there someone with him."

Megan began to quiver. "Papa was by himself."

Suddenly, it occurred to Adrian what to say. "But there was someone waiting for him, wasn't there?"

Megan almost shot out of his arms. Her eyes flew wide open. "Yes! Yes! There was a man waiting for my papa! A man on a horse!" Her eyes were wide. Her face was frozen with the dreadful knowledge she'd finally won. Then it crumpled in the agony of remembrance. Her voice rose to a keening wail. "And he p-p-pushed my papa . . ." Her shrill voice filled the room. "He pushed my papa over the cliff!"

Huge wracking sobs shook Megan's small frame.

Her words were lost in an incoherent babble of pain. She slumped against Adrian.

Cradling the child, Adrian looked to Lettie. He may have solved the riddle, but what had he done to the child?

Seeing the stricken look on Adrian's face, Lettie reached for Megan. Adrian let the child go and Lettie, crooning some ancient lullaby, walked back into the bedroom, rocking the child as she went.

Closing his eyes a moment against his own pain, Adrian sat silent. Recriminations made a private hell for him.

Lettie returned after a while. Crossing to him, she smiled. Seeing his haunted eyes, she placed her hands on his shoulders and shook her head at him. "No, no, Mr. Ashe. You're not to feel like that. Meggie said"— she bent down to look him full in the face—" 'Now, it's over,' and she went right off to sleep. I think you've done a wonderful thing, Lord bless you."

With that she kissed him gently on the cheek and went back to her dishes, humming. Hal gave him an approving smile.

Adrian let go a gusty sigh. He felt like a man reprieved from the gallows. Leaning back with his pipe again, he let his mind enjoy its triumph.

A man on a horse, the child had said. Only the gentry rode horses in these parts. He had one of his answers. Megan Frost's father had been shoved over the cliff to his death by a so-called *gentleman*!

Chapter Fifteen

❧

Elise sat frowning at the blank piece of crested notepaper on the desk in front of her. Bright bars of sunlight striped the broad surface of the tooled leather-topped desk, Lawrence's desk, for the storm had washed the skies to clear blue and sent the clouds scudding off to the west.

Only a few dust motes danced in the sunbeams.

Unfortunately, there were too few to serve as a distraction. There were simply not enough of them to make an interesting, shifting pattern. Too much space between motes. Sometimes her staff was more than efficient.

She really needed a distraction, too. She was trying to phrase a letter to Adrian Ashe, and it was proving difficult.

What was she to say to him? For that matter, how was she to address him? Further—and she threw up her hands—how the devil was she supposed to know if the man could even *read*!

Frustration drove her to pace the Oriental carpets strewn about on the parquet floor of her study. She

ought to be glad that Adrian Ashe had agreed to represent the miners for her. And she was. Really she was.

She took a deep breath and talked sense to herself.
"A miner, Elise," she told herself firmly. "Adrian
Ashe is a laborer. A common laborer."

She remembered all the strictures taught her from
the nursery. Remembered well all the tales of highborn
ladies who had lowered—and ruined—themselves by
running away with coachmen and grooms.

Especially, she remembered the oft-told tale of a
distant cousin who'd run away with the younger son
of an impoverished baronet who was working as her
father's secretary. How many times she'd been told
that Clarissa had lived a life of poverty and shame!

She continued to pace as she recalled her inability
to understand how her cousin could have done such a
thing. Now she felt . . . tangled, like a ball of yarn
used as a kitten's plaything. Except the magnitude of
what she was feeling transcended anything a kitten
might do. For an instant, she imagined a whimsical
picture of a lion playing with a ball of yarn.

Then her smile died slowly, and she stamped her
foot. "Enough!" She had absolutely no intention of
following in her cousin's footsteps. She was no green
girl fresh from the schoolroom. She'd been a happily
married woman. She was perfectly capable of controlling this foolish fascination for Adrian Ashe.

After all, it had come upon her in that moment of
weakness when Ashe had carried her out of that horror
of a mine, and it would leave her as quickly as it had
come. She'd been vulnerable. And she'd been foolish.
She would not be either one again.

Fleetingly, though, a wistful thought from her girlhood intruded. She remembered how she had often
wondered, while growing up, whether her cousin
Clarissa had been happy and in love—while in
poverty and disgrace.

A long moment passed, while Ashe's face filled her
mind's eye and her heartbeat quickened. Then Elise
laughed aloud. Deriding herself for being foolish, she
denied the longing she felt—ignored the fervent
wishing that he might have been of her own class.
Sharply, she told herself, "Behave, Elise Danforth!
There's no such thing as a fairy godmother."

Decisively, she returned to her desk and got back to
the task of writing the note. Forcing herself to think
impersonally, she settled on "Mr. Ashe" as the
address. After all, she was elevating him by asking
him to be her representative; he deserved the dignity
of that form of address. She could afford to give him
the polite form of salutation, as well. She had often
used it with Ethan Frost; she had no idea why she
wanted to withhold it from Ashe.

Dear Mr. Ashe, she wrote—then bogged down
again. She needed to meet with him, but where? He
was certain to remember—and resent—his last visit to
Danforth House. Somehow another didn't seem quite
the propitious thing to arrange. Where then? She could
hardly be expected to meet him at the inn. The
resulting scandal would rock the neighborhood.

She was momentarily amused at the thought.

Inspiration came. Betsy's! The Squire and Betsy
would be glad to have her visit, and the childless
couple were so indulgent where she was concerned

that she'd no doubt they'd tolerate Adrian for her sake, as well. They'd be the perfect chaperons for the meeting, and most important, it would be a safe place for Adrian to come.

Of course, she didn't want to risk his arriving there and perhaps having another unpleasant experience. She'd have him meet her at the crossroads just before, or at the foot of Squire Jepson's lane. Then they could go on together, and he would be safe.

Safe. Yes. She'd learned at the top of a smoking mine shaft that his safety had become her primary concern. Now, she didn't delude herself about wanting a safe meeting place. She was well aware that what had happened to Ethan Frost could just as easily happen to Adrian Ashe.

Even while her whole body chilled at the thought, she assured herself that she simply didn't want the responsibility of another tragedy. She would be as concerned for any man in Ashe's new position. That was only natural, simple human concern.

She sighed. So why did it have to be so much more with Ashe? Why did she have to be so attracted to a man who could never be anything to her?

Writing quickly, before she could become any more entangled in her own nonsense, she requested Adrian Ashe meet her just past the crossroads at the foot of Squire Jepson's lane at eight the following evening.

Rising from her desk, she crossed to the bellpull. A minute later, she was handing her note to the footman who answered her summons. "See that this gets to Mr. Ashe, please, Louis. He lives in the house that used to be Mr. Frost's."

"Down to Malfont's cottages. I'll do it, milady." He fought to keep his expression noncommittal, but he was the youngest of her footmen, and couldn't repress his grin. He bobbed her a half bow. "Right away, milady."

Overcome by embarrassment, he spun away from her and almost collided with Agnes at the door. "Heavens!" Agnes turned to watch the footman rush off down the hall. "What kind of fire did you light under him?"

"He's just young." Elise smiled. "This is the first commission I've ever given him. I think he's just eager to please." Her eyes were warm as she met her abigail's regard. "It's rather a nice feeling to be served with such enthusiasm."

"All of us like to please you. You're very easy to work for."

"Come now, Agnes." Elise frowned lightly. "Surely you don't put yourself in the category of servant?" She linked her arm through her friend's as they left the study.

"Right now, I do. I need you to come up to go through your wardrobe. The clothes you sent to London for have come, and there's nowhere near enough room to hang them up."

"Oh, good. I've been looking forward to their arrival. I want to see if Madame Denise understood my wishes."

"*Hmmmm.*" Agnes gave her a wry glance. "I think by the look of some of them, she understood better than you did yourself."

Elise asked with a voice full of laughter, "Now just what do you mean by that?"

"You'll see." Agnes tried to say it darkly, but her smile spoiled the effect.

When they reached her chambers, Elise cried out in delight. Every color imaginable filled the room. Fabric of every description covered every flat surface. Agnes had made a display of the new clothes Elise had ordered from London. Elise turned to hug her. "How wonderful! After two years of mourning—all these beautiful colors. I'd forgotten how much they lift the spirit!"

"A year of blacks and another of nothing but purples and lavenders can do that to you, milady, and that's no lie." Agnes smiled at her employer. "The only other colors you ever wore were those of your riding habits, and lately your one blue morning gown and your green evening gown. And thankful I was that you had those. I hope you never have another thing black, purple, or lavender!"

"*Hmmmm.*" Elise's very feminine attention had already been captured by the array of fabulous clothes. She picked up a diaphanous sea green gown. The silk clung to her fingers. The dress was cut to perfection. "Have necklines been lowered this much, Agnes?" Holding the dress up to her, she walked over to the pier glass and studied her reflection.

Agnes smiled at the picture she made. "You're young, my dear. On you it will be lovely."

Before she could stop herself, Elise wondered if Adrian Ashe would find her lovely in the green gown. For an instant distress showed on her face.

Agnes had no trouble reading her former nursery charge's thoughts. Deftly she turned them to more acceptable channels. "Both Sir James and Deverill will find you completely enchanting in that . . . and in all the others." She swept the room, with a broad gesture. "They're all masterpieces. All designed to show you off to perfection, whether at the dinner table or at an assembly."

Elise didn't care about dinners and assemblies, though. *His* was the only admiration she sought, and that made her gnash her teeth. How could she let one totally unsuitable man, a lowly stranger, spoil her emergence from her widow's weeds?

She vented a huge sigh of frustration. "That reminds me, Agnes. I've asked Adrian Ashe to meet me on the road to Squire Jepson's tomorrow night at eight. Will you accompany me, please?"

Agnes nodded. "Yes. Of course. If you're to meet that great brute of a man." Her eyes twinkled, but before she could say more, there was a light tap on the open door.

"Come in."

The crippled maid, Mary, sidled through the doorway, smiling. "Would you like anything, milady?"

Agnes frowned. Mary's devotion to Elise was so deep it was almost doglike, and it was beginning to irritate her. She knew Elise had rescued the woman from certain starvation, but still she wished Mary were not *quite* so grateful!

Surprised at herself for such a waspish thought, Agnes chided herself for jealousy and told the young woman, "I'm glad you've come." She forced a smile.

"I shall be grateful for your help hanging all these clothes." By the time she'd finished her sentence, her smile had genuine warmth.

The three of them set to work. Deciding which garments of Elise's extensive wardrobe to discard gave them no difficulty at all. With great enthusiasm, Elise pulled black, lavender, and purple out of the armoires in her dressing room by the armful rather than by the item. "These, and these, and this one."

Agnes straightened from where she bent over a storage trunk from the attics. Pushing a wayward strand of hair back under her cap, she started laughing. "Lissie! For heaven's sake. Go a little slower. Mary and I can't fold this fast."

Elise stopped pulling the past two years' clothing out of the cherry-wood armoire she was currently attacking and turned to Agnes, smiling. "I *am* in an awful rush to be rid of them, aren't I? Perhaps I should do penance for such unseemly haste by selecting something from among them to wear tomorrow night when I go to meet Adrian Ashe. We'll be picking him up at the crossroads, I'm afraid."

Neither of them heard Mary gasp.

"I'm sure Betsy Jepson would rather see one of your new fashions, Lissie. She loves pretty clothes, and you know she refuses to leave that husband of hers long enough to go to London and order any for herself."

"Yes, you're right. I shall wear this new rose velvet riding habit." She held the jacket of the habit against her chest. "How bold it is with my dreadful red hair. It will give me courage."

"As if you . . ."

But Agnes's reply and all else faded out of Mary's mind, she was so appalled by what she had heard. *Courage!* Lady Elise would need *courage* to meet Adrian Ashe? A brute, Agnes had called him, she had. A brute. And now her poor brave benefactress had to méet with him at the crossroads. Vaguely she'd heard that the man had agreed to help her mistress with the miners in some way. She hadn't listened carefully after she'd heard her mistress say, "I'm afraid . . ." Anger and panic filled Mary. Anger that this Ashe would force a meeting—and one at night, at that—on her cherished employer, and panic that she might be unable to stop him from keeping that appointment.

Her mind burned with the effort to come up with a solution. Her thoughts chased around in her head like foxes. She had no idea what it was she was supposed to do. Her hands began to shake with the strength of her inner turmoil. She must save Elise!

Elise noticed her servant's distress. "Mary. Are you all right?"

How like *her* to see and care. Mary managed to stutter, "I'm fine, milady." She couldn't control the shaking, however, and under the stress of her anxiety for Elise it became more pronounced.

"No, you are not all right." Elise came close, touching her shoulder, looking down into her face, her own full of concern. "Go and rest, Mary." Her mistress's voice was soft and gentle. "Get Cook to give you a cup of tea with lots of sugar." Her tone took on authority. "And don't do another thing for the rest of the day."

Mary didn't dare look up to protest that the day was young yet. She didn't want Elise to see the frantic determination in her eyes. There was only one thing she could do. "Yes, milady," she agreed meekly, and quietly left the room.

Once the door closed softly behind her, she ran, hobbling, down the hall. She had to get to her beloved lady's friend to get help. She had to. It was a long, long walk, and walking didn't come easy to her, but she had to go. If it took her all the rest of this day, she had to go.

Elise rang for Agnes to help her dress to meet Adrian Ashe. She'd had only a light supper, and it was a good thing, too, because butterflies in her stomach threatened to make even that sit poorly.

Agnes arrived, her bright brown eyes indulgent, a fond smile on her face. "Now, now, Lissie. Didn't we decide yesterday morning that you were going to wear the rose velvet riding habit?"

"Oh, that was sheer foolishness. Of course I don't need a riding habit when you and I are going together in the carriage." Her voice sounded a little tentative. "And the nonsense about needing that color for courage was all in fun as well. I have no need of courage to face Adrian Ashe."

Agnes wondered if that were so. She certainly found the large man intimidating in his scowling intensity and his newly-won heroic stature. Just now, however, she knew Elise was in a quandary because of the way the handsome Adrian Ashe pulled at her emotions. There was nothing surprising about that. She sighed heavily. Why must he be so unsuitable?

Her heart almost broke for the young woman in front of her. She knew society would never let them be together. She knew Elise's conscience would never let her have an affair. The whole thing was impossible.

With another gusty sigh, she turned to the task of choosing clothes with her employer. "I think that your new—"

A firm knock sounded.

Elise and Agnes looked at each other, startled. It was past suppertime. Any knock that firm had to be Helmsley's. Whatever could have happened to send the butler to Elise at this hour?

They both went to the door, Agnes curious, Elise worried that there might be some crisis. The last thing she wanted was a domestic accident that required her to linger at Danforth House. She would, of course, stay if one of her servants needed her attention, but oh, how she hoped she wouldn't have to be late meeting Adrian. He was such a prideful man. He'd take her tardiness as an insult, and he was difficult enough to deal with already. Offended, he'd be worse. She could certainly do without that!

"Yes, Helmsley?"

"You have a visitor, milady." Exasperation edged his voice. Clearly, he felt whoever had arrived, uninvited, at this hour was sadly lacking in good manners.

"Oh. Dev." Elise let the exclamation go before she'd thought. All three of them knew it had to be he. No one else would be so presumptuous.

Disappointment flooded her. She would be late.

Whatever Dev—who had always been there when she needed him—wanted, she could hardly send him away without seeing him, much as she wanted to. "Tell him I'll be right down, please, Helmsley."

With a carefully controlled, "Very good, milady," her butler turned and stalked off down the hall.

Agnes closed the door behind him. "Helmsley does not approve," she said, her voice full of amusement.

Elise huffed a disgusted sigh. "Neither do I! What can Dev want—tonight of all nights? It's almost as if he *meant* to make me late for my appointment." Her eyes flashed rebellion.

Agnes tried for a soothing tone. "Let's get you dressed, at least, dear. Then we can leave as soon as he does."

As soon as Elise appeared in the drawing-room doorway, Dev shot out of the ivory-brocade chair he'd graced with casual ease. "My word, Elise. Out of your mourning clothes . . . and you look smashing!" Smiling broadly, he took both her hands and kissed her cheek. "Thank you for seeing me."

Elise fought down her impatience and tried not to register the fact that the ormolu clock over the fireplace showed she had barely enough time left to make her appointment with Adrian. Smiling as sincerely as she could manage, she asked, "What is it, Dev? Is something the matter?"

"Must there be something the matter for me to visit my dearest friend?" He frowned lightly, an eyebrow quirked.

Recognizing in his cajoling tone that he needed her,

she sat on one end of the settee, and gestured for him to take the other.

He chose to sit in the middle. Turned toward her as he was, his knees pressed against her skirt. "You look exceptionally lovely. That is my favorite color, you know, yellow. So cheerful a color. Why, m'dear, it's almost as if you were expecting me."

To her own surprise, Elise blushed. She'd certainly been at pains to look her best, but not for Dev, and not telling him so made her feel as if she were somehow being dishonest. "No." She managed to keep the irritation out of her voice even as the tall clock in the hall chimed the half hour. Now she would certainly be late. "I have an appointment with the new head of the miners' group at eight." She had always confided in Dev; he was her best friend. She could hardly lie to him. Why then had she failed to name Ashe?

"Ah. Yes. The surly Mr. Ashe, is it not?"

Elise's eyes flashed. "He's not surly."

"You'd have your work cut out for you if you tried to prove that by me!"

"The man's a hero, Dev. He went into Malfont's mine and saved all the men trapped down there." She glared at her friend. "I hardly think calling him surly is a just reward for so selfless an act."

"Such heat, m'dear." Dev grinned at her.

Elise felt herself blushing again, and, not for the first time, heartily consigned her fair complexion to the nether regions. "I grow weary of you and James denigrating the man just because he isn't gentry. He's a man for all that, and a brave one to boot."

"To boot? Really Elise." His grin was affectionately

derisive. "Consorting with the lower classes is certainly adding interesting expressions to your vocabulary." He raised a teasing eyebrow. "I wonder if your family would approve?"

It was as if he'd thrown cold water on her. The approval of her family had always weighed heavily with her. Perhaps too heavily, in the light of their indifference to her. And she was certain that Dev knew it.

With a new clarity, she saw that he was not merely teasing. Dev was warning her. Was she so transparent, then? The thought brought her up short. Dearest God. She hoped not!

Deverill seemed to sense her sudden discomfort. Instantly he was contrite. Holding her at arm's length, he pretended to study her gown. "So this is one of the new gowns you ordered from Madame Denise. It's vastly becoming, my dear."

The clock chimed the three-quarter hour, and impatience leapt in Elise.

Dev was still speaking. "You wore your purples and lavenders better than any widow I've ever seen, but it's wonderful to see you in something else for a change." He laughed indulgently.

Rude or not, Elise looked directly at the clock on the mantel.

"Oh, Elise!" Dev gave it up. "I can feel the tension in your hands." His tone was injured. "Are you so anxious to go meet your lowly stranger?"

"Yes." Elise frowned severely at him. "Yes, I am," she told him firmly. "It's a business meeting, and it is for a cause that you know has long been dear to my heart." Anger raised her voice. "And I wish you would not imply that it is something more. I find your insinuation insulting, Dev. Mr. Ashe is not *'my lowly stranger,'* as you put it. He is a community-minded associate." She stood. "And I am now inexcusably late for my meeting with him."

Dev stood easily beside her. His eyes searched hers. "Ah, m'dear. *Never* speak to others of the estimable Mr. Ashe. You give too much away." He leaned forward and kissed her on her heated forehead. "Perhaps far too much," he whispered against her skin.

Pulling back, he kissed each of her hands in turn, and released them at last. "You know I love you, Elise, and I want you to be happy." He regarded her solemnly for a long moment, then said softly, "But this is not the way."

He turned then, and sauntered to the door. Pausing there he called back softly, "Go carefully, my dear." Then brusquely, "I'll call again at a more convenient time." He bowed, and was gone.

Elise stood still as a statue for a long moment. Then she rushed to the front door. Snatching from Helmsley the light cloak that matched the pale yellow gown she wore, she ran out of the house and down to the waiting carriage.

When she was safely seated across from Agnes, the coachman gave the horses their office to start.

From the lighted hallway behind the exasperated Helmsley, came the chime of the tall clock striking eight.

Agnes ignored the tears on her young friend's cheeks.

Elise clenched her hands into fists, the nails biting into her palms, and tried to tell herself her tears weren't caused by Dev's quiet warning. Instead, she told herself that they were tears of frustration.

Chapter Sixteen

∽

Adrian swung along the road toward the distant home of Squire Jepson. The night was pleasant, cool but without a chill, and the stars hung low in a clear sky. Full of an eagerness that he could explain all too well, he pushed on a bit faster.

When he passed the place where the road from the village joined the one he walked, he knew he was over halfway to his destination. The mouth of the next lane was it. He strode on purposefully.

Elise Danforth. He was about to see her again. See her in a quiet place and almost alone. Her image filled his mind. God, what a beauty she was. He felt warmth suffuse him at the mere thought of her, his gallant, glorious Elise.

She was brave and intelligent, too, and that more than pleased him. He'd known that from the moment he'd first looked into, and been completely captivated by, her marvelous green eyes. It had given him a great deal of satisfaction to have his estimation of her courage verified by her servants as well as her own actions at the mine disaster.

Since the accident at Malfont Mine, he'd made it a

point to buy drinks at the inn for the three footmen who had been of such help to him at the chimney shaft—the three men who'd saved him from falling back down the shaft with the unconscious Egan boy on his back.

The idea had been to thank them for his life, but it had garnered an additional benefit. They'd talked of little else but their mistress's attentiveness to the trapped men and to the operation to rescue them. Once the subject of Elise had come up, he'd encouraged them with pint after pint.

He felt his chest swell with pride to recall it. Elise Danforth was magnificent! He grinned recklessly as he let himself admit it. There at the very end, in those last horrible moments when he'd hung on that rope with hands that refused to obey his next command, he'd learned something.

When his hands were cramping and he began believing that he'd failed the boy on his back—that in the next moment he was going to lose his grip, let go, and plunge them back down into the collapsing mine to their deaths—truth had come. He was in love with Elise Danforth, and he was probably never going to get to tell her so. His overburdened, laboring heart had pained him at the thought.

He recalled vividly how one hand had slipped, sending him swinging wildly by the other. How the bound hands of the boy he was attempting to rescue had cut off his breath. How black despair had overwhelmed him. Worst of all, he remembered how he'd felt when he'd thought he was never going to see *her* again, never going to get to tell her that he loved her.

Then, just as his last vestige of strength had failed, Rafferty and Mudge had grabbed his wrists and pulled him and his burden over the edge to safety! He owed them far more than dinner and a pint of ale whenever he ran across them, but a greater reward would have to wait until his masquerade was over and he had taken his place as Earl of Haverford.

He let his mind dwell on those superlative moments when he had gotten up from where he'd lain, panting and spent on the rain-sodden ground beside the shaft and gone over to shelter under the overhang of the rock face. There Elise had been drawn to him. Against her will, but drawn surely, just the same. She'd been powerless not to come to where he sat, shaking with fatigue, sheltering under the lee of the rock.

Bless her. Blast her! She'd been unable to keep her hands off him, try as she would. Remembering, he could still feel the whisper of her touch on his hair. She'd been unable, too, to keep her feelings for him out of her eyes. But her words, when she'd addressed him, had been another matter altogether. The insufferable little snob had spoken to him as if he were infinitely beneath her notice.

His smile twisted. He was still determined to make her pay for that. He laughed aloud, a full-bodied, joyous laugh such as he hadn't laughed in years. He had such delectable tortures in store for her. His plan was simple. He intended slowly to drive her wild with kisses and tantalizing caresses—to force her to refute her snobbery.

Elise! And in a few more minutes he'd see her. Looking ahead, he saw the gate to the lane that went up the long slow hill to the squire's. With an odd little jolt he noted that there was no carriage waiting there as she'd promised. Odd. He frowned. He hadn't thought her the kind of person to be late. Remembering her men's enthusiastic praise of her punctuality, he found her absence doubly strange.

Suddenly his attention flew to a figure that had appeared on the path ahead. All his senses went on the alert. Somewhere in the back of his mind, a warning stirred.

The man meeting him in the road hardly seemed a threat. Slender and bent, he hobbled along, leaning heavily on a cane. He passed into the deep shadows cast by the trees at the entrance to Squire Jepson's lane and seemed to falter. Then he came slowly on, barely moving at all.

As they neared each other, the man looked up. His eyes completely hidden by the darkness under his hat brim he rasped, "Good evening, sir."

Something about the situation raised the hair on the back of Adrian's neck, but when the man stumbled and began to fall, he leapt forward to steady him.

The man's wiry arms closed around him, and he shouted, "Now!"

At his shout, two men rose from the ditch beside the road. Heavy clubs raised above their heads, they sprang at Adrian.

He shook the slender man off him and turned to meet his brawnier attackers. Instantly, the man he'd sought to save from falling leapt up and threw himself on Adrian's back, striving to hold Adrian's arms.

One of the clubs descended on Adrian's shoulder,

numbing his left arm. He turned in a flash to avoid the other, swinging his first attacker into its path.

With a howl the skinny man fell from Adrian's back. He lay in the dust of the lane, screeching curses.

"Quiet, you fool! Do you want to bring help for Ashe?"

The men with the clubs came at their victim again. The giant swung at him. The blow, deflected by Adrian's right forearm, failed in its intent to crush his skull, but left that arm useless. Still Adrian remained standing.

The frustrated bull of a man flung himself on Adrian and pinned him to the ground by sheer weight.

The second man stepped forward. "Got you!" He kept his voice low, but his victim heard every word. "Got you at last, damn you!" He danced around the two on the ground, watching for his opportunity. "Thanks to the beautiful redhead, we've got you!" Aiming as well as he could as the two men struggled and writhed, he struck a glancing blow to Adrian's head.

Dazed, Adrian stopped struggling for an instant.

It was all the advantage the man above him needed. Laughing triumphantly, he brought his club down again.

Evil blackness closed over Adrian Ashe.

Elise called impatiently to her coachman. "Faster! We're already late!"

Agnes grabbed a strap and hung on for dear life. The road to Squire Jepson's was hardly as smooth as a turnpike! She threw Elise a reproachful look. "He'll wait, dear." Then she bounced two feet into the air.

"Lissie!" she said sharply. "There's no need to get us killed!"

Elise just hung on to her own strap and let John Coachman take them on.

In Squire and Betsy Jepson's pleasant large, low-ceilinged parlor, Betsy Jepson waited. She and her husband were delighted at the prospect of a visit from Elise.

Betsy glanced at the tall clock beside the door. She frowned slightly. Elise would come soon now, surely. It was already ten minutes past eight. It wasn't like Elise to be late, and she was impatient to see her.

So was the squire; even if he wasn't about to admit it. She could tell by the frequency with which he pulled at his pipe. She smiled fondly. He was just as eager to see the dear girl as she was.

"Husband?"

"Yes, Wife?"

"You don't suppose anything has happened to her, do you?"

He shifted in his chair. "Now, Betsy." He sounded faintly exasperated. "What on earth could possibly happen to her between here and Danforth House? This isn't Hounslow Heath, you know."

Betsy colored faintly, put down her needlework, and came back at him with some heat. "Of course I know that this isn't—"

The door burst open. "Squire! Squire!" The disheveled man in the doorway was panting from his run to the house. "Moss and Yarborough . . . and me was . . . coming from the pub . . . when we saw some roughs beating a man half to death in the lane back yonder! He's in a bad way. You better ... you better come quick!"

Betsy sprang to her feet. The blood drained from her face. Faintly, she managed, "Not Hounslow Heath, indeed!"

Squire Jepson grabbed an antique blunderbuss from a hidden nook beside the chimney. A quick peck on his wife's cheek, and he ran out the door with the messenger. "Lock the door behind me, Betsy!" He pounded off down the drive behind his farmhand.

Betsy stood wringing her hands, and hoping now for all she was worth that Elise would be too late to see the mayhem that had been perpetrated at the foot of the drive.

Ten more minutes crept past, and still her husband hadn't returned. She was on her way to the kitchen for Cook when there was a rattle of wheels on the drive.

She threw back the bolts and rushed out the front door, heedless of any danger.

Elise's carriage stood at the foot of the steps.

Before Betsy could get to it, the door was thrown open and her husband jumped out. Turning, he reached for Elise to hand her down.

Elise was out of the carriage in a flash, Agnes hard on her heels. "What is it? What's going on?" Elise's eyes were huge. She looked from one to the other of them. "What is it?" Her voice rose. "Betsy! Squire won't tell me what's going on!" She very nearly shouted. "What's happened?"

"Now, Elise, dear." The squire tried to calm her. "It's nothing to trouble yourself about." He patted her hand absently. "Just a little altercation down in the lane."

Even more apprehensive, Elise demanded, "Is Adrian Ashe here?"

"No." The squire paused as if considering something.

"Oh, dear." Betsy's eyes grew wide. "Oh, dear! You don't suppose that Mr. Ashe was the man they killed at the foot of the lane, do you?"

Elise couldn't breathe. Her sight failed. Her knees buckled.

Squire Jepson caught her up in his arms as she fell. "Now see what you've done Betsy!" He carried Elise into the house and almost flung her on the settee, shouting, "Cook! Cook, bring the brandy!"

Elise popped up. She swayed dizzily.

Agnes pushed her head down toward her knees.

"Stop, Agnes. I'm all right. I have to think." She turned bright emerald eyes on the squire. "There wasn't anyone at the foot of the lane. Only you."

"Yes." The squire pulled at his neckcloth. "Well, I had sent them on, don't you see. I was just coming back to the house to tell Betsy what happened when you came barreling up. I'd sent my men along with some miners from the inn to help if they were needed."

"Needed?"

"Well, a clear attempt had been made to murder the man, after all!" The squire was ready to get testy, now he was certain his precious Elise was all right.

Elise locked her emotions down hard. There was no time to mourn or to fear right now. Her brain was awhirl with plans. She responded vaguely, her mind elsewhere, "Yes, yes, of course. Quite right of you, to be sure."

She'd have to send for help. Tomorrow, she'd send a messenger for the Bow Street Runners from London. She'd have to get in touch with the local magistrate, too. "Has the Earl of Haverford arrived yet, Squire?"

"What?" Confusion flustered the squire. "Were we supposed to be expecting him here tonight, too?"

"No, no." Elise was impatient in her despair. "I meant to ask if he had arrived in the district. He's magistrate, you know."

"Oh." The squire grew calmer faced with something he could answer. "Not that anyone knows. There was a rumor he had come and sent his secretary into a tizzy, but that must be wrong. He must have written him a letter. Must have." He frowned in concentration. "Had to have. Nobody's seen a coach. No, nor have there been any strange horsemen in the neighborhood. He must have sent a messenger to set Lewis all on his ear."

Elise wasn't listening. No Haverford. Oh, damn it. That meant there was no magistrate in the district. She'd have to send to London.

But not right now. She could feel the dam breaking. The iron will with which she'd pushed her major concern aside was fast weakening, and she could no longer hold back the fears she had for her love. Right now she had to find Adrian! Snatching at the squire's sleeve she demanded, "Where were they taking him?"

"Who? Oh, you mean the injured man. To the village to the doctor, I'd suppose. Or maybe to his cottage. No one said."

Elise said, "If he's wounded, they'll have need of the carriage to move him!" She kissed Betsy absently on the cheek. "Good-bye. Thank you, thank you very much indeed for your kindness."

She said the words by rote—they surfaced from a lifetime of good manners—then she was flying out the door, Agnes on her heels. *Make him be all right! Let him recover. Let him be all right,* she prayed desperately. "John!" The coachman had had the foresight to turn the carriage around, bless him. "Try to find the group of men who left here just before we came." She shoved Agnes unceremoniously into the carriage.

"Yes, milady!" John Coachman sang down from his box.

"They may have gone toward the village. Perhaps toward the Malfont cottages." She leapt in behind her abigail.

"Yes, milady." He whipped up the horses the moment the footman closed the carriage door behind her. The lad was lucky to grab a space for himself before they were flying down the lane.

In a nightmare racked with pain, Adrian Ashe was carried toward the village. With every step of the men who bore him, his body screamed agony through his dazed brain.

None of it compared, however, to the torture his soul suffered as again and again the words surged through his head, "Got you at last . . . thanks to the beautiful redhead. Thanks to the . . . redhead . . .

thanks to ... the redhead ..." Blackness closed out the voice.

Elise hung out the carriage window trying to see ahead—trying to find Adrian. Now that she wasn't making plans, her emotions had taken over and her thoughts, what few she seemed able to marshal, were in chaos. She could hardly think at all, she was in such a panic.

Betsy Jepson's words haunted her. But she refused to believe Adrian was dead in spite of Betsy's statement that a man had been murdered at the foot of the lane. Betsy hadn't been there! Betsy hadn't seen the man!

Betsy hadn't seen Adrian, she told herself. She *couldn't* know that he was dead.

And the squire had said that the men were taking him to the village. Surely that meant that he still needed a doctor ... that he still was alive.

Agnes pulled her bodily back into the carriage. "There, there," she said in a loud firm voice. "That's enough of that, Lissie. You can't expect to see anything from down here that John Coachman doesn't see first from up on his box. So, sit down and be a good girl." She patted Elise soothingly on the knee as she would a child. "We'll be at the village soon."

Before Elise could argue, the coachman yelled "Whoa," set his brake to keep the carriage from running up on his horses, and brought them to a halt. Six men walked carefully to one side of the road.

Elise was out of the rocking vehicle in a flash.

The six men halted their slow progress. She recognized four of them as miners, and the other two as Squire Jepson's farmhands. But her whole attention was riveted on the man they carried on their shoulders: Adrian!

Adrian's head had fallen back, his chin was thrust toward the sky, and his mouth half open. Her heart lurched as she saw by the moonlight that there was blood all over his face.

She felt Agnes slip a supporting arm around her. But she didn't need coddling right now. She needed action. "Would two of you go for the doctor, please. Tell him I want him." It wasn't a question, it was an order, and the two farmhands said, "Yes, milady."

The miners' grim faces told her they had no intention of leaving Ashe. "Take him into the carriage," she ordered them. She said "take" so that they would understand that she had every intention of letting them accompany Adrian. "We'll take him to Danforth House." Her lovely mouth set in a grim line. "He'll be safe there."

The farmhands, certain now of where to send the doctor, ran off toward the village.

The miners lifted Ashe into the carriage with infinite care. Even so, Elise's heart twisted when Adrian groaned aloud as they moved him.

With Ashe's murmur of pain as his battered body settled on the velvet squabs of her carriage, iron came into Elise's heart. Whoever had done this, or caused it to be done, was going to pay for it.

And they were going to pay dearly. She swore it!

Chapter Seventeen

❧

Elise removed the cloth from Ashe's forehead and placed her hand on his brow. "Ah, thank heavens." It was cool. The fever she'd feared might come after such a beating had not materialized.

Smoothing his unruly dark hair back from his forehead, she bent and closely studied the abrasion there. Clean. She had gotten every trace of dirt out. Perhaps that would keep it from leaving a scar. She hoped so. And it seemed to be a lot less swollen. She shook her head in pleased admiration. He certainly healed quickly!

Gratitude flooded her. He was healing well, and there was every indication he'd be himself again by next week. Tenderness overcame her, and she ran her hand along his jaw, gently smoothing the whiskers that had grown there in the past two days.

He seemed to be sleeping peacefully. It was safe. She thought with a smile, *He'll never know,* and leaned down to kiss him lightly on the forehead.

Straightening, she took a deep breath, pushed her own hair back, and retied the ribbon that secured her light wrapper over her thin linen night rail. She was exhausted. All night long the first night and on through the weary day just ending, she had refused to leave Adrian Ashe's side.

Now she was reassured. Her patient was going to be all right. Now she could go get one of the footmen to watch over him for the rest of the night.

She stretched and yawned. She could almost feel the bones in her spine popping as she straightened her back.

Rising, she stood looking down at his poor battered face. She was grateful beyond measure that he was safe and going to get well. Because this was her fault. All of it was her fault. Ethan Frost's death and now this. Her conscience demanded an accounting.

She stood and looked down at Adrian Ashe. His face was still devastatingly handsome, even with the scrapes, bruises, and the cut lip. She let her gaze drink in his features. She'd never been given the opportunity to do so before. When his eyes were open, they were so commanding that she'd never been able to look away from them to study the rest of his face.

Studying it now, she remembered how she'd feared for his eyesight when she'd seen the awful blow he'd taken on the right side of his forehead. The doctor had promised her that all was well, though. Thank God.

And all *was* well. He was safe here in Danforth House. He was recovering rapidly. And everything would be even better after *she* had had a good night's sleep. The prospect was delicious. She yawned again, daintily this time, her slender fingers covering her mouth.

Then, as she turned away from the bed, a hand grabbed her wrist.

Startled, she whirled back to face the man in the bed.

"Is that you beside my bed, milady?"

"Ashe, you're awake!"

"I have been for some time."

She remembered the kiss she'd bestowed on him and blushed. "You could have spoken," she said sternly.

"I think not."

Watching him, she had the uncomfortable feeling that something was wrong. She heard the taunting laughter in his voice and knew that all was not as it had been between them. There was a hard edge to his voice, a harsh glint in his gray eyes. They challenged her, mocking.

Then, with a strength that surprised her, he yanked her toward him. Suddenly she was in the bed, and his weight was pressing her down into the mattress.

"How dare you!" Surprised outrage was so strong in her that she trembled with it.

"Oh, I dare, milady. I dare." He smiled lazily down at her, his face inches from her own. "Lying here as your hands smoothed salve on my hurts and bathed my cuts, I've built up quite a lot of dare."

"I sought only to see to your welfare, Ashe." She moved slightly to signify that she wanted him to let her up. "Is this how you repay those who care for you?"

Anger flamed in him. Care for him? When it had been she who had betrayed him into the hands of his enemies. Enemies he'd not even known he had until they struck him down. Fine care!

When he looked at her, he heard again the soft, triumphant voice of the leader of his attackers. "Thanks to the redhead," he'd said, leaving Adrian with no doubt as to whom he owed thanks for the beating he'd taken—for the death that would have been his if the Jepson farmhands hadn't happened along when they had.

Anger wasn't what he wanted to show her, however. As furious as he might be, he still adhered to his original plan for her. He'd been determined to force the proud Lady Elise to admit that she loved him as a punishment.

Now, doubting such a perfidious woman was capable of love, he was determined to force her to admit that she wanted him . . . and to take her. To take her as payment for the rough handling he'd endured because of her.

"Are you comfortable, milady?"

Elise glared up at him, disdaining to answer.

"I'd hoped you would join me in a little love play," he told her, intending to insult her.

He was successful. Her eyes widened with shock.

"The first moment I saw you, I recognized the passion behind those glorious green eyes of yours." His own eyes darkened. "All today and into this night I've felt that passion in the way your hands lingered on my body as you bathed my hurts."

His smile disappeared and his eyes devoured her, blazing. "You have built my hunger for you quite skillfully, Lady Elise, but in doing so you've given yourself away. You want me as badly as I want you, Elise Danforth."

She struck out at him, fear tearing through her. What had come over him? She was trapped under him by his weight, and she was frightened. Frightened by this abrupt change in him. Frightened, too, that he was telling the truth: she did want him.

"That wasn't much of a blow, Lady Elise."

She felt his arousal, hard against her. And, shamefully, she felt her own body's eager reaction to it.

"I want you, Lady Elise. God, how I want you! It's been torture, exquisite torture, to lie still as you tended my hurts, to pretend to be asleep under the caressing touch of your hands."

"Trickster!" Her voice was husky. "How could you so deceive someone who sought only to help you?"

"I stood the torture as payment for the pleasure." His grin was reckless. "When, however, you bent over to kiss me . . . and your breasts all but fell out of your night rail, the torture became too much for a mere man to endure."

She struck out at him again, but he caught her hand. Bringing her other hand up to join it, he easily kept them both captive in his left one, stretching her arms high above her head.

Elise was acutely aware of how his action lifted her breasts toward him. Acutely aware of the way his gaze locked on them. Her heartbeat quickened. Then all her awareness centered in the place where his right hand rested, casually, on her rib cage just under her left breast.

His eyes dark with passion, he leaned down to

whisper against her lips, "I want you, Elise Danforth. I want you more than I've ever wanted any woman in my life, but I won't take you until you're crying out for me."

Her breath stopped in her throat, choking her. "Then you'll never take me," she gasped. In the spinning chaos of her mind sanity babbled inanely. Did he think that she would give herself to a common miner? A man with coal dust under his fingernails? She'd never surrender to a common laborer, no matter how devilishly handsome she found him, no matter how much she . . . "Never," she said more firmly. But the word was a lie. Her body was already begging for him.

"If never, milady, why are you not screaming for help?"

She gasped as he lowered his lips to hers again. Why wasn't she? Oh, God! Why wasn't she? Surely there were servants somewhere about. She snatched a breath to shout, but he covered her mouth with his own, hot, hard, and demanding. The cut on his lip reopened. She could taste the blood from it.

Adrian's hand left her rib cage to rise to her breast. He soothed her murmur of dissent with his tongue, passing the tip of it lightly across her lips. Her mouth softened under his touch. He took it again with his own, moving his lips over hers in a gentle persuasion that promised so much more. When she relaxed and he knew he'd caressed warmth from her, his hand left her breast and trailed slowly down to her knee, savoring the silken skin of her inner thigh.

His kisses deepened, dizzying her. Slowly, with

exquisite patience, he trailed his hand lightly up from her knee. As he did, he pushed her night rail up. His hand found the place he sought, and he lifted his head to laugh his triumph as he found the evidence of her wanting.

"Well, milady?"

She locked her teeth. She was on fire, and her body had told him how much she wanted him, but she refused to speak.

How hard it was to resist him! Her feelings for him ran so deep, so strong. She'd been so long without loving. She'd been a passionate wife, and she missed the love play she and her husband had shared. Ashe made the longing unbearable. Heroic, magnificent Adrian Ashe. She'd known from the moment she'd first seen him at the inn that Ashe was the man who would capture her heart . . . and that Ashe must be denied. At the memory of that Ashe, she writhed and almost cried out to him to end her yearning.

But this man *wasn't* that Ashe. This man was a mocking, cold-eyed stranger. So her pride held. She was silent. This was no gentleman pawing her, she told herself, seeking to brace her will. This was a miner, a common laborer. He wasn't even a yeoman!

Ashe shifted so that more of his weight was on her, his tongue plundering her mouth as his hand plundered her body.

She fought to keep her mind from telling her how much she was enjoying the weight of him, to keep from arching to meet him . . . but she lost. Her treacherous body moved toward his.

Groaning at this evidence of her response to him, he thrust a knee between her legs, parting them.

Elise waited for him to possess her, still with breathless anticipation.

Ashe lay still as well. He, too, was waiting, Shaking with the effort not to take her, he looked deep into her eyes. "Not yet, milady?"

His voice was a husky rasp, but she heard the drawl in it and told herself that she was infuriated at this attempt to ape his betters.

Straining, she tried to buck him off.

His breath was drawn in a hiss, "Careful, madam. I'm not made of marble."

"No," she threw at him, her eyes blazing, "you're nothing but a lump of coal!"

He kissed her, hard, hoping to crush a whimper from her, wanting to punish her soft lips. He tasted his own blood. He'd ground his lips against hers hard enough to reopen the cut on his lower one. Oddly sorry that he'd bloodied her, he drew back and soothed her lips free of his blood with the tip of his tongue.

He was dizzy with need of her. He had all but forgotten that he sought to punish her for her betrayal at the foot of the squire's lane. To punish her for luring him there with no intention of meeting him so that his enemies could vanquish him like a mad dog in the dirt of a country road.

His thoughts raised in him a brief anger, but the sight of her beautiful, dear face so near his own defused it. Her glorious hair was spread out like a mantle under her and across the pillow, and her white face was, in spite of her best efforts, full of passionate yearning.

It was all he could do not to tell her how much he loved her. No matter what she had done, God help him, he loved her!

When he spoke, his tone was almost pleading. "Ask, Elise. You have only to ask."

Elise shook her head wildly, denying the hunger for him that stormed through her. Never would she ask. He had tricked her and now he had put himself in a position to take her by force. She would never ask this—she sought words to give her strength to resist him—this common laborer to ease her burning need. Never!

"Very well." His mouth dropped to one of her breasts. He nudged it gently with his chin. "We shall just have to go on," he whispered against it. The bristles from his two-days' growth of beard touched and tantalized the supersensitized skin of her breast through the fine linen night rail.

Elise thought she would die with desire for him.

Still he held her hands stretched up over her head. Kissing aside the lace of her night rail, he brushed his lips across the silk of her bare skin. It nearly drove him out of his mind. Quivering with the effort to wait for her invitation, he built her need.

His tongue touched it once, then he took the tip of her breast into his mouth and did magical things to it. Elise found herself rocketing out of any hope of control. Ashe was driving her beyond anything she'd ever felt. Flames of desire consumed her.

He took his mouth away to look at her again. He

smiled to see her passion-glazed eyes. With an awful effort he kept his voice calm. "Perhaps, now, milady?"

She bit her lip until the blood ran. Her body was stridently demanding what she could never permit. She would never say the words, never! She might love him with all her heart, might want him with every fiber of her being, but she'd never give in to this . . . this stranger.

Somewhere in the back of her mind, she recognized the black force warring in him. Never would she surrender to what she recognized as some incomprehensible desire to punish her.

Then, he sucked gently at her other breast. His fingers caressed her inner thigh, and rose to tantalize unbearably.

Elise thought she'd go mad with desire. She threw her head back, unable to stand another second. At that instant, he released her hands. "No!" Panic seized her. *Ah, God! Why did he have to release her hands?* Now she had nothing to brace against, nothing to fight. She said again, panting with the effort, "No." Her eyes begged him . . . but not to stop. She managed to force out the words, "Oh, no."

But she knew that her eyes and the hands she was helpless to keep from his body conveyed a very different message.

So did he.

Chapter Eighteen

ॐ

He was gone, and Elise lay there in the tumbled, damask-draped bed spent and replete and more satisfied than she had ever been in her life. She stretched and felt every part of her body vibrantly alive, tingling with remembered sensations.

Adrian Ashe had made love to her with a fury that had lifted them both to the heights of rapture and held them there—passion-linked, clinging, soaring, until they'd cried out together and plummeted back to earth deliriously sated.

The rest of the night, he'd led her tenderly down paths of ecstasy she'd never known existed. She'd willingly followed, avidly followed, relishing every moment.

And she hated herself. She hated herself for letting him—for he'd never said he loved her. He'd not even said it in the way she'd always been warned that men lied to gain access to a woman's body. He'd said he wanted her. That he needed her had been his most tender utterance. But never, not once, had he told her he loved her.

Her only consolation was that, in the end, he'd been

the one to surrender. She'd never said the words he
sought to pry from her with his masterly love play. It
had been he, who, with a groan of passionate anguish,
had given way. He'd taken her by storm once she'd
touched him, in spite of his not having been able to
force a verbal request from her.

There was small satisfaction in that, for she'd met
him with a passion that matched his own, but at least it
was a sop to her pride. Whatever he'd tried to do to
her last night, he'd failed. But what had he been trying
to do? And why had he done it?

In the cove after he'd rescued her from the mine,
he'd been gentle, caring. She'd fallen in love with that
man. She'd *wanted* to love him in spite of their difference in station!

But *this* Ashe! This arrogant Ashe who had taunted
her and derided her and . . . she refused to give the
thought words. This Ashe she hated. Deliberately,
meaningfully, he had attempted to humiliate her and
she hated him.

Now he was gone, he and his masterful lovemaking, and she was left with only her loathing—not
just for Ashe, but for herself.

How could she have done such a thing? How could
she! Seeking to buttress her self-condemnation, she
dug deep for words that would do it. She was Lady
Elise Danforth . . . and she'd given herself to a lowly
miner.

She faced the truth unflinchingly. She hadn't
screamed for help. She'd given kiss for kiss, touch for
touch . . . all there was of herself . . . to the beautiful-
bodied, devilishly handsome Adrian Ashe. She lashed

herself mercilessly with her next thought . . . and he was nothing but a common coal miner, a lowly stranger. And none of that had mattered to her.

The only scrap she had left of her pride was that he'd been unable to force her to invite his lustful invasion. Softly her mind added, *no matter how desperately she'd wanted to.*

"Enough!" Teeth clenched, she leapt from her bed and yanked hard at the bellpull. With an effort, she refrained from tearing it out of the wall.

She must have a bath! She must wash every trace of him and his lovemaking from her body. Then . . . she sought wildly for her next move . . . then she'd ride the cliffs until she'd driven his mocking smile from her memory.

No common laborer was going to conquer *her.* No man she loved was going to humble her like this! He might have possessed her body, but he wasn't going to haunt her mind!

Standing high on the promontory that thrust farthest out into the sea, Adrian watched as Elise rode recklessly along the cliffs. She drove her mount mercilessly, and they flew out of sight.

He tried to feel triumph. Obviously his possession of the beautiful Elise had driven her to this heedless career along the cliff tops. The feeling wouldn't settle, though. Instead of victorious, he felt . . . ashamed? Damn it. Why the hell should he feel shamed?

Elise Danforth had betrayed him, blast her. She'd asked him to meet her far from the village, far from the safety of his friends, and he had come in good faith. He'd come only to find that she hadn't. To find men waiting in ambush. To find pain and intended annihilation!

Why she'd done it, he couldn't imagine, but he knew from all that he'd learned about her from her male servants that Lady Elise Danforth was punctual to a fault. That meant that her absence at their meeting place could only have been deliberate.

Anger flared in him afresh. Why? Why had she done it? If the men from Jepson's farm hadn't come home from their drinking at the inn when they had, he would be lying in his grave now. Or at the bottom of the sea.

He smiled grimly to remember how swiftly he'd recovered from the fierce beating he'd taken. And how he'd used that swift recovery against Elise. Years before the mast had toughened him past most men's endurance, thank God.

His smile twisted as he called vividly to mind how that toughening had enabled him to punish Elise. Punishment? Heat flooded him. His teeth grated as his jaw set. Against his will, he remembered how desperately he'd wanted to cry out to her that he loved her. Loved her more than life itself, the little traitor!

With all the might he could muster he'd fought down the feelings that had threatened to riot in him last night. Even now, he would die before he'd admit to the one that kept pushing against the firm barrier of his will. He'd die before he'd admit that he was hopelessly in love with the magnificent woman who'd so foully betrayed him!

He stood stock-still and fought his emotions. His

body braced as for a hurricane, he held his mind
against the force of the powerful truth that battered it.
Like a statue he stood. The wind tossed his dark hair
about his head, but there was no other sign of life
about him.

Only his eyes seemed alive. And his eyes showed
the agony of his spirit.

Finally, he moved, a living creature again, returned
from his own private hell. His mind had won a modicum of victory over his heart, and his smile was once
again cold and cynical.

Quietly, he watched the cliffs. Watched for her.

Elise's gelding was lathered by the time he saw
them return. His chestnut sides were heaving, and
Elise was walking him to cool him down.

One look at the rigid way she sat her horse told him
that Elise had not found the release she sought for
herself from her wild ride. Elation filled him, and he
sent his laughter ringing skyward to the wheeling
gulls. The release she sought she could get from only
him now.

He was glad she hadn't broken her pretty little neck.

Megan met him walking home from the sea. From
where she knelt in her little nest of wild, sweet-
smelling grasses, Adrian Ashe looked twelve feet tall!

For just an instant she quailed before the thunderous look on his face. Then she reminded herself
that this was Ashe. Her Ashe. The very same Ashe
who had brought "My Lovely" up out of the mine that
day when she'd been so affeared.

Dropping the wildflowers she'd gathered, she rose

and ran to meet him. "Ashe! Ashe!" she shouted. "It's me, Megan!" She held her arms wide, running straight at him.

Suddenly, Adrian smiled. Megan. Her welcoming presence was warm sunlight on a freezing day. Stooping, he grabbed her up in his arms and rose, hugging her. "Ah, Megan! How good it is to see you. What have you been up to?"

"It's good to see you, too." Then she reared back in his arms. She frowned at him. "Why do grown-ups always want to know what we children have been up to?"

He pretended to give the question serious thought. Finally he told her, simply, "Because we care."

She smiled as quickly as she'd frowned. "That's exactly what My Lovely says!"

Adrian didn't comment. There was nothing he could say about her Lovely that was fit for the ears of a child.

Megan traced her finger over his lower lip, lightly touching the cut there. "What have you done to yourself?"

He grinned at the thought that he might have split his own lip. "I got in a fight with some bad men."

"Did you win?"

Ruefully, he shook his head. His eyes momentarily darkened. "I'm afraid not, Poppet."

"Oooh." Her eyes were grave. "And you so big and strong." She peered down from the superior height his embrace gave her. "I'd have thought you'da banquished them 'thout any trouble atall."

"Well." He pretended to give her remark deep thought. "There were three of them, you see."

"Only three?" She looked puzzled.

He suppressed a chuckle. The child's faith touched him. Quickly, he tried to be worthy of it. "They had big clubs." When that didn't seem to do the trick, he added, "And they struck me down from behind." That did it. He watched her eyes grow wide and hastened to add, "I was not being sufficiently attentive, you see."

"Whyever not?" She was reproachful. Her knight had failed her.

"Well," he told her without thinking, "I was going to meet your Lovely, you see. And I had my mind so much on that, that I got careless." With a start, he realized that he'd just spoken the truth.

"And did you meet her?"

The child obviously didn't understand that he'd been incapacitated. It was just as well.

"No," he told her. Then, striving to keep bitterness out of his voice. "Your Lovely didn't come."

Megan's brow lowered. "That's not so!"

He was struck dumb by the vehemence in her tone.

"If My Lovely said she was going to do something, then she did it!"

He had nothing to say.

Megan did, and she said it hotly. "She is the only person in my whole life who never, ever, not one single time didn't do what she said she was going to do." She accented her next words by poking her finger into his chest with each one of them. "My Lovely doesn't break promises, and if she wasn't there, then *you* were early. Or *you* went to the wrong place.

Anyhow"—she looked at him truculently, highly agitated, and gave him the coup de grace—"it was all *your* fault!"

He set about soothing her, murmuring nonsense, stroking her hair, agreeing to anything.

His mind, however, wasn't agreeing to anything.

He knew damn well he'd been at the place Elise had specified. It had sure as hell turned out to be the wrong place for him all right! But he'd been where she'd told him to be. He'd been there at the time she'd set, too. Bitterly he wondered with whom else she'd set that particular time.

It was *she* who hadn't been there. *She* who hadn't kept their rendezvous. And it was she who'd left him to be struck down by three thugs who'd obviously known exactly where he was going to be.

Why else would three such men wait at the foot of Squire Jepson's lane? There were no toffs coming that way to be robbed, no farmhands with a week's wages—not at that hour, when they'd have spent it all at the inn's public room.

No! There was only one reason those men had been there. They'd been lying in wait for him. And there was only one person who could have told them he'd be there!

He closed his eyes in pain against the next thought. The thought that sealed it. And one of them had said, ". . . Thanks to the redhead."

"Ashe!" Megan pushed at his chest.

He looked at her, his mind still miles away.

"Your hug hurts!"

With quick apologies he loosened his angry grip on

the child. "I'm sorry, Angel." He smiled down at her reassuringly, vowing not to think of Elise Danforth's treachery. "Is that better?"

"It's always better to be able to breathe!"

Stormy-eyed, she reared back in his arms again and scowled at him. "Now you apologize for 'plying that My Lovely didn't come meet you when she said she would."

He could feel his teeth grate at that one. Anger surged fiercely through him.

He looked away for an instant. When he looked back he was in control. "All right, Megan," he managed, "I apologize."

"Say . . ."

He diverted her before she could demand a stronger apology, certain he'd choke on one if he tried to deliver it. Settling her on his left forearm, he raised his right hand and pointed. "Look. Isn't that Lord Deverill coming over the hill?"

Megan looked up. Her body began to shake. Clutching tight against him, she buried her face in his neck.

Holding the quivering child close, Adrian cursed himself. Of course. Her nightmares involved a man on a horse. Damn, he'd been thoughtless!

"There, there, Meggie." He patted her back soothingly. "We'll just pretend we don't see him and go down to the cottages this way."

The child didn't speak. She just hung on to him for dear life.

Adrian turned and strode swiftly down a path that took them away from the sight of the man on horseback. With every stride, he chided himself for upsetting the little girl he carried.

Where the path split, he ignored the one that would have taken them to their homes. Instead, he took the one that led to Haverford Village.

What was the good in owning a village if you couldn't take a child into it to buy her some candy?

Remembering the way Megan had reacted to the sight of a man on horseback, he decided to give up his search for a reason to own a horse.

That evening, as the birds settled themselves noisily for the night, Adrian left his cottage. He was dressed from head to toe in his darkest clothes. Carefully keeping to the shadows, he entered the woods behind the cottages.

The smell of damp earth and growing things surrounded him the moment he entered its confines. He had to stand awhile to permit his eyes to adjust to the dimmer light here under the dense canopy of leaves.

As he stood, rustles made by the quick movements of small forest creatures sounded all around him. Memories of his assailants kept him on the alert.

Damn, he wished he hadn't given up the idea of finding an excuse to keep a horse. A man on a horse was a hell of a lot less vulnerable than a man on foot, and he'd no great desire to repeat the experience of the other evening. Not the evening on which he'd taken such a beating, at any rate.

The one that had shortly followed was another matter, however. His body quickened achingly at the memory of his night with Elise. Stopping to stand quietly with his back against one of his oaks—for these were his woods, he reminded himself—he listened intently for signs of any other thing as large as he.

The woods were so quiet, and his senses so sharpened by the darkness that he could hear a leaf fall from the tree over his head. It whispered its leisurely way down through its fellows to fall with a tiny dry sound to the forest floor at his feet. Farther away, he could hear the gurgle of a stream. Hearing only those and the tiny sounds made by small creatures, he shoved away from the tree trunk and went on.

In spite of his attempting to avoid it, desire hung heavy on him. Recalling, however briefly, that night with Elise had been a mistake. He didn't need his body distracting him from his mission.

He moved on, cursing under his breath.

Within half an hour, he reached Delacourte. The huge mansion lay quiet, dreaming in the moonlight. There were no lights in any of the windows except those of the entry hall and those down in the servants' domain.

Stealing up to the place along the vine-covered wall that his butler and his secretary had shown him, he took out the key Perkins had provided. Slipping it into the newly-oiled lock on the hidden gate in the garden wall, he turned it easily, and passed quietly through.

Standing in the shadow of the wall, he closed and relocked the gate. He waited for clouds to obscure the bright half disk of a moon. When the moment came, and the moonlight dimmed, he sped across the garden to the tall French doors of his study, a shadow among shadows.

Letting himself in the window left open for him, he stood a moment waiting for his night-acclimated vision to sharpen enough to let him see in the almost total blackness of the luxurious room. When he could comfortably make out the outlines of the furnishings of the room, he moved to the double doors that led in from the hall, his feet noiseless on the deep Oriental carpet.

Trying the door, he found it locked. "Good." All was going according to plan. Perkins and Lewis had locked the door to keep any servant from finding him by chance and raising an alarm. No doubt, they'd pushed something against the bottom of it to keep light from being seen in the wide corridor outside it as well.

Confidently he moved to the massive desk on the left side of the room. Sliding his hands across the top to the richly tooled leather edges, he found the flint and steel there. He narrowly missed knocking them to the floor.

"Damn!"

Lighting the candles with a taper from the fireplace would have been easier, but Lewis and he had agreed that even the faint light from a small fire might give him away, and tonight the wide hearth was cold. Secure in the knowledge that the men who patrolled the estate had been given the job of catching a nonexistent poacher on the far side of it, he struck flint to steel and lit the candles, one by one.

Taking a small key from his pocket, he unlocked the top drawer of his desk. The papers were there. Lewis had been more successful than he had hoped, if the plumpness of the package under the young secretary's explanatory note was any indication.

With a smile of satisfaction, Adrian lifted the package to the desk's surface, and opened it. Avidly, he went through its contents, piece by piece. Half an hour later, he settled back in his chair, a deeply satisfied smile on his face.

Carefully, he put the many papers and pieces of paper and scraps of paper back into the neat package Lewis had prepared for him. Replacing the package in the desk drawer, he took a moment to reread the list of contents and the respectful note his secretary had fastened to the top of the package.

Lewis's note ended, *". . . I sincerely hope these are what you required of me, and I fervently pray that they will prove to keep you safe."*

"Aye, my young friend, so do I. So do I." With that and a mental reminder to congratulate his secretary, Adrian closed and locked the desk drawer, blew out the candles, and slipped back out into the night.

Chapter Nineteen

✦

"You *cannot* be serious!" Elise shot out of the huge, heavy chair behind her desk and rushed to stand almost toe-to-toe with him.

Adrian stood easily before her. His face was expressionless, like that of an American Indian she'd seen in pictures.

"Oh, yes, Lady Elise. I assure you, I am, indeed, most serious."

"No!" She turned from him so abruptly that her skirt whipped against his legs. "No! Absolutely not. I forbid it."

A crack of laughter was his only reply.

Agnes, sitting chaperon in one of the window seats across the study shivered involuntarily. What a nasty laugh the man had!

"Ashe," Elise said firmly, her voice lightly edged with something akin to panic, "you mustn't do this! You know the law. If you go through with this . . ." She paused almost imperceptibly, searching for a word that would convey no hint of admiration for the brave man who was volunteering to put himself so at risk. ". . . foolhardy plan, you *will* undoubtedly bring

215

the plight of the miners to the whole of the gentry in the district. You will *also* put your neck in a noose."

"Surely"—sarcasm was heavy in his voice—"your friends and neighbors are too civilized to hang me in Malfont's ballroom."

She turned on him in a fury. "Stop it! Stop it!" Balling her fists, she shook them at him. "This is no light matter, Adrian Ashe. It's a capital offense for a miner to speak out against his employer, and you know it." A bleak look passed fleetingly across her lovely face. "That was one of the laws Ethan Frost and I had hoped to get changed."

Jealousy tore through Ashe at her mention of his predecessor's name. Even though he was certain there had been nothing more than admiration and friendship between them, he was incapable of controlling the fierce possessiveness he felt toward Elise Danforth.

Elise spun away from him, frustrated beyond measure. "Until the law *is* changed, I can't let you do this."

"You can't *let* me?" His voice held such an incredulous note, it bordered on the comic.

Somehow Agnes didn't feel amused. She felt mesmerized by the drama being played out in front of her.

Elise whirled back to face the man who towered over her. "In God's name, Adrian! Why must you throw away your life like this?"

For an instant, he almost forgot what she had done to him. For a brief moment, he wanted to sweep her into his embrace and reassure her. To kiss away her fears and to tell her that he had put safeguards in place—safeguards that would act as guarantees even if he weren't the Earl of Haverford and a mine owner himself.

But Elise stood silhouetted against the window behind her desk, and in the light of the westering sun, her haloed hair was as red as he'd ever seen it. Insidiously, the exultant voice of his would-be murderer slithered into his mind, whispering "Thanks to the redhead" and no power on earth could have bent him to comfort her.

Firmly, he told her, "I have one other matter I intend to take care of this evening. Then, I shall see you at the ball."

She flew at him then, all restraint forgotten. "No! No, Adrian." She grabbed fistfuls of his shirt and hung onto him.

Agnes rose from her window seat, upset to see her usually calm Elise lose control like this. Her needlework tumbled unnoticed to the floor.

Elise cried, "Promise me you won't do this!" Sobs shook her slender frame. "Promise me!"

Adrian couldn't stop himself. Snatching her to him, he kissed her with brutal urgency. His mouth forced her trembling lips open and he kissed her deeply, intimately. Possessively. She was *his*!

When he'd kissed her till his own head was swimming, he raised it and looked down into her face. Her eyes were brimful of tears, and he kissed each in turn. Then he kissed her lips again, gently.

He took one long, searching look, as if he would imprint her image on his mind forever. Then he thrust her away, spun on his heel, and stalked from the room.

Lost in misery, Elise moaned, "Adrian. Oh, Adrian. God keep you safe."

Agnes sat back down, paralyzed with astonishment. She knew she should go to her Lissie. She wanted to go to her Lissie. But the power of the scene she'd just witnessed held her motionless.

Her eyes began to burn. If she didn't blink soon, her eyeballs would dry out! She hadn't been able to take her gaze off them long enough to do so.

Her poor, poor baby! Her disastrous fate was surely sealed. There was no doubt in Agnes's mind that as long as she lived, Lady Elise Heatherington Danforth would be bound to the magnificent brute that was Adrian Ashe.

Adrian strode through the woods that separated Elise's estate from a larger, but far less well-run one. He was going to confront the man who was behind the death of Ethan Frost. What he was going to do or say when he got to him, he wasn't quite certain.

Oh, he knew what he *planned* to say. He knew he'd inform the blackguard that he'd come in his capacity as district magistrate. Come to see to it that he paid for the murder of Ethan Frost and the attempted murder of Adrian himself. That was his plan, but he must take into consideration that he'd no idea how the man would react, and thus, no idea how this impromptu attack on him would go.

Still Adrian smiled with grim satisfaction as he swung along. It had taken him several days of careful questioning—questioning that was possible only because he was Adrian Ashe, coal miner, not Haverford, District Magistrate—to determine beyond any possibility of doubt that his quarry had been the only *gentleman* of the district to take a horse out on the night of Ethan Frost's murder.

After he'd discovered that, Adrian had found an old man who had been awake that night, attempting to walk away the pain of his rheumatism, and had seen the gentleman in question riding in the direction of Malfont's cottages. Now he was ready to accuse him of his crimes. In another twenty minutes he would do so.

Again he cursed his lack of a mount. He'd have the bastard by now if he'd not been on foot! With every stride his anger burned brighter.

The man who had led the attack on Adrian Ashe had already arrived at Ashe's destination. He'd come to tell his hoity-toity employer that he was through.

"The game is no longer worth the candle, my aristocratic friend," he told the man glaring at him from his thronelike chair on the other side of the desk. "My men and I shall be on our way as soon as you have paid me what you owe."

"Why should I pay you anything? You're leaving before your job is done." Though his face remained cold and haughty, his eyes burned at the man who stood, completely at ease, across the desk from him.

Fraley smiled evilly. "Well, I feel as if I've done quite a lot, after all. I've murdered a viscount for you, caused a bunch of nasty accidents at several mines, and tried to murder the man called Adrian Ashe." He spread his hands and shrugged. "The murder was easy. The accidents not especially difficult. But Ashe"—he slewed his head to one side so that he could look at his soon-to-be former employer out of the corner of one eye—"Ashe was a different proposition."

"I don't see—"

Fraley went on as if his employer hadn't spoken. "Ashe survived. What's more, he's begun asking a lot of questions. A lot of very disturbing questions. And I, for one, have no intention of waiting around until he finds the answers."

"I hired you to do a job, Fraley, and—"

Fraley cut him off. "And I did a job. Yes, and several other jobs."

"Damn you, Fraley! I'll . . ."

Fraley dropped his mask completely, and the half-mad face of the animal he truly was showed as he snarled, "You'll do nothing, my fine friend. You'll do absolutely nothing!" He put his knuckles down on the desk and leaned across it. "It was you who pushed Frost over that cliff, Mr. High and Mighty. And it was you who planned the accidents in the mines." His eyes glowed triumph at the other man, and he almost crowed as he brought forth his final accusation. "And it was you who planned the death of Viscount Danforth . . ." His eyes glittered with sadistic glee, and he emphasized each word, ". . . *because you wanted his wife.*"

"Damn you!" The host leapt from his chair, his hands stretched out for the other man's throat like talons.

Fraley jumped back. His laugh was a little breathless. "No, no, my friend. I know too much. You daren't make an enemy of me. *I watched you shove Ethan Frost to his death, remember?*"

That stopped him. The bastard was right. He didn't dare. His word would stand against one, but the man and his two henchmen made three. He dare not risk it. Slowly, as if the effort cost him dearly, he settled back into his chair.

After a long moment, he took a deep breath and opened the top right-hand drawer of his immense estate desk. A pistol gleamed dully in the candlelight. He sat looking down at it almost wistfully. For an instant, he considered using it.

Good sense prevailed in the end, however, and, instead, he took out the bag of gold that rested beside the firearm.

Looking up he saw the wide grin on his hired killer's face.

"Good choice." Fraley pushed his own pistol back into his pocket and took the bag of gold coins. Smiling a crooked smile, he said, "I'll be about my own business, now." His smile changed subtly and became a leer. "She's waited long enough." He crossed the oak floor with barely a sound, opened the door softly, and was gone.

The man at the desk stared into the fire. Fury had all but robbed him of reason.

Fraley had left. Blast him! The lowlife he'd hired to help him sabotage the other mines so that his own coal would fetch higher prices had left.

"Damn Fraley!" He struck the desk with his fist, and the inkwell jumped, sending dots of ink over the immediately surrounding surface. "The bastard. The sorry bastard." He plopped his elbows on the desk and dropped his head into his hands.

That was where the housemaid found him when she could move again. Struggling to reach him, she clutched her torn clothing around her and staggered to the door of the study. She scratched at the door, but her need to reach her master was so great that she entered in spite of the fact that he hadn't given his permission.

"Oh, sir . . ." Her voice was little more than a croak. "Help me, please, sir."

His head came up and he looked at her. Seeing her there with blood on her face and her clothing all but destroyed brought him out of his morass of self-pity.

He leapt to his feet and hurried to her. "My God, Phoebe? It is Phoebe, isn't it?" He put an arm around her as if she were made of glass and led her over to his chair. "God in heaven, child, what happened?"

She couldn't hold back the tears then. Not when he was taking off his very own coat to put 'round her to cover her nakedness. She sobbed as if her heart would break.

"Phoebe." Keeping a steadying hand on her shoulder, he poured her a glass of his own special brandy and pressed it on her. "Take this. Sip it. It'll help."

He sat on the edge of his desk and watched her drink. When the color returned to her cheeks he would ask her to talk. In the meanwhile, he took stock of her condition and was appalled.

The little maid's mobcap was gone, and her pretty red hair hung down about her shoulders. Tatters of it that someone had yanked from her scalp, their ends still tangled with the rest of her tresses, hung even lower. Her mouth was bruised as if someone had bitten at it—or battered at it with their own lips drawn back from their teeth.

Even though she clutched his coat close, he could see long, deep scratches on her thin chest. Scratches that ran down to the tips of her breasts . . . scratches that oozed blood.

"Phoebe. Dear child." He grabbed the bellpull and gave it three hard tugs—his prearranged signal for trouble. That would bring the entire household running. "Who has done this to you?"

" 'Twas 'im. That Fraley what comes here only some nights." She hiccuped a sob, then rushed on, her news of such import that she could rush through her own nightmare. "Caught me near the library door, 'e did. I was finished seeing to the fire in there and comin' out, ya know." Her eyes refilled with tears. "Pushed me back inside 'e did and tore near all me clothes orf. 'Urt me with 'is 'ands . . . 'urt me where 'e'd no right to touch me." She took a deep breath to calm herself. "Then, he got 'isself out of his britches like he was agoing to force me . . ."

"Did he . . ."

"Ah, no, sir," she interrupted him quickly. "I was that scared he was gonna, but 'e didn't 'ave 'is way wif me." Her eyes puzzled, she met his gaze. A frown creased her brow and she told him earnestly. "And then 'e said what I think you should know, sir." She frowned, concentrating. "Said he shouldn't 'ave bothered wif me"—her frown deepened— "*even if I was a redhead.* That's what 'e said, sir. Then 'e buttoned 'isself back into his trousers and said 'e was asaving of 'imself for another redhead. One 'e was going to stop on 'er way to a fancy ball."

Her voice became plaintive. "I'm not sure what he meant, sir, but I do know 'e's an evil man." Her eyes entreated him. "He's fair cruel, sir. And if you know of a lady with red 'air what's going to a ball tonight, then she needs your help."

She reached up to grasp his shirt. His coat fell away, and he saw that her breasts were covered with savage bites. Paralyzed with horror, he could only stare.

The little maid gave him a shake. "Please, sir!" She shook him again, until his shocked gaze returned to meet her own. "Oh, sir, she *needs* you!"

Everything began to happen at once. The servants stampeded into the room in eager answer to his summons.

He rebundled the little parlor maid in his coat and helped her stand. Frantic with the knowledge that there was only one ball tonight, and only one red-haired gentlewoman in the neighborhood to attend it, his usually graceful movements became clumsy with haste.

Desperate to get to Elise before she left the safety of her home, he hurried everybody out into the hall.

Thunderous pounding sounded at his door as he gave the little maid over to the care of his women servants. Chance had put him nearest the entrance, and this was no time to stand on formalities.

Adrian Ashe, something close to murder in his eyes, stood in the doorway. Instant understanding flashed between the two men. Ashe accused, the other admitted guilt.

But guilty or not, he hadn't time for this now. He shook his head and shouted, "Blast you, Ashe! Not now!" Thank God the man had come; he could use him. He opened his mouth to tell the big miner of Elise's danger.

With an inarticulate snarl, Ashe leapt toward him, his speech about being district magistrate forgotten in a blaze of feral instinct to revenge himself for the beating this man had ordered. His hands closed around his enemy's throat.

Gasping, Deverill pried at the iron grip that was choking the breath out of him. Blackness gathered at the edges of his vision. A high singing sound buzzed in his ears.

He tried with all his strength to say, "Elise! She's in danger!"

No words came.

As soon as he could speak after being choked half to death by Adrian Ashe, Deverill shouted to his footmen, "Let . . . him go!" He coughed and clutched at his abused throat. "It's all right. Let him go."

His servants stared at him as if he'd lost his mind. "No. No," he gasped. "I'm all right."

Glaring at the struggling Ashe he snapped. "Stop

fighting, you stupid bastard! My men aren't going to let you go so you can murder me!"

Adrian stopped his efforts to fight free of the five footmen clutching him and stood, head down like a charging bull, glaring at Deverill.

Deverill wasted no time. God alone knew when Ashe was going to explode again. "It's Elise. She's in danger!"

Adrian straightened from his half crouch. His brow cleared. "Then why the blazes are we standing here? Have you a mount for me?"

Deverill gave orders for his fastest horses to be brought from the stables. "Hurry! There's no time to waste!" Then he began a hasty explanation of what was going on.

Adrian listened in horror as Deverill told him the fears he had for Elise based on what had happened to the little parlor maid, Phoebe.

There was a shout from outside. A shrill neigh sounded. Wasting no more time, Ashe and Deverill ran out the huge front door and down the wide steps Ashe had stormed up what now felt like a lifetime ago.

Flinging themselves on the excited horses brought 'round for them by wildly curious stable boys, they tore off down the drive at a breakneck pace, knee to knee. Neither man had any thought but to get to Elise and to keep her safe. Each was ready to murder to keep the woman he loved safe.

Deverill rode with consummate skill, pushing his horse to the limit.

Adrian rode like a demon.

Ten minutes later, they came to the limestone-pillared entrance to the long drive leading to Danforth House.

"It's too early for her to have left for the ball," Deverill told Ashe.

Ashe nodded agreement. It was far too early for Elise even to have called for her carriage, so they knew she was still safe. Safe, and ignorant of her danger. They had only to find her enemy and stop him to keep her that way.

Ashe called in a low voice, "Watch the gate." They'd waylaid him at Squire Jepson's gate.

Deverill nodded to show he'd heard, even over the sounds of pounding hooves and creaking leather. By unspoken mutual consent, they drew rein and proceeded cautiously.

There was no sign of the three ruffians.

Adrian pointed to a graceful curve that had been artistically designed into the drive. In its loop, a stand of trees pooled dark shadows under their branches.

Again a careful approach, pistols drawn. Again nothing.

"Where the hell can the bastards be?" Deverill burst out.

Adrian didn't trust himself to speak. He had to find Fraley before that animal came within reach of Elise. But where the hell was he? A glance at his companion showed him that Deverill was as confused and anxious as he was.

Together they charged another decorative stand of trees. Empty!

"Nearer the house! Search the area nearer the house."

Ashe pointed to the right, gesturing for Deverill to search in that direction, then he swept off to the left.

When he reached the mansion, he rushed his excited thoroughbred into the perfect landscaping grouped to the right of Elise's front door.

Spurring his mount even as he cursed himself for doing so, he sent it trampling through the well-tended beds that bordered her home. Elise's gardeners were going to hate him, but when he met Deverill at the back of the mansion, he was going to be certain there were no would-be abductors in the shrubbery that banked the foundation of Danforth House.

Frustration nearly choked him. He glared at Deverill and demanded, "You saw no one?"

"Where the devil could they be?" Deverill was as frantic as Adrian was himself.

Inspiration struck Adrian. "The carriage house! They're in the carriage house!"

"Of course! They intend to take over the carriage!" Deverill looked at Adrian with admiration.

They turned their exhausted mounts and sent them flying down the gravel drive. As they drew their horses to a halt, they saw a dark form sprawled on the ground. Dismounting hastily, Adrian went to where the man lay half out of the doorway.

Deverill leveled his pistol at the heart of the darkness just inside the wide-arched entrance, while Ashe knelt beside the fallen man and felt for a pulse. He nodded to his companion with relief. But the man was Elise's coachman! Obviously the plan was to take over her carriage and spirit Elise away!

"Run to the house and spread the alarm!" Adrian told Deverill.

Deverill's answer was a disgusted snort.

Adrian half turned his back on the barn. "Damn you, Deverill . . ." It was all he got out before Jenks, the giant who had decked him that night in Squire Jepson's lane, was on him. The huge man's superior bulk took them both to the ground with a bone-jarring thud, and Adrian lost his grip on his gun.

At the same instant, the skinny member of the group of thugs, the man who'd distracted Adrian at the foot of the lane, leapt forward from his hiding place and slashed a buggy whip down across Deverill's wrist. Deverill dropped his pistol and cursed.

As Adrian and his huge opponent fought for an advantage, Deverill grappled with his attacker. Adrian slammed his fists into Jenks with wild satisfaction. Most of his punches were telling; the giant grunted, snarled, and tried to dodge. Wildly he landed clumsy punches of his own. He was heavier, but Adrian was the better fighter. A smashing blow to his jaw, and Jenks was momentarily dazed.

Adrian seized the advantage and heaved his huge attacker off.

With an enraged bellow, Jenks scrambled to his feet, snatched up a pitchfork, and charged Adrian.

Deverill scooped up the gun that had fallen from Adrian's hand when he'd been thrown to the ground and shot the man.

Rolling out of the spot into which the giant was sagging, Ashe leapt to his feet . . . to find the muzzle of another gun inches from his face.

Holding the weapon in a hand that was rock steady, Fraley sneered at Deverill without taking his eyes off Adrian. "Well, your high and mightiness." His voice was full of scorn as he addressed his former employer. "Looks like I *am* going to finish that last job you hired me for, after all!" A nasty smile lit his face. "And this time we make our own luck. Adrian Ashe is right here. We don't need Elise Danforth's little cripple running to us behind her mistress's back to tell us where he'll be this time. Even without that little whiner," he said tauntingly, "we can save Lady Elise from the big bad Adrian Ashe."

Adrian saw Fraley's finger begin to tighten on the trigger. Elise hadn't betrayed him! Her *servant* had told these animals where he'd be . . . probably in the mistaken belief that he posed some sort of threat to Elise. His heart soared.

The icy fear that would have seized any man in his right mind who found himself looking down a gun barrel never figured into Adrian's present feelings. He felt no fear and was about to leap at the man with the gun when Deverill gave a hoarse shout, flung his empty pistol at Fraley, and launched himself at the man. He was clutching Fraley's wrist, bearing his arm down, when the gun went off.

Deverill staggered back, his hand pressed to his side.

Fraley pulled a wicked blade from his boot top and lunged toward the wounded man, the knife pointed at Deverill's chest.

With a shout, Adrian snatched up the pistol Deverill had dropped when the buggy whip had struck his wrist. He shot Fraley. The knife fell from the man's lifeless fingers scant inches from its target.

Adrian dropped the smoking pistol and rushed to Deverill. Catching him, Adrian helped him to sit on a nearby harness box, then strip off his coat. Out of the corner of his eye, he saw the last of the villains— the man with the raspy voice—slip out the door of the barn and hightail it toward the woods.

He let him go. The danger to Elise lay dead in the moonlight flooding through the doorway. Deverill was his urgent concern now. He owed this man his life.

Deverill gasped, "Let be."

"I've got to stop this bleeding."

Deverill tried weakly to push Adrian's hands away. "No, I don't fancy . . . being saved for the hangman."

Adrian looked up at him sharply.

"You heard that scum." He gestured toward Fraley's sprawled body. Drawing a tentative breath, he found it painful and managed on a whisper, "I hired him. I brought . . . him here."

Adrian grunted that he'd heard and went on tearing the wounded man's fine linen shirt into bandages.

"When Haverford finally gets here and finds out, he'll have me hanged."

"No, he won't."

"Are you mad? Of course, he will. Things of this nature have a nasty way of getting out."

Adrian's gray eyes, dark with anger, bright with the remnants of the fight, pinned him, then narrowed. "I might not like you, Deverill, and I hope to heaven I never find out all you're guilty of, but you saved my life. I won't see you hanged."

Deverill laughed a bitter bark of a laugh, then clutched at his side cursing.

There was a lot of blood. Adrian tried to see if the ball was still in the wound, but there wasn't enough light in the dark cavern of the barn.

Deverill had regained control of his breath by then. "Very nice of you, I'm sure, Ashe"—he sneered— "but you're *nothing*! Nothing but a damned coal miner." His eyes, full of the contempt bred into him, blazed at Adrian.

With a little more roughness than was absolutely necessary, Adrian finished knotting the bandage.

"Damn you, Ashe!" Deverill glared.

Adrian crooked an eyebrow and smiled coolly. The bandage had to be tight to do its job. He tendered no apology.

After a moment, he sat back on his heels, fixed Deverill with a level look, and told him very softly, "I'm Haverford."

Chapter Twenty

∽

Elise arrived at Malfont's ball with her nerves strung tight. She was hoping against hope that the crush of people attending and the large number of carriages outside would serve to discourage Ashe. That they would show him that there were many more people here than he could hope to interest in their cause. She hoped he would reconsider.

No. It was much more than that. She was desperate for him to reconsider. She *prayed* that he would come to his senses and refrain from putting his neck in a hangman's noose!

Distracted with these worries, she didn't even hear herself announced, but Sir James met her at the foot of the sweeping staircase.

"You are breathtaking, my dear."

Elise saw that his compliment was sincere. "Thank you, James." Her own voice sounded vague to her. "I'm glad at last to be out of mourning." Her gaze ran over the assembled guests.

"Looking for Deverill, m'dear?" Sir James's voice was tight with aggravation. "He has not yet arrived."

His patent jealousy of their mutual friend served to

bring Elise back to herself. Smiling, she said, "James! You sound like an old bear. And no, I'm not looking for Dev." She could hardly tell him who she *was* looking for.

At just that moment there was a commotion at the French doors open to the garden terrace. People pressed back to form a corridor to accommodate a tall figure stalking into the room.

It was Ashe, of course. Elise stepped back up on the lower step of the ballroom stairs to see better. Adrian moved confidently across the ballroom to the raised platform on which the musicians sat. Ascending in a smooth step, he raised his arms for silence. Except for a surprised murmur that was instantly shushed by those who were too curious about this handsome stranger to listen to their neighbors' mutterings, the room grew still.

"Ladies and gentlemen," he began.

Sir James tore away from Elise's side. His black look boded no good for the interloper in his ballroom. With singleness of purpose, he headed for the hallway and his small army of footmen.

Elise clutched the banister beside her and wished with all her heart that she'd never asked Adrian Ashe to take over Ethan Frost's post as head of the miners.

Fear for Adrian's safety all but kept her from hearing what he'd come to say. Her gaze locked on him. She was powerless to look away . . . and not at all certain she would if she could.

She listened breathlessly, straining not to miss a single word from across the wide ballroom. He spoke about the flooding in the lower levels of Mr. Tate's mine, and she saw with relief that her neighbors took that fairly well.

Some of them even clucked at the shame of it, and she began to breathe easier. She even began to hope—as she never had found cause to hope before—that there might be some sympathy for the miners' cause here.

But when Adrian said that Lord Effers was mining coal from the support pillars in his spent galleries and voiced his well-considered criticism of the practice—and the danger it meant to the miners—it was a different matter. Elise's small ray of hope dimmed and disappeared.

Just in front of Elise, old Baron Chase was rigid with indignation. "What does this young whipper-snapper think he's doing, trying to tell Lord Effers what he can do with his own property? I'd like to know!" Effers was nobility, after all. If he wanted his coal mined more completely, then it was certainly his right!

The last bit of sympathy for the sinfully handsome commoner creating excitement died when he criticized Dev, and Elise's anxiety deepened to fear. Just then, James appeared at the top of the stairs behind her with a large number of footmen.

Ashe saw and raised his voice above the clatter of the men rushing down the stairs. "The timbers shoring up the walls and ceilings of the corridors and rooms in which Lord Deverill's men work are rotten and spaced too far apart for safety."

Adrian's gray eyes, dark with the anger he felt at the indifference of these people, burned them with scorn. His rich baritone rang out across the room, challenging them. His tone scathing, he asked, "How would you like to have your sons and brothers working in a mine that might cave in at any minute?"

There was a murmured protest, but not against dangerous working conditions in mines owned by some of the elegantly dressed men in their midst. The assembled gentry were outraged that, even for a moment, Ashe could suggest one of their number would ever lower himself to such menial labor.

How dare this upstart imply that any one of the sons or brothers of the distinguished company gathered here tonight would sink to do any work at all, much less toil with their hands! And shoulder to shoulder with miners in the filth of a mine? The gravest of insults. Their sons and brothers, indeed!

Moreover, their resentful comments ran, Deverill was a completely charming and a sporting gentleman of the first rank. No one had the right to criticize him. Of what concern to them was it if his shoring timbers *were* half-rotten and spaced too widely? Who in the world expected him to care for such mundane matters? And just who the devil did this ... this *commoner* think he was to come here and presume to speak to them?

Elise held hard to the banister she'd been clutching. A wave of disgust swept strongly through her. Were these the people whose approval she had long lived in fear of losing? Slowly, she let her gaze sweep the assembled guests in Sir James Malfont's glorious ballroom. Had she really cared for the good opinion of these shallow, unfeeling men and women? Well, she cared no more. Guarding her expression, she returned her gaze to the magnificent man on the platform. He stood, head high, like a noble stag with the hounds baying all around him.

Calmly he accepted the scorn and scathing remarks of those berating him. Calmly he watched Sir James and his six footmen pressing their way through the crowd of guests. Just as his captors reached him, Adrian turned and looked full at Elise. His eyes unreadable, he kept his gaze riveted to her face until Malfont's footmen pulled him roughly down from the platform into the crowd and Elise could see him no more.

Elise never knew how she had gotten through the rest of the ball. She had been berated for having appointed such a man spokesman for the miners. She'd been chastised for having a spokesman for the miners at all. The gentler among them had sought to persuade her that she should abandon her cause—let some *man* take over the championing of the miners. It was simply not the sort of thing a *lady* did. Not the sort of thing a lady did at all.

A messenger from Dev was waiting for Elise when, completely drained by the turmoil of her emotions, she arrived back at Danforth House. Startled by the man sitting his horse at the foot of her front stairs, her immediate response was sharp concern for her dear friend. "Deverill! Has something happened to him?"

The messenger, schooled by his master, replied evenly, "No, Your Ladyship." His color heightened at the telling of the lie, and he thanked his stars Lady

Elise couldn't see his face well in the torch-lit semi-darkness of her drive. "The master ordered me to see that you got this letter the minute you arrived home. He ordered me to sit right here and give it into your very own hands."

Helmsley, who was standing just a little way up the steps, rigid with righteous anger, said icily, "This *person*"—he shot the lad on the horse a glance that should have felled him—"has steadfastly refused to give me the missive, Your Ladyship."

"The master said then I was to leave, as there is no reply expected. So, please," the boy asked plaintively, "can I go now?"

Elise, breaking the seal on the letter even as she was helped from the carriage, told him absently, "Yes. Yes, of course."

The boy turned his horse and started off down the drive.

"Thank you!" Elise called after him.

Agnes came running to escort Elise up the steps. They were accompanied by a thoroughly miffed Helmsley.

Elise was so absorbed in what Dev had written that she didn't even hear Helmsley mutter, "I am perfectly capable of taking the mistress into the house without your assistance."

Agnes ignored him.

Elise, her eyes glued to the letter, headed for her study like a zombie. Agnes walked beside her, Helmsley majestically behind. When they reached the study door, the butler signaled one of his footmen to open the door. If he hadn't, the distracted Elise might have walked right into it.

She raised tragic eyes to Agnes the moment the door closed. Incredulously, she told her friend, "He's leaving England. Dev is leaving England, Agnes."

Her attention returned to the letter in her hand. Tears formed, clung briefly to her lashes, and spilled down her cheeks. "Listen, Agnes. He says that there were men watching in the carriage barn to take over my carriage and abduct me." She skimmed the letter. "He doesn't know why." She looked up at her abigail, bewildered. "Who would do such a thing, Agnes?"

She looked down again. "He says that Adrian Ashe got wind of the plot, came to him, and together they foiled it. He says they rescued John Coachman and eliminated the perpetrators." She shivered slightly. "Eliminated?"

Agnes just looked at her, wide-eyed. She'd get the story from Seth Timberwite—who, of course, was John Coachman—in the servants' dining room tomorrow morning. If men had tried to abduct her Elise, she hoped she'd hear a tale of mayhem and clandestine burial!

"Dev assures me all is well, and that I should look him up if ever I get to Philadelphia in the Colonies." Pain at the cavalier way in which her best friend was deserting her edged her voice. "He says that he is going there to live with an aging cousin who has great need of him."

She looked up at Agnes, hurt showing plainly in her eyes. "How kind of him. But I shall miss him sorely."

Agnes bit back the scornful sound that threatened to erupt from her. If ever she had known a selfish man, that man was Francis Joseph Deverill! If he was putting himself out to go to the Colonies—weren't they the United States, now? Seems like they were— then it was because *he* needed to go, not because someone needed him. Agnes wondered what could have sent him from Elise's side. He loved her. Of that she'd not the slightest doubt. Uneasiness filled her. Something very strange was afoot.

Elise sat down and leaned back in her chair. She never lifted her gaze from the stiff vellum in her hand.

Agnes took the chair on the other side of the desk and waited to learn more. When Elise offered no more information, she prodded, "What else does he have to say?"

Elise was caught up in the end of Dev's letter, and could only manage, "Nothing. That's all he . . ."

Agnes recognized futility when she saw it. Rising, she walked around the desk to give Elise's shoulder a loving pat. "I'll go up and get your bed ready. You have your cry and hurry up to me. You need your rest."

Elise patted the hand that was patting her shoulder. "Yes, dear. I'll be up presently." She sniffed daintily, to show her abigail that she was ready for her cry. The moment the door closed behind Agnes, however, she was on her feet pacing the floor.

Dev was leaving England. She didn't believe for a moment that he'd do that unless he had to. No doubt his creditors were too hot on his heels for comfort.

Oh, if only he'd let her help him with his finances

and estate management! She could have . . . But her attempt to do that had aggravated her masculine best friend to the point of nearly ending their friendship. It had been hopeless. Dev had kept right on living in his own reckless fashion. Now, no doubt he was ruined and fleeing the country before he was sent to debtors' prison.

She felt so helpless. She felt so deserted! What would she do without Dev?

And the rest of the letter. On top of losing Dev, she had a second and worse heartache. Dev had written:

I have it on very good authority that Haverford has arrived in the district. So, if anything should ever happen to that upstart who heads up your miners, you might look to that quarter.

I am not precisely certain that he will help you with your cause, but if you go to him seeking Adrian Ashe, the results could prove interesting.

Lastly. You know that I love you, and that I probably always will. All my problems would have been solved if only you had married me. Alas, it was not to be.

At least, I feel a great deal better about your penchant for the annoying Adrian Ashe now that I have met the elusive Haverford.

Pray that I find a wealthy widow in the Colonies that will want to marry and reform a profligate rogue of the first water, won't you?

Elise, believe me utterly sincere when I say that I regret all that I have done to hurt you more than I can say. When you think of me, please try to

*remember that I loved you as deeply and completely
as I was capable of loving.*

I beg you never to forget

Your Dev

Tears finally came, just as Agnes had expected. But
Elise couldn't have said for what she cried the most.
She'd lost her dear friend and confidant, Dev. She'd
been told she might have saved him by marrying
him—a service of which she'd never been capable—
and she'd been as good as warned that Haverford was
going to go after Adrian Ashe.

About her own attempted abduction, she cared not a
whit, as it had not been successful. Since it had all
happened without her being the slightest bit aware of
the whole thing, she would have been hard pressed to
care less. The thing she cared desperately about was
whether or not harm had befallen her rescuers.

Adrian had looked all right and had certainly
spoken with firmness and power at Sir James Malfont's ball, so she was certain he was fine—or at least
had been fine when he'd been forcibly escorted, head
high, from James's ballroom. Dev she had missed at
the ball. Had he been hurt?

No. His messenger had already assured her on that
point.

She would miss him dreadfully, but Dev had always
chosen his own path, and gone down it willfully and
willy-nilly. Everyone in the neighborhood had told
him again and again that it would someday come to
this. Now it had, and she was so busy feeling sorry for

herself, that she had very little sympathy to spare for her wayward friend.

She sighed deeply and hiccuped once, her bout of tears over. The thing that loomed, monstrous, in her mind, was Dev's implied threat about Adrian Ashe.

When Dev had written this letter—she placed it on the desktop and smoothed it absently—he hadn't known that Ashe had spoken out against the mine owners. Still he'd intimated that any appeal she made to Haverford as district magistrate would prove ... What had Dev written? She looked for that part again. Dev had penned that he didn't believe Haverford would help her with her cause. Did he mean to imply that Haverford might take a position that would harm Adrian? She found that fear hard to deal with.

She rose from the chair and went to the bellpull to summon messengers. Her hand was on it when she realized that there was very little she could ascertain at this hour of the night. . . .

"Tomorrow," she told herself.

"He ain't nowhere to be found, Your Ladyship." Her stableman's face was deeply troubled. He wasn't simply following an order, he was looking for his friend. "It looks like Adrian Ashe has dropped off the face of the earth, begging your pardon, milady."

"Thank you, Mudge." Elise's response was automatic. Her heart had plummeted to the bottom of her shoes, and her mind was completely occupied with the fright his words had given her. She knew that Mudge and Rafferty all but worshiped the ground Adrian walked on. They had done so ever since the taciturn hero of the mine disaster had made it a point to befriend them.

If anyone could have found Adrian, she was certain it would have been Mudge or Rafferty. But Rafferty had reported his lack of success just a few minutes ago, and now . . . Mudge had been her last hope.

This must have been what Dev had tried to warn her about. When he'd written his lighthearted farewell, he'd tried to tell her that Haverford was back—possibly summoned by one of her irate neighbors—and would probably arrest Adrian for his speech against mine owners. James had assured her that he had merely had Adrian Ashe escorted to the edge of his property and thrown off it.

If James told her he'd let Adrian go, then he had let Adrian go. So where was he? Even the messengers she'd sent to Hal and Lettie and to Squire Jepson—the only other person who might have befriended Ashe—to inquire of Adrian had returned with no news.

Where could he be? It was a cry from her heart.

All day she'd had her men out searching. Now she was toying with her supper and leaving it all on her plate. She was unable to rest. She was unable to pacify herself by pacing one more mile of any carpet in her spacious home.

She was fast approaching the end of her sanity. She was frantic.

Snatching her pristine damask napkin from her lap, she threw it down on the table beside her plate. She'd decided to take matters into her own hands.

If Haverford were in residence—and the rumors were conflicting on that subject—then there was the chance that he had Adrian. If someone who'd been at the ball had told him that Adrian had spoken out against the mine owners of the region, Haverford would have no other recourse than to arrest Adrian Ashe. It was his clear and simple duty.

She closed her eyes against the agony in her mind. If one of her neighbors went so far as to insist that the law against Adrian's actions be upheld, then Haverford would be forced to arrest Adrian *and* charge him with the crime he'd so recklessly committed in front of a ballroom full of witnesses. And then . . .

Elise clutched her empty stomach. Oh, God! The punishment for that crime under present English law . . . was death. Adrian would be hanged!

She let the horror of it wash over her as she clung to the back of the chair she'd just quitted. What could she do? She must do something! Oh, dearest Lord, what could she do?

A half hour later Lady Elise Danforth drew rein and slipped down from the saddle of her lathered mount. She rushed up the broad stairs to the palatial front doors of Delacourte and seized the huge brass knocker with both hands. She was prepared to pound the house down if she had to.

The door was opened almost as soon as she hammered her first blow with the brass sculpture of battling sea serpents. The butler, Perkins, if she recalled correctly, looked momentarily surprised to see her. "Lady Elise!"

"Yes, it is I." Slipping past him she began tearing

off her gloves. Impatiently she asked him, "Is the earl at home?"

Perkins tried to see around her without appearing to do so. He was looking for her abigail. Not seeing a female servant of any sort attending Lady Elise on this most improperly late and unheralded visit, he was scandalized, and asked in a shocked tone, "Where is Agnes?"

Elise colored, but said sharply, "Haverford. I must see Haverford immediately, Perkins."

"Yes, milady." Perkins bowed, again the perfect butler in spite of his disapproval. "He is in his study. I shall inform him you are here." His back as stiff as the proverbial poker, he stalked off down the hall that led off to the right.

Elise made an impatient sound and snatched her hat from her head. She wadded its veil into an untidy ball and stuffed it into the crown of the fashionable shako. Ignoring the fact that her gloves had flecks of foam from her hard-ridden gelding's mouth on them, she dropped them into her hat on top of the veil and plopped the whole on the nearest table. Then she fell to pacing the huge hall like a tigress in a cage.

"What if he refuses to see me at this hour? What if he refuses to see me at all?" She muttered to herself as she paced; she was so upset, she had no idea she was doing so.

Taking three deep, calming breaths, she stood and wondered how she'd allowed herself to get in such a state. Nothing in her life had *ever* caused her to so forget herself in such a fashion!

"The earl will see you now, Lady Elise."

* * *

The study was in total darkness except for the light from the fire burning brightly on the hearth. Not a single candle illuminated the spacious study.

Her host stood silhouetted against the fireplace, his legs spread, his arms locked behind his back. It was impossible to do more than to ascertain that he was a very tall, very large, well-shaped gentleman with his hair styled in the latest fashion.

As for what else she could see, Elise could make out nothing more than the spill of rich colors on the luxurious rug before the hearth, a glint or two from firelight reflected on shining silver and brass items around the room, the twinkle of firelight play in the cut-crystal decanters on a side table, and an edge of deep blue highlighting the superfine that clad the earl's broad shoulders.

She stopped dead on the threshold, astonished. What manner of man entertained guests—especially a lone woman guest—in a room without lighted candles? Into what sort of situation had she thrust herself?

Before Elise could whirl around and absent herself, Haverford spoke. "How may I be of service to you, Lady Elise?"

Transfixed by the hauntingly familiar timbre of his voice, she froze in place, then she gave herself a mental shake and used her common sense. She was perfectly safe. Perkins would never be a party to . . . to anything scandalous. Just remembering the butler's presence braced her.

"I've come to ask if you know anything of the whereabouts of . . . of a friend of mine."

"And just why would you imagine that I should know the whereabouts of a *friend* of the Lady Elise Danforth?"

Obviously, this insulting man intended to play cat and mouse with her whether or not he knew anything about Adrian. The thought angered her. She was no green girl to run from the first insult a man offered. Not with all she had at stake.

She drew herself up to her full height and hoped she fixed him with a haughty stare. Without being able to see his face, she wasn't certain of her target. "I have come here at this unseemly hour, unannounced"—there that ought to tell him that she was completely aware of what she was doing, and that she considered herself of sufficient consequence to do it without harm to her reputation—"because I'm interested in whether or not you have recently . . . detained anyone."

He shifted easily, the movement as graceful as a cat's, and lay his arm along the mantel. He kept his face turned so that it was still in shadow too deep for her to make out his features. "Detained anyone? What a curious question."

Elise clenched her teeth against the words she wanted to utter, saying instead, "If you mean curious in the sense of wanting information, then my question is surely that." She regarded him with bright annoyance. "If you mean curious in the sense of strange, then you must be unaware that you serve the Crown as district magistrate here. In which case, I find *that* quite curious."

She glared at him across the room, refusing to play whatever game he sought to put in motion here. "Have you or have you not taken anyone into your custody in your office as district magistrate?" she demanded.

"Why should I answer you on that subject, Lady Elise? Surely that is man's business in general, and mine in particular." He turned his back on her, looking down into the fire. "If you want such information, send your husband."

She received the blow without flinching. She answered him in insultingly even syllables. "I am a widow. I have no husband to send to you to make my inquiries."

"Ah." He turned again to face her, still silhouetted against the firelight. His voice became silky with insinuation. "Is that the reason you seek this man you think I may hold in the dungeons of Delacourte?"

She was utterly infuriated by his implication that she was seeking her lover. She'd die before she let him know that, however. "Please do not be absurd. I, in addition to the whole of England, am well aware that there are no dungeons here at Delacourte!" She picked up the train of her riding skirt, in preparation for her departure.

With a single word, he detained her just as she turned to go. "Ashe." He let the name hang in the air between them.

Elise dropped her heavy train and took an involuntary step forward.

"Ah, yes." He almost hissed at her. "It is Ashe you seek, then? How very interesting."

She clamped her lips shut against the world of questions that rose in her. "How is he?" "Is he all right?" And the one that tore at her heart and brought tears to the back of her eyes was, "Have you hurt him?"

But the last and most important question she could not hold back. In a voice she barely recognized as her own she demanded, "What do you intend to do with him?"

The man at the fireplace regarded her a long moment before telling her in a voice full of insinuation, "That, my dear depends entirely on you."

She felt her lips part, and her breathing quicken. Was this creature saying what she thought he was saying?

"If the continued comfort and good health of your Adrian Ashe depended on your . . . shall we say, *generosity* to another gentleman . . ." The words trailed away and he waited, head cocked inquiringly, for her reply.

Fury such as she had never known erupted in Elise. "You swine! You utter swine!" She rushed half across the room toward him before she caught herself. Even if this animal in front of her did illustrate all the dire warning Agnes had given her about how some men treated widows, she had no intention of demeaning herself to the point of striking him—no matter how fiercely she wanted to.

"Oh, no, my dear." His tone was derisive. "It really isn't a good idea to call the person responsible for the health of your lover names."

"Adrian Ashe is not my lover."

"Your words lack sufficient force, milady." He held

up a hand to still her outburst. "I shall accept your claim as truth, however, and ask you instead why you are so concerned about this man."

She was without an answer for longer than feasible. She heard him laugh softly at the length of her pause. Finally, she managed, "Adrian Ashe is a hero. He risked his life and nearly died saving miners from a disaster at Malfont Mine. Such a man deserves everyone's concern."

"Lame. Very lame, my dear. A letter sent by messenger could have given me those cold facts. But you. You come here, hasty and disheveled . . . and quite beautiful, I might add." His voice became husky. "Too beautiful, perhaps, for a mere man to resist." Then his tone hardened. "Why? What is this man to you?"

She looked at him with absolute loathing. Her lovely face was distorted by the contempt she felt for the Earl of Haverford and his lewd suggestiveness.

But Adrian was hard put not to stride across the room to snatch his goddess into his arms. His whole body ached with love for her. His heart yearned to comfort her, to reassure her. Dearest God! Was there ever such a woman?

She was so brave, standing there defying a man twice her size—a man in a darkened room who had let her know beyond any chance of doubt that he had lustful designs on her person.

And Elise had endured it all. All for him. His heart was full to the point of bursting with the joy that knowledge brought him. But still he wanted more. He *had to have* more!

He curled his hands into fists and rammed them

down to his sides to keep himself from reaching for her. He clenched down with his toes into the soles of his boots to keep himself rooted to the hearth as he sought to draw from her the one admission he had to have. The one admission he could no longer live without. He had to hear her say she loved him! Loved *him*, Adrian Ashe. That she loved *him*, coal miner, lowly stranger.

He had to!

In a voice strangled with emotion, he demanded hoarsely, "Just what are you willing to do for *me* to keep your Adrian Ashe safe . . . and perhaps guarantee him a happy old age?"

He watched, on her inexpressibly beautiful and dear face, the awful interior battle raging in Elise. It was all he could do not to shout, "Enough! I'm here! I'm safe . . . and I adore you." The pain of holding back the words was almost more than he could stand.

Then he saw her surrender, and his soul wept for her.

"Anything," she said numbly, "I'll do anything."

It was everything he'd wanted once, this humiliation of the proud woman who refused to acknowledge his true worth as a man because he lacked the outward trappings of a gentleman. But that was in the past. A past so overshadowed now by the love he felt for her that it seemed distant.

He drew a deep breath and thanked His Maker that the other thing had been resolved. Fervently, he gave thanks that he'd learned the other night from the dead Fraley that she had not betrayed him to the thugs. It had been Deverill's doing that she was late for their rendezvous. Deverill had deliberately detained her.

The perverse Irishman had sent him a note here to Delacourte telling him so. At least the angry beast raised in him by the thought that she had had something to do with the beating he'd taken was laid to rest.

So now, all he had to win from her was the admission that she loved him for the man he was. Simply for the man he was. The man who loved her.

He knew well that it would take all the strength left in him to force her to admit she loved a commoner. Nevertheless, he brought it to bear—mercilessly.

"Why?" He made the single word one of accusation.

She was bewildered. "Why?" Then anger began to grow in her, and she demanded, "What do you mean, 'why'?"

"I mean, *milady*"—he gave her title an insulting emphasis—"that I am curious to know why you, a lady, one of the gentry, are willing to grant me"—this time it was an insulting pause—"your favors . . . to save a common coal miner."

Elise could contain herself no longer. "You cur! How dare you demand explanations from me? Isn't it enough that I've consented to be your whore?"

He held his silence for a long moment, while he died inside for her.

Then, he demanded fiercely in a rasping whisper that was the best sound he could force from his emotion-clogged throat, "Why? You must tell me why!"

Elise flung the words at him like daggers, her face aflame with the blazing truth of them. "Because I love him!" she shouted. Then, staggered by her own statement, she said in a voice soft with wonder, "I love

Adrian Ashe." She smiled then, a gentle, beatific smile that seemed to light the room.

Her arms went around herself, and she hugged her new hard-won knowledge to her. She could tell the world. It was all right. She didn't care who knew. She *loved* him. And that was all that mattered. It was everything in the whole world that mattered to her now.

She raised her eyes to him and told him as if she was declaring she was safe from anything he might choose to do to her—kept safe by the blazing intensity of the love that burned bright in her. "Do what you will."

He was strangled by the strength of love for her that rose in him. No words would come. If they had, they would have fallen over one another in his desperation to tell her how magnificent she was. And how much he loved her.

So he reached out a hand in a gesture that bid her come to him. Desire for her overwhelmed him as she threw back her head and marched toward the fireplace at which he stood with her shoulders back and her face set as if she were mounting the very steps to the guillotine.

When she raised her hand imperiously and placed it in his own, flames engulfed him. Reason fled, and he swept her into his arms. He heard her gasp as he crushed her to him and she felt the hard evidence of his need for her. Ignoring her struggles, he bent his head and his lips devoured the firmly set line of her own.

Instantly, her struggles ceased. She snatched back from his slackened grip. "Adrian!"

Shock shuddered through her slender body. Then wondrous relief flooded her. Then fierce anger erupted in her. "Adrian Ashe!" It was a hiss, an accusation. "You!" The word was full of condemnation.

She worked an arm free of his embrace and slapped him with all her strength.

He didn't even feel the blow. His head bent to her again. He whispered against her lips, "You love me. Ah, God, *you love me!*"

"I *hate* you!" Rage made her words breathless. "How could you do such a thing to m—" Her words and her breath were cut off as his mouth closed over hers.

His hands roamed her body fiercely, frantically. Passion long denied had set him aflame, and he was burning out of control.

He felt the firm roundness of her hips as he caressed them, the narrowness of her slender waist. Then his hand was rising to her breasts, and it was as if he had never touched a woman before. His hands were shaking like a green boy's with his first woman.

Desperate to feel her silken skin beneath the frustrating layers of her clothing, he hooked his fingers in the V at the top of her riding jacket and yanked down. Buttons went flying.

Moaning from the very depths of him, he touched the fine linen of her shirt with the tips of his fingers and felt the warmth of her body under it. And it was too much.

But it was not enough. Not enough! He hooked his fingers at her neck again, his other arm holding her close against his hard body, stilling her struggles, foiling her attempt to escape him. This time when he pulled downward, her shirt ripped apart, and he had only the silk of her chemise as a barrier to that which he sought.

Slowly, he lowered his mouth to her breast, his eyes locked with hers. He had to be certain, absolutely certain, that she would not object when he took her.

For he was going to take her. There was no way he could stop himself. He'd die here on the luxurious rug in front of this fireplace, killed by the ravening desire that racked him, if he didn't possess her!

His senses were reeling, centered entirely on the responses he was drawing from his beloved's unwilling body. His mouth closed over the tip of her breast and after an instant, he heard her add her soft moan of desire to those he uttered.

Her eyes, he saw before the weight of passion brought his lids down over his own, were glazed with her desire for him. Dark as the forest at midnight, they reflected the war that was going on behind them as her body begged him for the release he had neither the wish nor the power to withhold from her . . . and her mind demanded vengeance.

She might think she hated him, and perhaps just now she did, but she wanted him, and right now, that was enough. He would overcome this brief hatred with his lovemaking.

He never saw her hand reach behind her for the poker.

Chapter Twenty-one

❧

Galloping home, hatless and without her gloves, Elise vacillated between fervently hoping she'd *killed* Adrian Ashe and knowing very well that she had not. Her well-timed blow had merely put an instant end to the passion overcoming them both, and had sent Adrian reeling.

He'd certainly had the strength and the presence of mind to curse her while he cradled the side of his head in his hands, though. From his fluency, she knew she hadn't addled his wits, much less caused the rogue any lasting damage!

When he'd gotten over his initial shock, he'd called out to her, "Elise! Elise, wait. Don't go!"

Ignoring him, she'd rushed out as fast as she could run, fury lending wings to her feet. And unless she was very much mistaken, his last words, shouted in a voice that would have carried over a hurricane at sea, were, "Damn you, Elise Danforth! Come back here!"

She was still seething. Haverford! Adrian Ashe was Haverford! She was so angry, she was fit to be tied.

How *dare he*! How *dare* he pretend to be a lowly stranger, a commoner—worse, a common coal miner—

when he was the rich and powerful Earl of Haverford! How dare he so misrepresent himself? It was perfidy of the worst sort.

How dare he stand there in the dark and twist her into knots? Why had the odious man wrung from her a confession that she loved him—loved Adrian Ashe, that was—when there had been no such person?

Furthermore, his masquerade had cost her weeks of sleepless nights. And all of it had been for nothing. Nothing! The man she loved . . . had loved . . . wasn't even real. He didn't even exist. He was the invention of a . . . of a demented nobleman!

And she had been completely taken in. She had loved that figment of the Earl of Haverford's twisted imagination with all her heart, with every fiber of her being. Yes, and she had suffered the tortures of the damned because of it.

Her gelding leaned into the turn at the Danforth House gate so hard he nearly slung her from the saddle. Sensing her anger, hearing the little cries of indignant outrage she uttered now and again, the big horse, thoroughly confused, was heading for the safety of his stall as fast as he could go.

"Lady Elise!" Rafferty and Mudge came rushing out of the barn to meet her.

"Are you all right?" Rafferty demanded as he reached up and swung her unceremoniously from the saddle.

Mudge caught and calmed the sweating gelding, but his eyes were on his mistress, too. "Were you attacked, milady?" He stared at her disheveled state, wide eyed.

"No!" Her face flamed. "I'm all right." She took a deep breath and told herself it was time to be calm; at least, she must strive to *appear* normal. She forced a smile for the concerned men, and was pleased to feel it become entirely genuine. There was honest warmth in her voice as she said, "Thank you both. I was just distracted on my way home and forgot myself."

There were sounds of gravel crunching under hurrying feet, and Agnes came puffing up. "Lissie!" She took three great breaths and tried not to pant. "Helmsley said you . . . rode right past the . . . front doors." She took three great gulps of air. "Is everything all right?"

Elise slipped her arm through her friend's. "Everything is fine, dear." She looked back at her stablehands. "Thank you both for your concern." She added softly, "It means a great deal to me." Then, briskly, "I apologize for bringing my horse in so hot."

"Never fear, milady. We'll cool him out good before we puts him up for the night."

Agnes had caught enough of her breath to demand, "Lissie, what is it? What's happened?" She looked her mistress over and asked in a scandalized tone, "And where in the world is your hat?"

Elise didn't confide in Agnes. She couldn't tell her she'd nearly given herself to Ashe! So now she was paying the price of a guilty conscience. She tossed and turned all night.

When she slept the first time, she dreamt she was in the arms of Adrian Ashe. When she woke, breathless and aching with longing, she spurned such a dream and concentrated, instead, on Haverford and his perfidy.

She could still scarcely believe that it was true! Whatever would cause a nobleman, a very high-ranking nobleman, to go around pretending to be a coal miner, of all things?

She puzzled over that until she was drowsy. Worry at it as she would, though, she still couldn't imagine why he had done such a thing. Slowly, playing one guess about his possible reasons after another in her mind, she relaxed against her feather-filled pillows.

A moment later she was asleep again. When she slept this time, she relived her last few seconds in Adrian's arms. First there was the ultimate bliss of his kisses. Then she experienced again the suspicion that he was seeking to conquer her with his lovemaking. Not with the same cruelty she'd sensed in him that night after she'd tended his wounds. She'd seen in his eyes that night that he sought revenge. Tonight, he'd seemed to seek to dominate her.

She felt again her determination not to let herself become a victim of her own passion. A determination not to let her body rule her mind. She recalled the moment of her decision, and the difficulty with which she had forced her passion-drugged mind to rally and take charge. Then she was reaching for a weapon to stop his wondrous assault on her senses, and . . .

"Ahhhh! Nooooo!" Horror shocked her awake as, in her dream, instead of the thick brass handle, it was the sharper business end of the fireplace tool with which she hit Adrian . . . *and his head flew off*! His head flew off his shoulders!

Awakened by her own piercing cry, she shot bolt upright. Wildly she looked around her room, seeking reassurance from a dream too vivid, a fear too real.

The familiarity of her surroundings instantly calmed her. She wasn't really the savage murderer of a belted earl! With a sigh of relief, she leaned back against her lace-trimmed pillows and told herself, "What an awful dream. And why in the world am I turning into such a ninnyhammer?"

She looked toward the windows where the early dawn light was making her white damask draperies glow softly. "Thank heavens. It's almost time to get up. I've certainly had enough of this dismal attempt at sleep." She shook her head, her wild mane of heavy auburn hair shifting on her back and shoulders. "I don't think I want to risk sleeping again."

Adrian Ashe was fine, she was certain. He'd been on his feet bellowing for her to come back when she'd fled his house. Cursing as he did so, at that. No one could shout that loud if he were really hurt.

Could he?

She'd never struck another person before. How did she know that she hadn't done real damage? She didn't, obviously. Hadn't she heard of people who sustained a blow to the head, seemed just fine all day, and then died in their bed at night?

And he had staggered badly as he tried to come after her.

"Stop it, Elise! This is pure foolishness. What's-his-name is just fine. You may depend on it."

She sat up and straightened her shoulders. Besides.

He deserved it. He had deceived her. *He'd deceived the whole blessed neighborhood!*

He had lied to her about his name as well as his identity.

She hastily raised her hands to her flaming cheeks. Hadn't she mooned like a besotted idiot about the way the syllables of his name seemed to slip through her mind . . . "Like silk," hadn't she been ninny enough to say? Or at least to think? How aggravating it was to have been such a complete fool!

And then to have him try to make love to her there on the hearth rug! She blushed to remember how . . .

She wasn't going to think of that anymore. Her mind hesitated over one detail, though. She wasn't going to think about it except to remember that he had never once told her he loved her.

Wretch! Rogue! He'd possessed her once without any words of love. He had spoken then of want and need, but never love. He'd made love to her with what she could only call a strange cruelty. He'd mercilessly forced her to betray the fact that she wanted him then, and, now, last night, he'd forced her to humiliate herself to save Adrian Ashe. Why in God's name was she stupid enough to love such a man? She wished she could know *that* answer.

Last night he had been Haverford. He had been the deceiver. He had also been the aggressor. In stunning him with his own fireplace poker, she had merely defended herself. The entire sorry happening had been his own fault.

She felt much better now. In fact, she told herself, if

she *had* knocked his head free of his shoulders, it was no more than he deserved!

With that totally rational, coolly intelligent assessment of the situation, Lady Elise Danforth burst into tears.

Adrian Ashe, ignoring the grandfather of all headaches, changed back into his work clothes and set out for supper with Lettie and Hal and the enchanting moppet, Megan. He hadn't an invitation as such, but had been told so often that he was always welcome that he'd no qualms about dropping in.

He rode Deverill's thoroughbred, glad to have a horse under him again after six years at sea. He had an excellent chance to see if he remembered his equestrian skills, as he had a wild ride—thanks to the big hamper he carried in one hand. "Blast you, horse! I haven't time to retrain you to put up with baskets, so just behave, damn it. We haven't far to go."

His mount slewed around in a circle, bucked once and continued on, sidestepping joltingly every inch of the way. By the time they reached the Limes', Adrian's arm was ready to drop out of its socket. Holding the picnic hamper his chef had packed with everything imaginable away from the excited horse was beginning to tell on him.

His ignominious arrival did not, as he had hoped, go unnoticed. "Welcome!" Hal cried out, his voice full of amusement at what he interpreted as his friend's inability to ride. "Better get down before you get put down." He stood in the doorway, enjoying the spectacle. "Where'd you get that animal? Bit fine for a miner, I'd say."

Willem pushed past his father. "Here, now." He got eager hands on the sweaty thoroughbred, stroking it soothingly. "There, now." Taking the hamper from Adrian, he set it safely on the stoop at his father's feet and turned back to the nervous horse, crooning soft reassurances.

Adrian stepped down and let the boy have the animal. The lad had a way with horses, he saw. Willem was calming the fractious gelding nicely.

He'd given the horse a rough time asking him to carry a picnic hamper when the animal had obviously never seen one. He'd try to make it up to the poor beast on the way home.

That thought stopped him in midstride. He was incredulous. Was he really thinking of Delacourte as home?

"Come in here this instant!" His thoughts were interrupted by Lettie's glad order. She ran out to meet him, took his hand, and dragged him into her house. "You'll stay for supper, of course."

Adrian laughed. "Indeed I shall." He nodded back toward the doorway. "I've brought *you* supper, for a change."

Hal came in, pretending to stagger under the weight of the wicker hamper. "Feels like you've brought supper for an army!"

"Mr. Ashe!" Lettie was all flustered. "You didn't!"

"Well, if he didn't"—Hal laughed—"then he's brought us a fine-smelling collection of rocks."

"Oooh." Lettie rushed over to peer into the hamper.

"My, I've never heard tell of such vittles from the inn." She looked at him with great curiosity.

Adrian colored slightly. "They're not from the inn, Lettie," he said softly, as if the lack of volume excused the intent to deceive. "I—uh—I paid the chef at Delacourte to make you something special."

"Delacourte!" Lettie's eyes flew wide open. Concern for him shone in them. "You better stay away from there. The earl might not like a miner talking to his servants."

Adrian hated that. He hated the way she and Hal seemed just naturally to assume anyone had the right to object to them—any of them, him, Hal, or Lettie— talking to his servants. A new wave of appreciation for Elise and her fight to better the lot of the miners swept over him.

He touched the slightly swollen side of his head gingerly, and smiled. Shrugging off memories that might prove troublesome, he said, "Well, Lettie? Do I have to borrow your apron and serve dinner, too?"

They were halfway through their supper when there was a thundering clamor at the door. Both men sprang to their feet.

Neither had time to reach the door before it was thrown violently open and a group of eight men surged into the room. Ugly determination marred their faces as they headed straight for Adrian Ashe.

Elise was back in perfect control of her turbulent emotions by dinner time, and was glad Sir James had accepted her hasty invitation to join her for an early supper.

Handsome as always, he was amusing this evening as well. It was as if he were trying to make up for the lighter-minded Deverill's absence.

Calm in the candlelight until now, he looked up from his plate suddenly. "I say. Did you know that Haverford bought Deverill out, lock, stock, and barrel?"

Elise just looked at him. She hoped her mouth wasn't hanging open.

"Everything. The hall, the mine, stables, the farms—not that they're worth anything the way they've become run down—even his horses—everything."

Elise frowned slightly, not quite sure how she wanted to respond. Finally she decided to be ignorant of anything pertaining to Haverford. "That was very kind of him, I suppose. Since Dev had to leave for his cousin's so precipitously, I mean."

"Yes, he did leave in a rush, didn't he?"

"He didn't even say good-bye." She sounded forlorn to her own ears and tried to rally. "I shall miss him dreadfully, of course." She said it briskly, as if it were of no particular importance. "As shall you, I'm certain." She smiled at him a little too brightly.

"Yes," Sir James admitted slowly, "I shall, I suppose." For an instant, he looked surprised that it was true. Then he, too, rallied. "Right now, though, we have sufficient excitement with Ashe."

"With Ashe?" She was instantly alert. Her breath caught in her throat, and she felt as if Sir James was taking an age to answer.

"Yes. We've all had enough of that insolent upstart's interference. We've decided to put an end to it once and for all. Effers and Tate had the miscreant picked up by their men this evening." He took out and glanced at his watch. "About fifteen minutes ago, as a matter of fact."

As if the very skies protested, a blaze of light lit the window. It was followed by the crash of thunder.

"Well," he said, unaware of Elise's acute distress, "looks as if they were lucky. A few minutes later, and they would have been in for a good drenching from the looks of things."

There was another flash of lightning, another growl of thunder.

"What about Ashe?" It was only natural she would be interested. He worked with her after all. "What are they going to do? What are *you all* going to do?" Fear edged her voice lightly. "Do they—you—mean to hang him?"

"Don't be melodramatic, Elise. Of course we are not going to hang him."

She sagged a little in her chair, weak with relief.

"They're going to take him to the district magistrate."

"But the district magistrate is Haverford, and he is . . ."

"Not any longer." Sir James assumed she was going to say, "not in residence."

Interrupted, she let it go.

Sir James was looking a little smug. He was rather pleased to be the one to break the news about Haverford to her. Hitherto, Dev had always managed to get to her first with the latest news. "He's finally arrived, they tell me." He rose and placed his napkin beside his dinner plate.

"Well, m'dear. As I told you when I accepted your invitation, I have another engagement. And this is it. I must go to Haverford's and add my testimony to that of the others. Then *Haverford* can see to it that Adrian Ashe is hanged."

Elise's breath stopped altogether. She stared.

"We are all quite determined," Sir James told her calmly, "that any miner—no matter *who* he is—who speaks out against the owners shall pay the ultimate price demanded by the law." He looked at her closely. "You do understand that anything less would be anarchy, don't you, Elise?"

He bowed, finished pushing back his chair, and walked to the door. There he turned and said, "Thank you for a most pleasant meal, m'dear." Then he was gone.

Elise never heard his last words; she was still trying to tell herself that there was no way Haverford could hang Adrian Ashe. For pity's sake, they were the same man!

Or, at least, Ashe was the invention of Haverford, and possibly not a real person at all.

Then a terrible thought occurred to her. Ashe had been a miner when he'd spoken out at the ball. Perhaps her friends, not having any loyalty to Haverford because they didn't know him, would try to hang Ashe even if doing so included stretching the neck of an earl!

Or, worse yet, they might hang Ashe never knowing he *was* the Earl of Haverford!

She had to do something. She had to get to Adrian—Haverford—and try to help him, at least—no matter who he was!

Just then there was a commotion at her front door. The sounds coming to her down the hall indicated that the footman who'd opened the door was battling the person who stood outside it.

"Lady Elise!" It was Willem's voice shouting for her. "It's Mr. Ashe! They've taken him!"

She shot up out of her chair and ran from the room like a madwoman.

The footman who'd been stationed behind her chair caught it as it tumbled backward. He exchanged a startled look with the usually imperturbable Helmsley.

The butler, however, was almost as aghast as he.

Elise ran to the front door calling, "Let him go. It's all right, Hutchins!" She demanded of Willem, "Where are they taking him? Do you know?"

Willem was already retreating, going to see to the magnificent thoroughbred he'd ridden to warn her. He threw back over his shoulder, "To the magistrate, milady. To Haverford at Delacourte."

Elise, looking at the horse with an eye to begging its use from the boy, decided it was too far spent for her to ride. "Thank you, Willem!" She spun around and pelted down the hall to the grand staircase with her skirts clutched up over her knees.

Her footmen were scandalized. Helmsley was even shocked.

When the mistress, in an action totally out of character for her, so far forgot herself as to lean over the stair railing and yell down from the first floor, "Helmsley! Get me Columbine!" Helmsley looked ready to faint.

Outside, a brilliant slash of lightning lit the sky.

Thunder shook the doors and rattled every window in Danforth House.

"You can't do this, milady!" Rafferty held Columbine firmly. The mare's eyes were showing white rims and her ears flicked nervously from the clouds full of lightning back to Rafferty for reassurance. "Look at that storm!" He pointed with a careful movement, so as not to startle the mare. "You can't go out in this!"

"I must, Rafferty." She fixed her head stableman with a level gaze. "I have no choice." She gathered her reins.

Reluctantly Rafferty let go, but he kept his hand on Columbine's neck. "At least let me escort you, milady."

"No time!" She spurred Columbine and was off.

Rafferty clenched and unclenched his fists helplessly for a moment, then turned and ran for the barn. Two minutes later, he emerged on a big-boned, rangy gray gelding and took off in hot pursuit of his mistress.

Elise had no idea there was anyone following her. Her full attention was on getting to Delacourte before her neighbors made a drastic mistake.

Suppose they *hanged* Adrian Ashe? Or Haverford? Whichever he was? Surely they would come under the displeasure of the Crown if they hanged one of His Majesty's magistrates!

And she! What would befall her if she never solved the puzzle of which man was real, Haverford or Adrian Ashe? She chided herself for this proof that she still hoped against hope that Ashe was an actual man, and not the product of the earl's machinations.

Bending low over her horse's neck, she tried to avoid the light branch of a tree that blew out toward her. She lost her hat to it anyway.

The wind was rising, tearing at the bindings of her hair, now. That and the speed of her passage threatened to loose it completely. The temperature was dropping steadily. Low clouds threaded with silver flashes of lightning were scudding closer. Elise wished she'd worn a heavier habit.

She wished the skies were lighter so that she could see her way more clearly. She wished the storm were not so close . . . and that it were not going to be as severe as it looked. She wished that it weren't so far to Delacourte. Or that Columbine could fly!

Most of all she wished she could think of something more, anything more to keep herself from desperately worrying that she might not be in time to prevent a disaster. Her mind was working as fast as the tempo of her mare's hoofbeats, however; there was no way she could keep it from anxiety for the man she wished with all her heart she could say she didn't love!

At Delacourte, eight rough men dragged a battered Adrian Ashe up to the front door.

Perkins, already upset by the number of gentlemen who had demanded entrance in the past half hour, opened the door with more haste than usual. *When you already have a baker's dozen,* he fumed, *what are a few more?* His mouth dropped open when he saw his master, clad in his disguise as a coal miner, in the custody of eight grim captors.

"Lewis," Adrian commanded through bloodied lips.

"'Is name's Perkins, Ashe. And keep your trap shut!" One of the men snarled at Adrian.

Perkins blanched. He understood perfectly what he'd been ordered to do. "I'll call the earl's secretary." He saw the approval that lit his master's eyes and almost went limp with relief. "In the meantime, you lot bring that man inside. You can wait in the west anteroom."

Perkins led the way with every bit of frosty dignity he could manage. By his actions, he hoped to win a modicum of safety for his master. Men who would abuse another outside were simply a different story in the elegant confines of a great house. Cowed them a bit, he'd always thought. At any rate it was worth trying.

Adrian thought it a capital idea. As Perkins left to find his secretary, he shot him a grateful glance. He'd no taste for further misery to add to the headache his true love had given him.

By not so much as a twitch of his lip did the butler indicate he'd understood, but Adrian knew he had. He stood patiently, his arms held tightly by two brawny stablemen who kept checking to see if they had any mud on their boots.

Adrian had to smile. Perkins had known what he was doing. If they'd been left to wait outside the doors of Delacourte, these toughs would have pounded him occasionally to relieve their boredom. Here in the luxurious anteroom, they had other things to occupy their minds.

Adrian, now that it was no longer necessary to watch out for random blows, let himself listen to the noises dimly heard from the principal drawing room across and down the hall. It seemed that quite a number of men were gathered here under his roof.

These visitors, and the fact that he'd been dragged here so unceremoniously, indicated that the mine owners of the neighborhood had decided to do something about him. Obviously his impromptu appearance at Sir James Malfont's ball had inspired them.

The others must have come to offer their friends support. He could hear crusty old Baron Chase clearly, even here in the anteroom.

It should prove an interesting evening.

Lewis entered the anteroom at something just under a dead run. Warned by Perkins, he didn't acknowledge his employer as the Earl of Haverford, but he couldn't help the way his face blanched when he saw Adrian's bloody one. Before he was able to deal with the situation, the gentlemen mine owners of the district came in from the drawing room.

"Ah, you have him." Sir James nodded firm approval.

"There's the rogue who ruined your ball, Sir James." Lord Effers rubbed slender hands together in satisfaction.

"So," Tate demanded practically, "where's Haverford? We, and our friends in the drawing room, have come to see him about hanging this lawbreaker."

If anything, Lewis went even whiter. Now the pallor was due to rage at the treatment meted out to the man held captive in front of him. He drew his slender figure up to its full height. "Release this man to my custody, and I will bring you the Earl of Haverford."

"Nonsense."

"Ridiculous."

"Why should we do such a thing?"

Lewis answered the last man. "Because," he told them all in measured tones, "if you do not, I shall not bother to bring you the earl."

"We'll get him ourselves!"

Lewis said calmly, "I think not. Delacourte is an immense building, and"—he paused as he gestured toward the doorway into the hall—"its servants are many."

The assembled gentlemen looked into the servant-crowded great hall and decided to release Adrian to the earl's secretary.

Lewis took his master gently by the arm and led him to the doorway. Having won, he could afford to be hospitable. "There are port and brandy in the drawing room, gentleman. Perkins will see to you."

Perkins sent the secretary a slightly poisonous look. Then, having thus subtly registered his complaint, he walked majestically back to the principal drawing room, and intoned, "If you would be so kind as to follow me, gentlemen." Then he proceeded to lead them to the drink table in the earl's *second-best* drawing room.

The men of the neighborhood, satisfied that their demands were about to be met, moved after him. Suddenly they were completely affable. A comfortable

room, good port and brandy, and, if they were as
lucky as they were feeling just now, the assurance that
Adrian Ashe would be hanged along with it all. They
couldn't ask for a finer evening!

Their glasses full, they fell to speculating. "I say,"
Effers asked, "does anybody know who this Haverford is?"

"No, by George," Tate said, "and while I was
hardly the sort to hobnob with the family, I did think I
knew who they all were."

"Seems as if Dev or someone would have sent to
London to find out, doesn't it?"

Sir James entered in. "*I* did, gentlemen. In fact my
secretary was due back early today. These storms to
the south of us must have held him up."

"Well, we'll know soon enough, my friends." With
his glass, Tate gestured toward the hall and the magnificent staircase that rose from it.

Every man of them turned to see what he meant.
Listening, they heard Lewis speaking respectfully to
the man he was accompanying to the head of the
stairs, but at just that moment, the front door was
again assaulted. When Perkins opened it, a man in the
sober garb of a gentleman, though not one of means,
rushed through. His hair looked blown in all direc-
tions, and he clutched his hat in his hands. "I seek Sir
James Malfont!"

Immediately behind the man, Lady Elise Danforth
slipped through the door with her finger to her lips.

Perkins repressed a start of surprise. Understanding
that she wanted his silence, he pretended not to see
her, but see her he did. She was as windblown as the

man who had preceded her. Her bright auburn hair
rioted loose around her like a cloak. Her cheeks were
pink from exercise, her eyes bright with purpose.
Perkins had never seen anyone lovelier.

Fortunately the man was oblivious to Perkins's distraction. "Where, I say, where is Sir James Malfont?"
With a start, Perkins remembered his duty and escorted the newly arrived gentleman to the second-best
withdrawing room.

There Sir James indicated the man with a wave of
his wineglass. "My messenger, gentlemen."

The others recognized Malfont's secretary.

"Well, it seems you've arrived with the news just in
time, Smathers." Malfont smiled. "Have you discovered the full name of the new earl?"

The secretary swelled visibly with self-importance.
"I have, Sir James, and you will never believe who
it is!"

Malfont was out of patience. The earl and *his* secretary were already on their way down the stairs.
Perkins was moving to the doorway to announce his
master. If he were going to steal a march on his
friends, he had to do it quickly. "Who, you fool?"

"He's A—"

At just that moment, Adrian's butler took a deep
breath and announced his employer's arrival in
ringing tones, "His lordship, Peter Adrian Ashe Delacourte, Ninth Earl of Haverford!"

Adrian, his slightly battered face sardonic, walked
into the room.

"Ashe, by God!" Effers was stunned.

The babble that followed sounded as if it were

made by many more men than the dozen or so present.
Every man there was painfully reminded of his part in
the apprehending of the man they knew as Adrian
Ashe . . . and in the subsequent bruises on the Earl of
Haverford's face.

Malfont was the first to recover. Certain that he was
the only cool head left among the mine owners, he
said with icy civility, "What a pity, Your Lordship.
Here we have just made your acquaintance, and it
promises to be such a brief one."

Elise, standing just outside the door where she
could not be seen, went dizzy with the implied threat
in Sir James's words. Obviously, he meant to go
through with his plan to be rid of Adrian Ashe at any
cost—even this. She held her breath. Her mind
worked furiously trying to recall *anyone* she knew in
London who could help her stop this.

The earl merely raised an eyebrow.

Sir James's voice came to her clearly. His drawl
was more pronounced than she'd ever heard it.
"Surely, gentlemen, we must all agree that it is a
shame that, under present British law, Adrian Ashe
must have himself hanged by Peter Adrian Ashe Delacourte"—his voice filled with heavy sarcasm—"Ninth
Earl of Haverford?"

Hearing was no longer good enough. Elise tiptoed
to where she could see through the crack between the
edge of the door and its hinges. She watched as
Adrian, magnificent in black, moved to stand with his
back to the fireplace. He moved with the leisured gait
of a superbly confident man.

From his position on the hearth, he commanded the

room. Head high, his patrician face disdainful in spite of the damage it had sustained, he stood there and stared them down. For a long moment he simply looked from man to man.

Lightning flashed and lit the room twice and still he didn't speak. Thunder rumbled nearby.

Some of the men shifted restively.

Tate met Haverford's gaze ruefully.

Effers was deeply embarrassed and looked away.

The others, men who'd come without a second thought to condemn a cheeky commoner, were feeling that confronting a supercilious peer of the realm was altogether a different matter . . . and not precisely their cup of tea.

Finally, after a third clap of thunder, Haverford spoke. "Have you thought, gentlemen," he said in a perfectly casual voice that made Elise want to scream, "that if I die, my will will have to be executed?"

The men exchanged puzzled looks.

"What has that to do with anything, Ashe?" Sir James still wasn't willing to give this man his title. He'd worked in his mine, for God's sake!

"When I die, there are certain charges that will have to be executed, gentlemen. Certain mortgages, loans, and gambling debts that will have to be repaid to the benefit of the Haverford estate."

Lightning sizzled outside. A crack of thunder made a pause necessary.

"Well, gentlemen?" Ashe prompted softly, his eyebrow raised.

Tate sank back into his chair. An astute businessman, he understood instantly.

Effers saw the look on his friend's face and demanded, "What's he talking about, Tate?"

Tate smiled a twisted smile and told his bewildered companion, "He's saying he's bought up our mortgages and vowels, Effers." His face reluctantly registered his admiration. "It means he's got us." He chuckled, finding humor in the situation.

"I don't believe this!" Sir James looked like he wanted to pounce on each of them in turn. The men who weren't mine owners wouldn't meet his eyes.

"Would you care to have my secretary read the list, Sir James?"

When no answer came, he raised his hand toward the intense young man who was his secretary, and Lewis began to read.

"Lord Henry Effers, a mortgage of seventeen thousand pounds on an estate known as . . ."

"That's enough!" Effers had no desire to have his financial matters made public in this manner.

Lewis shrugged and skipped down the page. "Sir James Malfont, a mortgage on a town house in Mayfair, London, in the sum of . . ."

"Insolence!" Sir James looked ready to froth at the mouth.

Elise wished he would. It was no more than he deserved.

Adrian gestured to the length of the two-page list his secretary held. "Gentlemen, there are more. All of them will be made public and collected at my death. Surely you would prefer to know ahead of time which of your obligations I have acquired? There is a great deal of money involved and some of you may want to begin making . . . adjustments . . . in your style of living so that you may pay your obligations. Surely it would help to know for whom . . . and how much?"

His smile became as malicious as he intended his actions to be. "After all, there may be one or two I missed. I don't think so, but one can never tell."

"Damn you." There was a long pause as Sir James wrestled with his baser self. Then, his more prudent side won and he repeated, "Damn you, *Haverford*!"

Disquieted by James's long pause, Elise stepped into the doorway so that she could see what was going on.

Adrian caught her movement out of the corner of his eye, but he didn't remove his regard from Malfont. He had to finish this. "Very well, Sir James. But you must tell me. Am I to be hanged before being damned, or is yours merely . . . a social suggestion?"

There was a titter from somewhere among the gentlemen.

"You win, Ashe-Haverford." Sir James went so far as to hyphenate his two names but still he glared at him. Then, after a long hesitation, reluctantly he admitted, "I never particularly liked seeing a man hang, anyway."

Adrian smiled tightly and looked at the others. Both Tate and Effers looked relieved that Malfont, their leader, had solved their dilemma for them.

The spectators, as Adrian now thought of them, merely looked interested to see what developed.

Tate rose and walked to the man at the fireplace. "I'm a cit, Your Lordship. A plain man . . ."

Elise, relieved that Adrian had bested them, but still

fiercely angered by his deception, turned away. She knew what was coming. Indeed, it had already begun.

Thoroughly disgusted that men could be mortal enemies one moment and friends the next with no apparent feeling that this was in the least bit odd, she left them to it. She had no need to watch them make peace. She wanted no part of this. She wanted to be able to pretend absolute ignorance about the whole thing.

When she heard Adrian say cordially, "Gentlemen, it has begun to rain; I must insist that you stay the night," it was the last straw. She was, rain or no rain, going home!

Adrian looked quickly to the doorway. His battle won, the peace terms of his own dictating, he needed to share it with Elise.

Something had just happened in this room that Adrian didn't quite understand, and he wanted Elise to share it, and perhaps even to explain it. He'd won over these men of the gentry, and in doing so had finally found peace in victory.

No longer did he feel he had to exact revenge against the aristocracy he'd always blamed for turning their backs on the sufferings of his family. Somewhere, in the brief happenings in this room—probably in his having held the whip hand over the assembled company—he'd found release.

For the first time, he understood what had held him back from telling Elise of his love for her. Now, at last, he was free to tell her.

The wonder of it surged through him. He wanted to tell the world!

With a bold, loving smile, he turned toward her. "Gentlemen," he announced, gesturing toward the doorway where his beloved stood, "I would like you all to greet my betrothed, Lady Elise Danforth."

Elise gasped at his effrontery. How dare he assume that she would be willing to be his fiancée! How dare he make such an announcement without her permission!

Too angry to trust herself with words, she turned and fled the doorway. Fled through the great hall with its glittering array of armament. Fled out into the night and the bright, fitful illumination of the storm.

Adrian ran after her. "Elise, wait!" What the devil had gotten into her? Why the blazes was she so blasted offended at the thought of becoming his countess?

He reached the steps in time to watch Elise gallop off. Desperate to follow, he bellowed at the young groom who'd helped her mount. "Get me a horse!"

The groom rushed off toward the stables. An instant later, the skies opened wide and torrents of rain fell.

A gray horse charged up, almost knocking Adrian down. "What the devil?" He looked up at the rider. "Rafferty!"

Rafferty vaulted off the big gelding. "Here!" He thrust the reins into Adrian's hands. "I was waiting for Lady Elise to come out. Lucky I saw you run after her. Take him. He's Lady Elise's second-fastest horse. He won't catch Columbine, but he'll be close behind her when she can't run anymore."

Adrian clapped Rafferty on the back and leapt on the gray. "My thanks, friend!"

"Good luck!" Rafferty wiped the rain out of his eyes and shielded them with a hand so he could watch Ashe dash away. As the heavy rain obscured his friend, he told him softly, "You're going to need it."

Chapter Twenty-two

୶

Torrents of rain fell, viciously blown by winds approaching gale force. Adrian crouched low over the neck of the big gray gelding Rafferty had lent him and cursed like the sailor he'd been for six years.

Without a hat, he was having the devil's own time seeing where the big horse was taking him. The rain beat his hair down into his eyes and plastered it there. It sent cold rivulets down the back of his jacket, and soon every stitch he wore was soaked through.

Under the big gray's hooves, the ground was sodden. The footing was already treacherous, and conditions were fast worsening. Adrian's horse slipped twice rounding the curve in the drive. The surface over which he rode was already soft and uncertain, in another few minutes, it would be a quagmire.

As the going got more difficult, the gray gelding labored. Anxiety for Elise grew in Adrian. Where the blazes was she?

The world was a gray curtain. Rain from the sky met the rain bouncing back off the earth and the division between the earth and sky was mistily indistinct. Adrian felt as if he were in a fog back at sea.

He stopped cursing and began to mutter thanks to God that the horse he rode seemed able to sense and follow Elise's mare.

Finally, up ahead, he caught sight of Elise and her mount. It was just a glimpse, then a sheet of rain obscured her once more. He went icy cold but not from the chill of the rain. He could tell, even from that glimpse, that she was riding recklessly.

He could feel his stomach knotting. She could be killed. Damn it! Why didn't she slow down? Why was she fleeing him so madly? Didn't the little fool know she could break her beautiful neck out here?

Haunted by a picture of Elise lying like a broken doll in the mire, he drove his own mount onward. His heart in his throat with concern for her danger, he asked the big hunter to give him more speed.

The gray bunched his mighty hindquarters and hurled himself forward. In a moment they'd made enough headway to get within hailing distance of Columbine.

The wind precluded calling Elise's name—even if Adrian hadn't known it would do no good. Thunder rolled over their heads, and he saw Columbine toss her head nervously.

Adrian's heart all but stopped to see the gallant little mare soar over a hedge, then stagger in the heavy footing on the far side.

Elise was thrown forward in her saddle, and Adrian groaned aloud. Feeling, long kept at bay after the awful pain of losing his loved ones, returned with a vengeance. For years, he'd refused to allow himself to feel like this, to care like this—for anybody. Now, he was tortured by his fear that Elise might come to harm.

In a searing flash of recognition, he realized that he couldn't imagine life without her. Worse. He didn't want a life without her.

It was too late to protect himself from the pain of again caring desperately for another. It might be easier if he could return to his former state—the state he'd attained to survive the loss of his family—but it was hopeless, and he knew it. It was too damned late. Elise had broken through his defenses.

He cared. Oh, God how he cared! He cared for Elise Danforth desperately. As he rode, his soul cried out to her, pleading with her, begging her to slow her mare, to be careful!

The gray gelding slipped in the mud and went to his knees. Adrian threw his weight back, fighting to stay in the saddle. It was a near thing, but he was still aboard when the great-hearted gelding lunged back to his feet and on into the gallop again.

Somewhere off to the right, lightning struck. A bright glare, then there was the splintering, sizzling crash of a tree falling.

Up ahead, Columbine shied violently even as Elise cringed tightly down into her saddle. She was safe. The mare's startled leap sideways hadn't unseated her! All of Adrian's thoughts became expressions of gratitude.

That faltering movement of the thoroughbred mare gave the gray a six-stride advantage. Adrian's heart soared. They were closing the gap!

Still, there was nothing he could do to stem Elise's

headlong flight from his presence. If there had been, he'd have done it. Anything.

He'd have turned back if he'd thought it would have done any good—if he'd thought that there was even the slightest chance that it was only his presence that was goading her on. But he knew that it was not. There was a quality to Elise's headlong flight that told him she was not only fleeing him, but the strength of her own emotions, as well.

Too, he was certain there was no way she could know that it was he, and not Rafferty, who followed her. After all, Rafferty had been behind her all the way to Delacourte.

Then, with a single glance over her shoulder, she dispelled any hope he had that she thought he was Rafferty. Obviously, Elise was as electrically aware of him, and of when he was near, as he was of her. She *had* been from the first moment their glances had met. Achingly aware, just as he was, and he knew that.

Impatience flared in him. He'd waited long enough to secure her as his own, and secure her he was going to do. Why, then, couldn't she just surrender to the inevitable? Why couldn't she just draw rein and wait for him to take her in his arms?

He had, blast it! He'd admitted the inevitability of his love for her. Admitted life was empty without her. He'd given up fighting *his* love for *her*, given up resenting her for being one of the gentry.

He'd somehow gotten over his hatred of his own— finally realized that they were merely human beings with the same hopes, fears, distractions, and careless-ness of the rest of the world. He'd learned that from the foibles of his new neighbors. No doubt he would have done that early on if he'd been left with those of his own class when he'd been little better than a boy, instead of impressed into His Majesty's Royal Navy.

Someday he'd have to tell his uncle that he forgave him. That he'd learned to understand and to forgive.

Because he'd met Elise Danforth and her little waif, Megan, he'd been forced, even against his will, to learn to care again. To dare to love again . . . and to feel responsibility for those he loved . . . again.

His stomach in a knot, he brushed those thoughts aside. Important as they were, they didn't matter now. All of that had nothing to do with the physical safety of the woman riding hell-for-leather ahead of him. To rescue her from the possible consequences of this mad dash and to cherish her for the rest of his life were his only concerns.

Even in the chill of the driving rain and roaring wind, the thought of holding Elise again warmed him through and through. But first he had to stop her from breaking her neck!

Once he had her safely in his arms, he could rest. Could relive the soul-joining experience he'd had the first moment he'd seen Elise.

He'd known then, and he knew now, that they were meant to be. He could have fought it until the last trump sounded, but in the end, his end, it would have been as it was to be, *her*.

In an agony of spirit, he watched her dash on through the storm. She headed her mare straight at a stone wall that separated his land from that beyond.

Columbine hesitated.

Elise spurred her on.

The valiant little mare tried her best, gathering herself with all her might as she neared the foot of the wall. She chose the moment to lift her forehand perfectly, but her hind legs all but slipped from under her when she thrust upward. She nearly went down! Only by a quick turn away from the wall did the clever mare avert tragedy.

Her quick turn, however, almost spelled disaster for her rider. Elise kept her seat on the rain-slicked leather of her saddle only with the greatest of difficulty.

Elise glared back over her shoulder at Adrian and turned Columbine away from him. The ground under the horses was all mud now, and the lighter-muscled mare was tiring badly. She was finding it exceptionally difficult to keep up the speed her mistress asked of her. Stride by stride, inexorably, Adrian's gray began to catch up.

When he saw Elise wrench her mare around and head across a recently plowed bit of his land, he was exultant. There was no way the dainty Columbine could outdistance the huge hunter he rode in such footing. The mare began to lose speed, and he caught up with Elise before she had traversed half the narrow strip plowed for a new island of shrubbery.

Adrian let the gray have his head, satisfied with the pace the horses set now, knowing he'd overtake Columbine easily. When he did, he leaned from his saddle, locked an arm around Elise, and dragged her to his own saddle bow.

"Let me go!" She struck at him as best she could

with her back to him and his arm like a steel band crushing the breath out of her.

"No!" Thunder crashed and rolled, and he shouted over it, "Not now, not ever!"

Elise still had Columbine's reins, and the mare stumbled after the gray as Adrian sent him toward the vacant gatekeeper's cottage in the back wall of the estate. Abandoned for fifty years, the back gate had once served commercial traffic to Delacourte. Adrian had had the cottage cleaned and repaired with an eye to holding meetings with the miners there, as it was centrally located.

The ancient structure was hardly the bower of roses that he'd have chosen for his true love, but with the lightning striking ever nearer, and thunder drowning out his unwilling fiancée's vigorous protests, it looked like the best bet to him.

That decided—in his mind, at least—Adrian pulled the horses up at the door of the little stone cottage, swung down with Elise in his arms, and strode inside. Setting Elise down, he kissed her quickly—was resoundingly slapped for it—then went back out to lead the horses to shelter. He returned just in time to stop Elise from heading back out into the storm.

"What the deuce do you think you're doing, Elise?"

"I'm going home! Where have you put Columbine?"

"Don't be a fool." He saw the emerald sparks in her eyes, saw the determined thrust of her delicate chin, and added, "Your mare's spent. Why the devil do you want to kill her trying to get home in this?" He gestured broadly at the weather beyond the walls.

They could both hear the howling winds and slashing rain outside. Elise hesitated. Columbine was dear to her.

"Didn't I just tell you I'd never let you go?"

"I don't *know* you!" Her voice was firm, but her eyes told him she was unsure.

Adrian pressed his advantage. "Stay." His expression softened. "Stay and let me beg you to forgive me."

Elise was stunned. Whatever she'd expected, it wasn't this!

Her eyes wide with astonishment, she shook her head, but it didn't carry much conviction. Her voice had a plaintive note as she told him, "Forgive you? How can I forgive you? You've deceived me all this time." Now her eyes were stricken, as if by a great loss. "Indeed, you've deceived us all."

"Deceived you? How have I deceived you except not to declare myself as Earl of Haverford?"

Sadly, she reproached him. "I believed you were real. Really Adrian Ashe, a simple, brave, miner."

Adrian laughed harshly. "Never was I simple, Elise. Not in any sense of the word."

She colored. "You know what I meant . . ."

"Yes, damn it! I know precisely what you meant." He could feel anger stir. "You meant that I was a commoner, a *simple* peasant. Quite beneath your notice." He cocked his head, his voice insolent. "Am I not right?"

She stared at him an instant and her lips parted as if she would utter words that would make everything right between them. Then her eyes narrowed and instead she threw at him "Yes! Quite beneath my notice!" Her words were spoken in such a scathing tone that they both knew them for sarcastic lies. "You toasted me with your ale and I never noticed how your eyes smoldered at me. You brought Megan and me out of Tate's mine and I said 'thank you very much, Mr. Ashe' and rode calmly away."

She was working herself up into a fury. The only effect it seemed to have on her audience of one was to make the corner of his mouth twitch.

Adrian watched her as if he would never have his fill of watching her. Her eyes were emerald flames in a face colored high with anger. He'd never seen her more beautiful.

Elise wasn't half done. "You saved a dozen men at great peril to yourself and I thanked you again and serenely took myself off home to a warm supper without a second thought of you!"

He took one stride forward. "You've left out one memorable episode, my love."

She spun away from him, putting a stride's distance between them again before she turned back to hiss, "Oh, yes. There was one other *little* thing wasn't there? There was that time I nursed you until I was ready to drop . . . all the while dying of guilt for having brought that horrible beating on you by asking you to head up my miners! If I recall correctly, you used that opportunity to crush my body beneath your own and force me to accept your advances *in my own bed*!"

Adrian felt the anger in the back of his mind lash its tail. Elise had hit a nerve. "Force, milady?" His voice was sardonic, his eyes hot. "I thought the whole point of that little exercise was to have you ask nicely."

She hit him so hard she rocked him back on his heels.

He grabbed her hand as she aimed another slap at his jaw and used her own momentum to snatch her against him. Wet through or not, heat leapt between their bodies.

He locked her head in the crook of his arm and brought his mouth crushingly down on hers. His other arm tightened like a vise, molding her body to his.

She resisted, shoving at his chest with her trapped hands.

He kissed her all the harder.

With a helpless little moan, she pulled her hands free and wrapped her arms around his neck. Stretching up to his kiss, she brought herself even closer to him.

Suddenly, it was as if they couldn't be close enough, couldn't get enough contact between them. Adrian began to tear his jacket off with one hand while he held her pressed to him with the other. Then he began trying to get hers off.

As he conquered each damp, impossibly clingy piece of her clothing, he kissed the skin he exposed. Soon there was a pile of wet muddy garments on the floor in front of the cold fireplace. It might have been a bed of the finest eiderdown in a luxurious bed-chamber to the two lovers. Neither of them felt the cold draft from the chimney, both were lost in the glory of their coming union. Together they clung and strained to be one.

He kissed every inch of her body, his lips warm on

her cool alabaster skin—kissed her until she glowed with the radiance of her love for him. She held to him and begged with little moans and soft nips for him to come to her, to complete her.

When he could wait no longer, he took her. It was as if the lightning and the thunder of the storm had entered the cottage, filled it, and transported them beyond the stars.

Nothing in life had prepared them for the sweetness of their mutual surrender. In the end they had each spent every vestige of themselves on loving the other.

When it was over, he cradled her in his arms, his chest heaving as if he'd run for miles. A tiny tremor went through their bodies, and with a start, he realized they were cold.

She shivered slightly, snuggling closer to the warmth of his big frame. The still, chill air in the cottage was penetrating her consciousness.

With a sound that told her clearly how disgusted with himself he felt for not having done it when they'd first entered the cottage, Adrian reluctantly let her go and threw himself down on one knee on the hearth.

He struck fire into the tinder under the logs there and skillfully nursed the blaze to life while she lay and languidly watched the play of his muscles under his skin.

With dawning horror, she recognized the marks of a whip on his broad back. "Adrian!" Her cry carried a hint of the pain she felt at seeing him scarred so.

Instantly, he had her back in his arms, his bare flesh again warming her own as he held her close and demanded, "What is it? What's the matter?"

"Your back. I saw your back. Who has done such a thing to you?"

He laughed, and it rumbled deep in his chest. "Ah. That particular boatswain will be forever blessed. Those scars I will cherish from this moment forth."

She pulled her head away from the strong column of his neck where she had tucked it and looked at him questioningly. "Whatever do you mean?" Her eyes were bewildered.

"Didn't you say that you were confused as to whether or not I was the creation of the Earl of Haverford?"

"Yes."

"Well, the evidence I bear on my back should give you the proof you need to know that I am all that I say I am—simply your Adrian Ashe." He smiled down at her, and his voice became tender. "For who, my angel, would dare to introduce a belted earl to a cat-o'-nine-tails?"

She frowned slightly. "A cat-o'-nine-tails?" She reared up to a sitting position. Comprehension came. "A whip." Tears gathered in her eyes. "Oh, my poor darling." She pressed her lips to a scar that curled around his shoulder. "Why?" Her eyes were luminous with concern. "How . . . ?"

Instantly the flames ignited in Adrian equalled those dancing on the dry logs and filling the little room with warmth. "Hush. We've the rest of our lives for questions. Now is the time for promises. May I ask you again to be my countess?"

"You never asked the first time!"

"Then forgive me for my boorish announcement . . . and accept."

Elise gave up her pose of being offended and sank back down on the pile of their clothing with him. "I shall forgive Adrian Ashe. I seem to be able to forgive him anything." She looked at him with eyes that smoldered. "The Earl of Haverford, however, may be a different matter."

"What do you require from him, then, milady?" Adrian was cautious.

Elise leaned back in his embrace and looked deep into his eyes a long time.

Finally, she leaned forward slowly and said, very softly against his lips, "A lifetime."

Christina Cordaire

Elise gave up her pose of being offended and sank down on the pile of their clothing with him. "I

"A delicious stew of crime, passion,
high fashion, and tragic love."
—*Affaire de Coeur*

From Sally Beauman,
the bestselling author of *Lovers and Liars*,
comes a new tale of international intrigue
and fatal passion.

DANGER ZONES

A reclusive designer of originality and passion, Maria Cazarès is a legend shrouded in mystery. When the fashion glitterati assemble in Paris to breathlessly await the new Cazarès collection, a long-buried secret resurfaces and tragedy strikes. Two journalists, Rowland McGuire and Gini Hunter, pick up the scent of an unfolding scandal that will converge with the desperate search for an innocent girl who has disappeared. And at last, some blood red truths will be revealed....

Published by Fawcett Books.
Available wherever books are sold.